the
likeable
fraudster

BOOK NINE OF THE
SYDNEY HARBOUR
HOSPITAL SERIES

CHRIS TAYLOR

LCT Productions Pty Ltd
18364 Kamilaroi Highway, Narrabri NSW 2390

ISBN. 978-1-925119-41-1 (Paperback)

The Likeable Fraudster is a work of fiction. Names, characters, places, brands, media and incidents either are the product of the author's imagination or are used fictitiously. Any resemblance to actual persons, living or dead, events, or locales, is entirely coincidental.

Published in the United States of America.

BOOKS BY CHRIS TAYLOR

THE MUNRO FAMILY SERIES
(In order)

The Profiler
The Investigator
The Predator
The Betrayal
The Deception
The Negotiator
The Christmas Vigil
The Ransom
The Defendant
The Shooting
The Maker
(Available in Audio)

THE SYDNEY HARBOUR HOSPITAL SERIES
(in order)

The Perfect Husband
The Body Thief
The Baby Snatchers
The Final Bullet
The Debt Collector
The Lab Test
The Stolen Identity
The Cliff-top Killer
The Likeable Fraudster

THE SYDNEY LEGAL SERIES
(in order)

An Accidental Murderer
At the Hand of her Father
A Woman Scorned
Lies and Deception
Ordinary Evil
The Perfect Crime
Malicious Love
Toxic Inheritance

THE BARRINGTON FAMILY SERIES
(in order)

Broken Lives
Broken Promises
Broken Bonds
Broken Spirits
Broken Vows
Broken Minds
Broken Dreams
Broken Hearts
Broken Homes

THE CRAIGDON FAMILY SERIES
(in order)

Callum
Joel
Isabella
Nicholas
Sophia
Flynn
Noah
Logan
Elizabeth

Get a FREE book when you sign up for Chris Taylor's
newsletter at: www.christaylorauthor.com.au

Love Audiobooks? Check out Chris Taylor Books on audio
on Audible.com, Amazon.com and the iBooks store.

Join Chris Taylor's Facebook reader group/fan page and be
among the first to receive news of book releases, read and
review books prior to release and other amazing offers. Join
Now at: www.facebook.com/groups/1758023621144744/

Find out more about all of Chris Taylor's books, by visiting her
website at: www.christaylorauthor.com.au/about/books

Dedication

ACKNOWLEDGMENTS

As usual, no book comes into being without a lot of help and support by my friends and family. A world of thanks must go to my wonderful editor, Pat Thomas. Thank you for everything that you do to make my stories even more amazing than I could ever dare to dream. To Detective Superintendent Michael Kilfoyle, thank you for lending my story credibility. Any mistakes are wholly my own.

To Chrissy and all of the staff at damonza.com, thank you for yet another fantastic cover. To my sister, Nicole Guihot and to my friend, Ally Thomson, thank you for your excellent editorial comments, proof reading skills and suggestions. I hope you like the final result.

To Amy Atwell and her dedicated staff at Author E.M.S. who are so much more than book formatters. Amy, once again, thank you for your magic.

To the fantastic writer organizations such as Romance Writers of Australia, Romance Writers of

America and Romance Writers of New Zealand for all the help, support and encouragement they offer new and aspiring writers, including me.

To my readers, thank you for your support and love for my stories. Your encouragement and enjoyment make this journey all worthwhile.

And lastly, to my friends and family, especially my husband and children. Thank you for putting up with late dinners and even later conversations as I've emerged day after day from the sometimes scary but always enthralling world I've created on my computer.

PROLOGUE

Dear Diary,

I can't believe I've done it! I've killed a man! I'm not sure why I'm surprised. After all, he had it coming. It's just that...this was my first time. I didn't realize how easy it would be. I had a gun... I pulled the trigger... And just like that, he was gone...

I'm shocked and horrified by what I've done, but I'm also strangely...elated. It's wrong, so wrong, but it's done and there's nothing I can do to change it, even if I wanted to.

And like I said, he had it coming...

CHAPTER 1

Holly Greenwood adjusted her heavy shoulder bag. Pushing the hair out of her eyes, she juggled the load of files in her hands and then inserted her key in the lock that secured the front door of the medical clinic where she'd worked for the past two years. With an effort, she managed to unlock the door and make her way into the cool, quiet waiting room.

She dumped the files and her shoulder bag on her already cluttered desk then hurried over to the small security panel fixed to the wall near the entry like she did every morning. She had thirty seconds to disable the alarm. She usually needed less than fifteen.

Opening the small door that protected the keypad and screen, she stared at the illuminated panel. Her fingers hovered over the keys, but she made no move to put in the numbers. There was no need. The alarm had already been disabled.

Damn! She must have forgotten to set it on her way out the night before. Either that, or one of the doctors she worked for had arrived at the clinic early. *Had they finished their ward rounds and arrived ahead of their usual time?*

Occasionally, they'd come in early to go over test results or return phone calls. She wondered which one of them was in. Not Kevin Johnson, that's for sure. He was never in early.

Making her way over to the large windows that took up most of one wall in the waiting area, she tugged open the heavy, navy-blue curtains and then blinked against the bright summer sunlight that poured inside. When her eyes adjusted, she took a moment to look out on the streets below. They were filled with staff from the Sydney Harbour Hospital making their way to work, mostly clinicians and technicians who worked office hours. The nursing and medical staff had started their shifts more than an hour earlier, including the three doctors she worked for.

Doctors Jake Alexander, Kevin Johnson and Shane Cannington were college friends and after several years of employment at the Sydney Harbour Hospital, they had opened a private practice. She'd been their first and only receptionist and at the ripe old age of twenty, it had been something of a coup to be placed in the job straight out of secretarial college. But her bosses were also young and, unlike most men, they'd looked past the Barbie doll look she cultivated for fun and recognized the keen intelligence and quiet efficiency that made them confident she was a perfect fit. And she had been.

Over the couple of years since she'd started, she'd turned the medical clinic into an efficient war machine. She juggled appointment books for the three doctors, all of whom still attended patients on the hospital wards in addition to their private clinic. She pacified relatives when bad news was delivered, she offered cool drinks and cups of tea. She answered phones, she entered data, chased up test results—she kept the office running smoothly and she did it all with a genuine smile on her face. There was nothing Holly didn't love about her job—or the doctors she worked for. One doctor in particular had totally stolen her heart.

After taking a moment to stack the magazines that were spread across a low table in the center of the waiting area, she stowed her handbag in its usual place beneath her desk and then switched on her computer. While she waited for it to boot up, she wandered down the carpeted corridor toward the doctors' rooms. As she'd surmised, Kevin Johnson's office was empty. Next to it, Shane Cannington's door stood slightly ajar. A familiar surge of butterflies swirled in her stomach at the thought of seeing the man she'd come to care for so much. Out of habit, she gave a perfunctory knock and pushed it open.

"Oh my God!"

Shane lay in a crumpled heap on the floor. A dark stain had spread in a wide circle beneath his head. As Holly edged closer, she could see two bullet holes neatly spaced, both in the back of his head.

"Holy shit! Holy shit! Holy shit!" she murmured, trying hard to stem her panic as her heart kicked into overdrive.

He was dead. She could tell from the way he lay there, completely still and silent, and from the single unblinking brown eye that stared sightlessly across the room.

She looked wildly about her. The photo frames lined up along the window ledge looked undisturbed. The examination bed was neat and tidy, made up with a clean sheet and pillowcase, just like she'd left it the night before. In fact, apart from the man who lay in a pool of blood on the floor, the room appeared just as it always did.

Inching backwards, she made her way through the open doorway and hurried down the corridor to the reception area. With shaking fingers, she dialed the police. And then she called Jake.

Doctor Jake Alexander returned the stethoscope to its usual position around his neck and smiled down at his patient.

"Everything sounds good, Robyn. That chest infection has cleared up and it's all systems go. By this time tomorrow, the surgery will be over."

The middle-aged woman smiled back at him, although Jake could see it was an effort. Her pale blue eyes were ringed with fear. One of her hands was clasped tightly in her husband's, the other was fisted in the sheets. Jake could understand her apprehension. A double mastectomy was a serious operation and one that wasn't undertaken lightly. It would involve several surgeons and many hours of work.

Once again, he felt the need to reassure her. "We've already spoken about the risks, Robyn, and if there was any other way to deal with this cancer, we'd do it. The mastectomy is the best way to go forward; the most reliable method we have of getting all of it and making sure it doesn't come back. We'll supplement the surgery with radiotherapy and chemo and we'll beat this thing. I promise you."

Robyn acknowledged his comments with a nod, her lips taut.

"How long will she be in the theater?" her husband asked quietly.

Jake turned his attention to the man who sat beside Robyn. Richard Bell looked almost as fearful as his wife.

"The mastectomy will take two or three hours. She's also undergoing a breast reconstruction, so once we've finished removing the breast tissue, the plastic surgeons will take over and begin the reconstruction. It could take another couple of hours. We'll let you know how she's doing as we go along, I promise. I don't envisage any complications."

He turned slightly and shot his patient another reassuring smile and was relieved when some of the tension around her mouth eased. Her hand relaxed against the sheets and a tiny sigh escaped her lips.

"Thank you, Doctor," she murmured. "I appreciate you telling us how it will go. I'm one of these people who'd rather know all the ins and outs of the procedure, all the risks, before I go under. It'll be too late when I'm in there, right?"

She followed the comment with a chuckle and Jake felt a surge of admiration. Despite their fears and the odds that were often stacked against them, his patients seemed to dig deep and bring forth courage and good humor from somewhere way down inside them during what might be the most critical moments of their lives. It never ceased to amaze him. That was one of the reasons he loved being an oncologist.

"You're right, Robyn," he replied and then gave her a wink. "You're going to be fine and after it's all over, you'll have the comfort of knowing the cancer's been removed and you can start getting on with your life, doing all those things you've been putting off."

"Yes, like buying a caravan and traveling around Australia," she said and smiled at her husband.

"I'm game if you are," Richard replied, patting her hand.

Robyn turned back to Jake. "So, about this reconstruction... I'm getting a double-D cup, right?"

Jake laughed. "You can have whatever cup size you like, but I thought when we spoke about this before, you were happy to replace what you'd had? Have you changed your mind?"

The woman smiled up at him. "No. I was just

having a little fun. Give me back my C cup and I'll get on just fine."

"Done," Jake beamed.

Robyn's color had returned to normal and the pinched look about her face had almost disappeared. He couldn't help but feel pleased that he'd managed to distract her from her worries, even for a little while.

His cell vibrated against his belt and he excused himself from Robyn and her husband and the nurse who had accompanied him to Robyn's bedside. He unclipped the phone and checked the screen. Holly Greenwood's name beckoned. Moving further away, he answered the call.

"Holly, what can I do for you? If it's about old Mr Germaine begging to see me again, just tell him I'll be in later this morning. I have a full list in front of me and—"

"Jake, it's not about Mr Germaine. It's... It's Shane."

Jake frowned. "What's wrong with Shane?"

"He... He..." There was a catch in Holly's voice. Jake's concern ratcheted up another notch.

"Holly, talk to me. What's happened? Is Shane all right?"

"Nooo!"

The word sounded like it had been wrenched from deep inside her. It was followed by a loud sob. Jake's gut clenched. He reined in his panic and forced himself to remain calm.

"Okay, Holly, you need to take a deep breath and tell me what happened."

His request was met with gasps and even more

tortured sobs. He bit down on his impatience and tried again.

"Holly, listen to me. Get a grip. Big breaths. Slowly. Okay, now, talk to me. I need to know what happened."

"It's Shane," she gasped softly. "He's...dead."

If she'd said Deborah Healy, the middle-aged general manager of the Sydney Harbour Hospital, had turned up naked and skipping a two-step across the waiting room, he couldn't have been more shocked. Blinking hard, he shook his head and sought clarification.

"I'm sorry?"

"I told you! Shane's dead, Jake! He's been shot twice in the head!"

Jake's legs nearly went out from under him. He reached out for the nearest wall and leaned on it for support. All the time, he tried to come to terms with what he'd heard.

"Shane's been shot? Where? When?" he demanded, his breath coming fast.

"Here. At the clinic. Sometime through the night, I think. He's lying on the floor in his office."

A fresh wave of shock ricocheted through him. *Had Shane committed suicide?* He couldn't bear to give credence to that thought. Shane had everything to live for. He was in the prime of his life, had a successful career, good friends... Life was treating him well.

But if not suicide, then what?

There was a loud buzzing in his ears. He managed to tell Holly to call the police and reassured her he'd be there as soon as he could and then he ended the call. He stowed the cell in the pocket of his white coat, reported to the nurses' desk that he was leaving to deal with an emergency and bolted from the ward.

The warm summer breeze ruffled his hair as he raced outside. People moved to get out of his way. The clinic where he and his college buddies ran their private medical practice was only two blocks away. With that thought in mind, he turned to the right and took off at a run.

He made it to the next intersection only slightly out of breath. Waiting for the light to turn green, he tugged out his phone and called Kevin. It took forever for the call to be answered.

"Hi, Jake. What's up?" a friendly female voice asked.

Katrina. Kevin's girlfriend. She sounded slightly out of breath, like she'd run to answer the phone. Jake drew in some air and tried to sound normal.

"Hi, Kat. I'm looking for Kevin. Is he around?"

"Yes, but he's in the shower. I just got out. I barely had time to dry." She laughed a little and then added, "We had a late night."

For a millisecond, Jake saw Katrina West standing naked and soapy beneath the hot spray. With a sound of disgust, he forced the image from his mind. This wasn't the time or the place. He cleared his throat.

"Can you ask him to call me as soon as he can? It's important."

The laughter faded from Kat's voice. "Jake, you sound so serious and it's barely eight-thirty. What's the matter?"

Jake opened his mouth and then closed it again. She was Kevin's girlfriend. It wasn't Jake's place to break the news. Besides, he knew very little, apart from the fact Shane was dead. He cleared his throat.

"Just get Kevin to call me as soon as he gets out of the shower. I need to talk to him."

Jake ended the call, feeling grim. A moment later, the light changed and once again, he took off at a run. The building that housed their private medical practice loomed in front of him at the top of the hill. The glass-and-steel structure was one of the newer buildings on the street and was modern and sleek. The sun sparkled off the bank of windows that made up the eastern wall, sending a thousand shards of light glittering through the air. The sight of it normally filled him with pride that he had an office inside this much-sought-after piece of real estate, but right now, the sight of the building filled him with dread.

Rushing across the pale gray marble-tiled foyer, he impatiently pressed the button for the elevator. Almost immediately, the silver doors slid open with barely a whisper. He bit back a sigh of relief and hurried inside. Less than a minute later, he stepped out on the fifth floor and jogged the rest of the way to the clinic door.

His name and the names of his two colleagues had been stenciled in a professional script across the glass entryway, announcing to the world that these were the offices of Doctor Jake Alexander, oncologist, Doctor Kevin Johnson, plastic surgeon and Doctor Shane Cannington, ears, nose and throat specialist. Shouldering his way inside, Jake was relieved to see the waiting room was empty of patients. He pulled up short at the sight of his receptionist sobbing quietly behind the front desk.

"Holly..."

She looked up at him, her eyes red and swollen. Her normally immaculately made-up face was now a mess of smeared eye shadow and rivulets of black mascara ran down her cheeks. Her bouncy blond hair hung loose around her face, like she'd been too distracted to do anything with it. He didn't think he'd ever seen her look so crushed. Knowing what had caused it sent a surge of dread through his veins.

"Have you called the police?" he asked quietly.

"Y-yes," she stammered. "I-I called them first."

Jake absorbed the information and then nodded, more to himself than to Holly. If Shane had been murdered, the clinic was now a crime scene. The thought filled him with disbelief. "Where is he?" he murmured.

"In h-his office, like I-I said."

With his lips compressed, Jake forced himself down the corridor, in the direction of the rooms that were used for patient consultations. The first door was open. He glanced through the doorway. Kevin's room was empty. Jake was flooded with a momentary surge of irritation. He still hadn't heard from his partner. *How long did it take to have a shower, for Christ's sake?* This was an emergency.

The next room was Shane's and his door was also open. Filled with dread, Jake forced himself inside. Shane lay on his stomach, surrounded by a pool of blood. His head was turned slightly to one side. Jake made himself move closer and crouched beside his friend, nausea rising in his throat. He'd seen death before, but not so personally, so close.

Reaching out, he felt for a pulse in the side of Shane's neck, but it was a useless gesture, and Jake knew it. His dead partner's skin was a mottled blue-gray color and he was cold to the touch. He'd been dead for some time. The two bullet wounds, visible in the back of Shane's head, put an end to any speculation that they were self-inflicted.

Shock and disbelief poured through him at the knowledge his friend and colleague had been murdered. Coming slowly to his feet, he moved away from the body and braced his hands against the windowsill. Leaning forward, with his head down, he sucked in some air, trying to come to terms with the awful truth.

Sirens sounded in the distance and their wail sent a shiver down his spine. Hearing sirens outside a hospital was so commonplace, he usually tuned them out. But not this time. This time, they were coming for his college buddy, a man Jake had liked and respected enough not only to go into business with, but to call a true friend. The thought that someone had callously murdered him was simply beyond belief.

Who could have done this? Why?

Shane was an excellent ENT specialist and an all-round nice guy. Everybody loved him. So what if he spent more time in his books than he did with anybody else? It didn't mean he deserved to be murdered. Nobody deserved to end up like that.

The sirens drew closer. Jake looked through the window and saw two police cars and an ambulance pull into the emergency parking bay below. A second later, doors opened and several first responders climbed out. He braced himself for the moment when pandemonium would prevail.

Where the hell was Kevin and why hadn't he called?

Chapter 2

Kat West walked into the bathroom she shared with her boyfriend of three years and called out to the man who still stood in the shower.

"Kevin, you need to call Jake."

He wiped the frosted glass with his hand and squinted at her. "What did you say?"

"Jake called. He wants you to phone him. He says it's urgent."

Kevin shook his head and his longish Matthew McConaughey curls went flying every which way. He grinned at Kat. "With Jake, it's always urgent. He's been working on the oncology ward for too long."

Stemming her irritation left over from an incident the night before, she raised her voice over the sound of the running shower. "He sounded pretty serious. I think you should give him a call."

A moment later, the water was silenced and Kevin stepped out of the cubicle. He shook his head again and she was covered in droplets.

Once again, her irritation with him flared. She cried out and turned on her heel to leave, but he would have none of it.

With the lean, taut body of an athlete and a cute and disarming smile that hid a multitude of sins, Kevin Johnson garnered his fair share of female attention. Kat wasn't immune, at least, she hadn't been in the early days. She looked back now and couldn't believe how easily he'd drawn her in. Now, his arms came around her from behind and he pulled her back hard against him. His hands cupped her breasts through her blouse.

"Kevin, you're getting me wet!" she snapped, not at all in the mood for his shenanigans.

"Who cares about a bit of water? You look mighty fuckable today, Miss West. Your tits look great in that top. Is it new?"

She made a sound of disgust in the back of her throat and batted his hands away, but to her annoyance, he merely chuckled and tightened his hold. As if oblivious to her irritation, he nuzzled the side of her neck and pressed his hips forward. She registered the feel of his erection against her butt.

"Kevin, we don't have time for this," she said, refusing to give in to his attempts at persuasion. In response, his fingers found her nipples and he tweaked them hard.

"Ouch! That hurt!" she cried, and twisted out of his hold, completely done with his attempts to manhandle her into submission.

His smile was full of practiced charm. "Come on, Kat. Don't play coy with me. You like it a little rough."

She glared at him. "Actually, I don't. You ought to know that by now."

His grin widened. "Excuse me if I don't believe you. I seem to recall it was only last night that you wiggled your cute little ass at me. I fucked you hard and fast and you screamed with pleasure. I rammed my cock so far up your—"

Kat's face flamed with embarrassment and anger. "Kevin! Stop talking that way! It wasn't like that, and you know it. I was barely awake. Besides, you were so drunk I'm surprised you were able to perform at all, let alone remember any of it."

He moved closer, his erection still full and hard. It jutted thickly from the nest of dark curls at the juncture of his thighs. He reached out and cupped her cheek.

"I remember everything." He growled. "And tonight, we're going to do it all over again. You pretend you don't like it, but the truth is, you can't get enough. Say it, Katrina. Tell me how much you love to suck my cock."

Kat screwed up her face in distaste. She was far from prudish, but hearing Kevin speak about their acts of intimacy with such crudity left a bad taste in her mouth. On top of that, she was still irritated at him for the way he'd allowed his friend to hijack their dinner the night before. Lately, it seemed he rarely had time for her, unless it was to have sex. Ignoring him, she turned her face away. "You need to call Jake," she said instead.

"Fuck Jake. No, don't fuck Jake." His expression turned calculating. "Then again, that might be fun. You could do the two of us at once. He's always had a hard-on for you."

Kat spun away from him, outrage pouring through her veins. "Kevin! Stop it! I don't appreciate you speaking to me like that. I deserve more respect. I'm not your plaything. It isn't funny and it sure as hell doesn't turn me on."

Kevin merely chuckled and once again sidled closer. Flinging an arm around her shoulders, he dragged her against him and bent his head to nip at her neck. "Are you sure?" he mumbled against her skin.

One of his hands stole up between them and pinched her nipple again. She slapped at his hand, now completely and utterly fed up.

"Go away, Kevin, and leave me alone."

Something in her tone finally registered. Kevin lifted his head and stared at her, his blue eyes filling with remorse.

"Hey, sugar, I didn't mean it. I'm sorry. There's no need to get so upset. I was joking."

Kat folded her arms across her chest and glared at him. "That's the problem, Kevin. You don't listen and when you do, you only hear what suits you. And if that's your idea of a joke, don't bother." She turned away and headed toward the open door to the bathroom. Before she exited the room, she turned and threw over her shoulder, "Now, would you please get dressed and call Jake."

———

Just like Jake had anticipated, the arrival of the

police and paramedics brought pandemonium. Removing himself from the steady stream of emergency personnel who traipsed in and out of the waiting area, he took a seat on one of the high-backed chairs normally reserved for patients.

At his request, Holly was on the phone to patients canceling the appointments of those scheduled to attend upon one or another of the doctors that day. With neither of them allowed to leave until the police had finished speaking with them, she'd begged Jake to give her something to do, anything to take her mind off what had happened. Calling the patients was a no-brainer. The last thing he needed was more people in the room asking questions.

The vibration of his cell phone caught his attention and he reached down and pulled it off his belt.

Kevin.

"About time. What the hell have you been doing?" Jake barked without preamble.

"I was in the shower. Is that all right? What's up?"

Jake dragged his hand through his hair and cast around for the right words. "It's about Shane. I'm sorry, Kev. There's no easy way to say this. He's... He's been murdered."

"*What the fuck...?*"

"Yeah."

"Where?"

"At the clinic."

"Fuck. How?"

Wearily, Jake filled him in.

"Who the fuck would do something like that?" Kevin exploded. "Shane's the nicest guy around."

"Yeah, that's what I told the police."

"What's their take on it?"

Jake blew his breath out on a heavy sigh. "So far, they say they have sweet FA, other than it's a homicide."

"Was there any sign of forced entry? Did they set off the alarm?"

"No. That's the thing. Holly was the first one here this morning. She said the alarm wasn't on. Shane must have stayed back, working late."

"Fuck. Poor Holly," Kevin murmured. "How's she holding up?"

"About as well as you'd expect. She found him."

"Shit, this is so fucked up."

Silence fell between them. Jake's thoughts went round and round in his head. It was as Kevin said. Everything was fucked up.

"The police want to talk to you," he murmured.

Kevin's voice sharpened. "Why me?"

"Relax. They want to talk to all of us. Holly and I have already told them what we know. You're next. We need to do whatever we can to help find Shane's killer and ruling ourselves out is a first step."

"Yeah, of course. I'll be there as soon as I can."

After ending the call and clipping the phone back on his belt, Jake stood and wandered over to where Holly sat behind the front desk. The phone was back in its cradle and she was staring dazedly off into space. Her expression was blank, her skin chalky. Dried tears and inky black still stained her cheeks. A surge of sympathy washed over him. He couldn't imagine how it had been, discovering Shane like that.

"How are you holding up, Holly?" he asked gently.

She lifted her gaze briefly to his and then lowered it again. "Not good."

"Thank you for making those calls. I appreciate it."

She offered him a tiny shrug. "It's okay."

He moved closer to perch on the edge of the desk. "I'm so sorry you were the one to find him. No one should have to go through something like that."

A rush of fresh tears filled her eyes and spilled over onto her cheeks. "He was so nice!" she cried. "He was always smiling, even when he forgot where he'd left his glasses or couldn't find his bag! He always asked after my cat."

Jake stared at her, feeling stupid. "You have a cat?"

"Yes. Chocolate. He's a chocolate point Siamese. Get it?"

She looked at Jake expectantly. He managed a nod.

Holly sighed. "Shane loves...loved cats, but he could never own one. He lived with his mother. She's allergic." She gave another tiny shrug. "He loved to listen to my stories about Chocolate's escapades."

Her voice drifted off. She sniffed and swiped at her eyes with the back of her hand. Jake didn't know what to say. He had no idea Shane loved cats, or for that matter, that he lived with his mother. He wondered how Holly had come by so much information and what else he didn't know about his late friend and colleague.

Kat glanced at the clock on the wall opposite the X-ray room and forced her attention back to the small boy who lay on the stretcher. She shot him a smile of reassurance and carefully repositioned his arm.

"How did you hurt yourself, Caleb?" she asked.

"I fell off the playground equipment. I was taking a turn on the flying fox. I only got halfway and my arms gave out. I landed on the ground."

"Ouch," Kat replied with a grin. "And I'm guessing you put this arm out to break your fall, right?"

The child nodded and smiled. "Right."

"Well, I'm going to take a few pictures and then we'll be able to tell if you've broken it."

The boy's eyes grew round and fearful. He glanced at his mother who stood nearby and then looked back at Kat. "Will it hurt?" he asked. "'Cause it hurt a lot when I fell."

She patted his hand reassuringly and smiled. "No, honey, it won't hurt."

"Promise?"

"I promise. But I do need you to stay very still. Can you do that for me?"

He nodded, even though his eyes remained wide. Kat winked at him. "Good boy." She turned to his mother.

"I need you to wait outside, if you don't mind."

The mother, who had introduced herself as Susan, acknowledged Kat's comment with a tilt of her head. After pressing a kiss against her son's forehead, she followed Kat out of the room.

"This won't take long," Kat assured her. "He'll be fine."

A couple of minutes later, it was done. Kat pulled the pictures up on her computer screen and scrutinized them closely. The left radius was broken clear through, but it wasn't displaced. A simple plaster cast to stabilize the arm for five or six weeks and the child would be as good as new. She found his mother waiting outside and gave her the news.

"I'll write up the report so it's available for the doctor who examined your son in the Emergency Department. He'll arrange for Caleb's arm to be set in plaster. I'll have someone take you both back there now."

"Thank you, Doctor. I appreciate everything you've done."

Kat smiled and waved off the thanks. "No problem. Just doing my job."

As the woman and her son were led away by one of the nursing staff, Kat returned to her computer. Quietly and efficiently, she reported her findings and then saved the file to the hard drive. The hospital's system allowed anyone on the medical staff to access patient records, including pathology and radiology results. Caleb's doctor would view the report and take the appropriate action.

Pushing back from her chair, Kat stood and stretched. She stifled a yawn. She'd been at work less than thirty minutes, but already she was tired. It served her right for staying out so late with Kevin on the night before an early shift, and then being persuaded to have sex when they got home. It had been well past midnight before she fell asleep.

The sound of her phone ringing snagged her attention and she paused to pull it out of her pocket.

Kevin.

Remembering their last conversation, she debated about whether to answer it. She was still annoyed at the way he'd dismissed her concerns. What she'd said was true. He didn't listen to her and when he did, he often didn't take her seriously.

The phone continued to ring. The screen with Kevin's name splashed across it taunted her and though she didn't want to speak with him she knew she should pick up. It wasn't like they'd had an all-out fight. Besides, she had to speak with him sooner or later. *Perhaps he was calling to apologize?* With a sigh, she answered the call.

"Hi, Kevin. What's up?"

"You're not going to believe this," he said by way of greeting.

Kat frowned. "What are you talking about?"

"Remember how Jake wanted to talk to me? Well, I just called him back. It's Shane. He's dead."

"*What?*" The word burst from Kat's lips. Her heart hammered.

"Yeah, and it gets worse. He was murdered. Shot twice in the back of the head."

Kat reeled from a second wave of shock. "*Murdered?* You're kidding?"

Kevin's tone was grim. "I'm afraid not."

"Where did it happen?"

"At the clinic. Jake's there now."

Kat closed her eyes against a wave of distress. Jake must have been at the clinic when he'd called Kevin that morning. No wonder he'd sounded so tense.

"How's he taking it?" she asked quietly.

"We're all shook up."

"Of course! I still can't believe it! Where are you?"

"I'm on my way to the clinic. The police are still going over the crime scene." He paused and then his voice turned rough with incredulity. "The crime scene. Christ, it's like something out of a movie or a scene from *CSI*."

Kat's chest tightened. She was filled with just as much shock and disbelief as Kevin. "Do the police have any idea who might have done it?" she asked.

"No, not at this stage, but they do know there was no forced entry. They're guessing whoever did this was someone Shane knew. Holly's certain she locked the door on her way out late yesterday afternoon, like she usually does even when one of us are still inside, so Shane must have let them in. The alarm was also off which makes sense if Shane was still there."

There was a pause and then Kevin sighed heavily in her ear. "Holly told the police she left at her usual time. Shane told her he was working late. She didn't think anything more of it until she arrived this morning."

Kat's breath halted as Kevin's words sunk in. "You mean, it was Holly who found him?"

"Yeah." Kevin's voice was grim.

Kat gasped. "Oh, my goodness! Poor Holly! I can't imagine how she must feel."

"You're right. It must have been awful."

"Has anyone told Shane's mother?" she asked softly.

"I'm not sure."

"She's going to be devastated. He's been taking care of her. She has multiple sclerosis. It's affected her vision and her ability to walk. She's almost totally dependent upon him."

"Hell," Kevin muttered. "I didn't know."

Kat frowned. "How couldn't you know? Shane told me about it months ago. The two of you worked together. I just assumed you knew."

"I didn't know," Kevin replied. "Shane never said anything to me about it. I guess he didn't want me to know."

Kat's phone began to vibrate, indicating another incoming call. She checked the screen and saw it was Jake.

"I'm sorry, Kevin. Jake's calling me. Probably about Shane. I'd better go."

"Yeah, all right. Tell him I'm not far away."

"I will."

Kat ended the call and then answered the next

one. "Jake, sorry. I was talking to Kevin. He'll be at the clinic soon."

"So, you know?" he asked.

"Yes. I can't believe it! Who would do such a thing? Shane was the nicest, sweetest man around. He wouldn't hurt anyone! I don't understand."

"You and me, both," Jake muttered.

His voice was dull and lifeless. Even over the phone, she sensed his devastation.

"Are you at work, Kat?" he asked quietly.

"Yes."

"I need to talk to you. Can I come over? The police just told me I'm no longer needed here."

The pleading in his voice tugged at her heart. He'd always been so big and tough and indomitable—in the physical *and* emotional sense. He was a highly respected oncologist who fought cancer head on. He didn't always win the battle, but his success rate was second to none.

He'd also been her good friend and confidante during the years she'd been with Kevin, often being a sounding board when she needed one. He was strong and dependable. And yet, the death of his friend and business partner had obviously left him shattered. At least, that's how he sounded. It was little wonder.

"Of course," she replied. "Barring an emergency, my next appointment isn't for another hour and a half. Tell Cindy to send you through. I'll be in my office."

"Thank you."

His relief was palpable. She compressed her lips

on a silent sigh. This wasn't going to be easy for any of them and there was a long road ahead filled with questions that might never be answered. With a murmured good-bye, she ended the call and waited.

Shortly thereafter, Jake stood in the doorway of her office. His face was drawn, his expression haggard. She couldn't imagine how hard the last couple of hours had been. To discover his friend had been murdered and then to be questioned by the police... That would be tough going for anyone.

"Hey," she said quietly and pushed away from her desk.

Without hesitation, she went to him and hugged him. At the thought of Shane, she was filled with a fresh surge of sadness.

"I'm so sorry, Jake. I can't believe it. Poor Shane!"

Jake stared down at her. "I can't believe it, either."

She moved closer, feeling the need to touch him, reassure him. She was a respectable five-foot-ten, but he towered above her. She'd always liked that about him. It made her feel safe.

She rested her fingers lightly on his arm, but he stepped away and swiped the back of his hand across his eyes.

"I just can't understand it, Kat! Why Shane? He didn't have any enemies. Nothing about this makes sense!"

"You're right," she replied. "Thoughts keep circling around inside my head. Shane was an all-round nice guy. I never heard him speak ill of anyone. Okay, so he might have spent a little too much time poring over finances, but he loved that kind of thing. Apart from medicine, we all knew numbers were his passion."

Jake nodded in agreement. "Yeah. When the three of us were first talking about going into private practice, Shane was the one who put up his hand to do the books. He was thrilled when Kevin and I agreed. Little did he know we were relieved he was so keen to do the accounts. Numbers have never been my strength."

She smiled softly. "I hear you."

A silence fell between them. Kat's mind filled with memories of Shane. A little while later, she spoke again. "Have you called his mother?"

Jake glanced down at her in surprise. "You know about his mother?"

"Yes. I'm not sure how the topic came up with him. I think I might have been talking about my parents back home in Maitland. Dad has advanced Alzheimer's. Mom cares for him at home. It's tough. Shane told me how his mother has MS. He's her primary caregiver."

Jake shook his head. "I didn't have a clue. We never talked about it. The long hours he put in at the hospital and at the clinic and then to go home to... The man was a saint." He cleared his throat. "I think the police are going to attend upon his mother and give her the news."

Kat thought about how the scene would unfold and blew out her breath on a heavy sigh. "Are you sure you and Kevin wouldn't rather do it? I never met her, but I could go along too, if you like."

"Yes, you're right. It would be better coming from us. I'll call Kevin and see if he's up to coming along."

"She's going to be devastated," Kat murmured.

"Like the rest of us," Jake muttered, clenching his fists.

Kat looked at him and once again, sympathy flooded through her. She'd known Shane, of course, but not as well as Kevin and Jake. She wondered how Shane's death would affect their business partnership and whether they'd even want to continue without him. It was almost like the three musketeers had become two. "What are you going to do?" she asked.

Jake sighed. "Holly cancelled all our appointments for the rest of the week. That gives us a little time to analyze the situation and consider future directions. At the moment, I can't imagine stepping foot inside those rooms again."

"Oh, Jake! Don't go making any rash decisions. Give it time. The three of you worked so hard for this. Shane wouldn't want you to throw it all away."

He shrugged and looked away. "I guess. I'll talk to Kevin. It's his business as much as mine but I'm not sure he'll want to continue either."

He sounded so forlorn. Kat's heart clenched with another wave of sympathy. Jake loved practicing medicine and helping as many people as he could. She was sure once he'd had time to come to terms with what had happened, he'd feel differently about continuing the clinic without Shane. In the meantime, she'd do all she could to help him.

She moved toward him and once again put her arms around him and hugged him tight. He pulled her close. He was so much taller than Kevin, and in that moment it felt a little strange, but it also felt warm and familiar, like she was where she was meant to be.

His broad chest was firm and muscular. She could feel the heat of him through her clothes. The scent of his cologne, spicy and masculine, tickled her nostrils. She tilted her head up and caught his gaze. Her heart stuttered at the pain she found there.

"I'm sorry, Jake. I'm so sorry. Poor Shane... I can't believe it..."

"*Shh*," he whispered and tightened his hold on her.

For another long moment, she relished the feel of him against her and then, realizing they were in an inappropriate embrace, gradually pulled away.

"Kat... I need..."

His plea was filled with desolation, like the bleakness that shadowed his eyes. She stared at him, caught between the desire to comfort him and doing the right thing. Before she could come to a decision, he lowered his head and kissed her.

His lips were whisper-soft and barely grazed her mouth, but even at the slight touch, fire exploded inside her. She stood perfectly still, shocked at the wonder of it and then he kissed her again. The second time was more forceful, as if a powerful surge of energy had been unleashed inside him. His firm lips moved over hers, seeking, searching, pleading—

With a gasp, she wrenched herself away. Flames spread across her face. She stared at him in embarrassment, her breath coming fast.

"Jake! What are you doing?"

From the tumultuous look in his green eyes, he was also feeling unbalanced. He pressed his fingers to his lips as if to stop the feeling. She wanted to touch hers, too. Her mouth felt like it was on fire and it wasn't the only part of her body that was burning.

A fresh wave of embarrassment washed over her. She couldn't believe they'd kissed. She was with Kevin. Even if it wasn't perfect, she was happy with Kevin. *Wasn't she?* Of course she was! She'd given him three years of her life.

Jake hadn't any right to kiss her. Then again, it had been a terrible day. He probably wasn't thinking straight. His friend had just been murdered. That was enough to set anyone awry. But had she really minded? And if not, why was that...?

The thoughts kept tumbling in her head. Straightening her clothing, she looked at him. "You shouldn't have done that."

He stared back at her, his expression now solemn. "No, I shouldn't have."

She opened her mouth to speak again, but he beat her to it.

"But I'm not sorry I did. I wish I could stay and

talk it through, but I have a lady waiting upstairs for surgery. It's the last thing I feel like doing, but I'm not going to let her down. I have to go."

Before she could utter a word, he shot her a look filled with an indefinable emotion that burned right through to her soul. Then, turning on his heel, he let himself out of the room.

On unsteady legs, Kat made her way back to her desk and collapsed in her chair, her thoughts in turmoil.

What just happened?

Chapter 3

How can you love someone and hate them at the same time? Even as a child, I couldn't work that out. I loved my mom and daddy, but I hated them, too. It hadn't always been like that. When I think really hard, I can remember a time when I loved both my parents unconditionally and they loved me that way, too. I didn't know what it was like to hate. Then my mom got hurt. She stayed all day and all night in her room and my daddy forgot I existed...

———

Jake let himself into the clinic and made his way down the now-silent and empty corridor to his office. The police and forensic technicians had left and Holly was nowhere to be seen. He presumed she'd taken the rest of the day off, like he'd urged her to do before he'd gone to see Kat.

Kat.

Flinging himself into his chair, he let out a groan of frustration and disbelief. As if the day hadn't already provided enough challenges, he'd gone and kissed his best friend's girl.

What the hell had he been thinking? That was the problem. He hadn't been thinking. At least, not with his head.

With the shock of Shane's death still weighing heavily in his gut, his only thought had been to seek comfort from someone he cared about, and no matter what he told himself in the harsh light of day, he cared about Katrina West. He cared about her a great deal. In fact, he'd been in love with her almost from the moment they'd met.

The memory of that night came back at him full force: the hum of the patrons who crowded the bar; the sight and sound of their laughter; the noise of the jukebox as it belted out tunes in the far corner of the room; the press of bodies as people found their groove on the small dance floor.

He and Kevin had pushed their way through the throng of people vying to get the bartender's attention and had found a space at the front. The bar was a favorite haunt for many young professionals who worked in and around the city, including a fair portion of the staff from the Sydney Harbour Hospital, situated nearby. The twenty-somethings that filled the place were well-paid, well-dressed and looking for a good time. He and Kevin fit in perfectly.

'Hey, see those girls over there?' Kevin had shouted over the din.

Jake turned in the direction his friend had indicated and spied a redhead and a blonde a little further down the bar. The redhead had her back to them. She was tall and curvy. When she spoke to the blonde, she flipped her long, wavy hair sideways and Jake was treated to a glimpse of the curve of one smooth cheek. Both women held cocktail glasses and were dressed in flimsy pieces of fabric that barely covered the essentials. The blonde laughed at something her companion said and the throaty sound of it hit Jake right in the gut. His body hardened instinctively.

He turned back to Kevin and said, 'Yeah, I see them.'

Kevin grinned at him. 'Let's toss for them.' And he'd given Jake a wink.

Jake shook his head in disgust. 'Are you kidding?'

Kevin pulled out a coin from the pocket of his pants. 'Your call, buddy.'

'Isn't this a bit juvenile? It's not like we're still in college,' Jake had replied dryly.

Kevin merely shrugged and seemed unperturbed. 'Who cares? We can't both hit on the blonde. I'm just trying to play fair. But from what I can tell, there will be no losers.'

Jake rolled his eyes, but grudgingly gave in. After all, it was harmless. It wasn't as if either of them were going to tell the girls how things had been decided, or whether the girls would even be interested in their company.

'Okay, fine.' He'd glanced again in the girls' direction. The blonde had moved slightly so that he now got a good look at her face. With wide green eyes, pert breasts and full lips generously coated in cherry-red lipstick, she looked just as delectable as her companion. Jake was filled with a sudden surge of anticipation.

'I'll call heads,' he said, his gaze remaining focused on the women. 'If I win, I get the blonde.'

Kevin tossed the coin in the air and slapped it down on the back of his hand. Lifting his hand slowly, he revealed the coin's surface to Jake's curious gaze.

'Heads it is.' Kevin had grinned and then punched him lightly in the arm. 'You lucky bastard. I guess the redhead is mine.'

Catching the eye of the bartender, they ordered drinks, and with glasses in hand they made their way to where the women stood. Within moments, they'd introduced themselves and it wasn't long before the conversation flowed almost as freely as the drinks. The blonde's name was Annaliese Brakenstock and she was a lab technician who worked at the Sydney Harbour Hospital. The redhead introduced herself as Katrina West and informed them she was a radiologist at the same hospital.

Jake knew immediately he'd made a mistake. Up close, the redhead was even more beautiful than he'd thought. Her voice was sweet and lyrical and she spoke in the cultured tones of someone who'd been fortunate enough to get a private school education. Beneath the lights from the bar, her hair shone more auburn than red and her skin glowed with good health and vitality. He was drawn to her, unable to look away, until Kevin cleared his throat and dug him surreptitiously in the ribs, reminding him that he'd chosen the blonde.

With an effort, Jake tore his gaze away and concentrated on the curvy blonde. Despite the strange connection he felt to her companion, Annaliese was bright and bubbly and kept him amused throughout the night with tales about the lab where she worked.

It was going on for one in the morning when they finally called it a night and the four of them agreed to head back to the apartment he rented with Kevin. He and Kevin had shared lodgings in college and when they both relocated from Brisbane to Sydney to take up positions at the hospital, it seemed only natural that they look for a place together.

With their promotions came better salaries and they'd managed to secure a lease on a comfortable two-bedroom unit that was not only within walking distance of their workplace, but also the harbor. Furnished with simple yet stylish pieces, it was a place Jake had been proud to call home.

That night, he deliberately avoided watching Kevin and Kat disappear into Kevin's bedroom and had concentrated all his efforts on enjoying all of what Annaliese had to offer. She was sweet and giving and surprisingly adventurous between the sheets, but every time he closed his eyes, it was Kat he saw spread-eagled before him, taking everything he had to give. Afterwards, he'd fallen asleep with Annaliese in his arms and Katrina West on his mind. It irritated him to think how quickly she'd infiltrated his being, like something about her touched him way down deep inside, all the way to his soul.

A few months later, he found the courage to break things off with Annaliese. Though she was funny and smart and pretty, he knew she wasn't the one. It hadn't been fair to lead her on, when all the time he'd yearned for another.

By then, Kat and Kevin were an item and it wasn't long before Kevin asked Jake if Kat could move in. Unable to bear the thought of cohabiting with the woman he'd unwittingly fallen in love with knowing she was sleeping with his best friend, he wished them all the happiness in the world and had packed up his things and moved out.

Three years had passed and as hard as he'd tried to forget about Kat West, it hadn't happened. After Annaliese, Jake had gone on a frenzy of dating, trying desperately to rid himself of his strange fixation on the one girl he couldn't have. Nothing had worked. He loved her as much now as he had in the beginning.

And now he'd kissed her.

The phone clipped to his belt rang, breaking through his somber thoughts and returning him to reality. His hand was smudged with black fingerprint dust. He must have come into contact with it when he'd opened the clinic's front door. The police had been thorough. Fingerprint powder covered every possible surface. They'd retrieved hundreds of prints. Not that Jake held out any hope it would help them find the killer. The place had been filled with patients the day before. Identifying one set that didn't belong would be nigh on impossible.

With a sigh, he forced the depressing thought from his mind and answered the phone. No doubt it was the theater staff informing him that they were almost ready for Robyn Bell. He needed to clear his head and concentrate on the job at hand. It was the very least he could do for his patient. Besides, performing the surgery would provide a welcome distraction to the tragedy that had occurred in the clinic and it could very well save a woman's life.

Detective Senior Sergeant Devlin Grayson of the City of Sydney Police Station shuffled the papers on his desk. The office was quiet. The work day was nearly over and yet he had precious little to show for his efforts to gather clues and information regarding the murder of a local doctor.

According to the preliminary autopsy report, Doctor Shane Cannington had died as a result of two gunshots to the back of the head. One of them would have sufficed. There were no signs of forced entry into the clinic or the room where Cannington had been found, nor were there any signs of a struggle. It appeared the victim had willingly allowed the perpetrator access and had been comfortable enough to turn his back on his murderer.

Detective Senior Sergeant Bryce Sutcliffe stretched his arms over his head and yawned. "What do you think?" he asked.

Devlin glanced across at his partner. "I have no proof, but my gut tells me it's an inside job by one of our vic's colleagues." He picked up a sheet of paper and read from it. "Either Jake Alexander or his buddy, Kevin Johnson."

Bryce nodded. "I agree. With no signs of forced entry and the receptionist certain she secured the lock, it's more likely someone he knew, or at least expected. Given that the last appointment that day was for five-thirty, I think we can rule out a disgruntled patient."

"The forensic pathologist put the time of death somewhere between nine o'clock and midnight. I can't imagine that our victim would open a door to a stranger during those hours," Devlin said.

"You're right," Bryce replied.

"Who's right?" Detective Sergeant Lachlan Coleridge asked as he entered the space and propped his hip against Devlin's desk.

Without waiting for a reply, Lachlan casually reached across Devlin's desk for a stick of gum that sat in a packet near his keyboard. He unwrapped it and popped it into his mouth while Devlin glared at him. Lachlan returned his stare, seemingly unperturbed by Devlin's scowl.

"We were talking about the murder of that doctor at the private clinic near the Sydney Harbour Hospital," Bryce said.

Lachlan nodded. "I heard about it on the police radio while I was out and about this afternoon. Nasty stuff. I called Ava right away and told her about it," he said, referring to his wife. "She was shocked. Her psychiatry consultation rooms are in the same building. She didn't know Doctor Cannington personally, but she knows of the clinic and the doctors who work there. All friendly, professional, nice... Things like this don't happen in places like that."

"Yeah," Bryce responded, straightening in his seat. "I spoke to my wife, too. Chanel knows all three of the doctors through work and she's also good friends with Katrina West."

"Who's Katrina West?" Lachlan asked, his jaws working the gum.

"She's the girlfriend of Kevin Johnson, one of the victim's business partners," Bryce replied. "She's also the sister of Isobel Donnelly. Sorry, Isobel Alexander, now. She remarried awhile back."

Devlin sat forward, suddenly alert. "Isobel Alexander?"

Bryce nodded. "Yes. She married Mason Alexander. She's a nurse at the same hospital where Chanel works. Kat works there, too."

"Is this Mason guy any relation to Jake Alexander?" Devlin asked.

Lachlan frowned and rejoined the conversation. "I think there might be a connection. I'm sure I remember Ava telling me something about the Alexander men. Apparently, they're the kind of tall, good-looking athletic men that make guys like us grind our teeth together at the unfairness of life. I'm not sure that they're brothers, but I have a feeling they're related somehow." He looked at Devlin. "Apart from Kat being the girlfriend of one of the doctors, where do she and Isobel Alexander come into your investigation?"

Devlin pulled the sheaf of papers toward him. "I don't know about Isobel Alexander or her husband, apart from the fact they might be related to one of my suspects. As for Katrina West, according to Kevin Johnson, she's his alibi."

Lachlan's expression was grim. "Just the kind of thing you want to be caught up in."

Bryce's expression also turned serious. "Chanel knows Kat pretty well. Doctor West is a respected radiologist. It'll be interesting to hear what my wife thinks when I tell her that her friend could be involved in a murder investigation."

"Let's not get ahead of ourselves. We don't know anything for certain, yet," Devlin interjected. "But it's interesting that the woman who can presumably verify Johnson's whereabouts at

the time of the murder is someone so well thought of."

"Except she's not exactly impartial," Lachlan murmured dryly.

"You're right," Devlin agreed, "but it's better than no alibi at all, which is the exact situation our other suspect is facing."

"You mean Jake Alexander," Bryce stated.

"Yes."

"Do we have a motive?" Lachlan asked.

"Not yet," Devlin replied. "We'll look at the

usual ones first: love and money. As far as we've been able to ascertain, Cannington was single and there's no ex-wife out to seek retribution. We're waiting for the partnership's financials. Our victim was the one who kept the accounts. It'll be interesting to see what we find."

"I've interviewed Cannington's mother," Bryce added. "I asked her for a list of her son's friends and acquaintances, but she couldn't come up with any names we didn't already have. Apparently he lived a quiet life. Went to work and home again and nothing much in between. Occasionally he went out for a drink with his colleagues. You're right about the lack of wives and girlfriends. When I asked the mother if he had either, she told me no. The only woman she mentioned was the receptionist, Holly Greenwood. She said Shane would talk about the girl every now and then, but the mother didn't think there was much to it and Shane never brought the woman home."

"Have you brought Alexander in for an interview?" Lachlan asked.

"Not yet, but I will," Devlin replied. "I'm going to check out Johnson's alibi first. If Katrina West doesn't confirm he was with her, I'll bring both suspects in. We'll play one against the other and see who turns on the other first."

Lachlan frowned. "You're that certain it's an inside job?"

Devlin compressed his lips and stared at his colleagues grimly. "I'm open to any possibilities, but at this stage, my gut is telling me yes. Two bullets to the back of the head? That's personal."

Kat pulled the pins from her hair and released the band that kept her bun firmly in place. Running her hand through the long strands to loosen them, she sighed in relief. It had been a long day full of shocks and emotional upheavals: her growing realization that Kevin might not be the one for her; discovering Shane's murder, followed by Jake's unexpected kiss...

She'd always known he had a soft spot for her, but he'd never said or done anything to make her uncomfortable. An awareness was just there, in the shadows—in the way he looked at her sometimes when he didn't think anyone was watching. It hadn't bothered her. In fact, she'd always thought it was kind of sweet. He was easy to talk to and spend time with, but she'd been in love with his best friend. She'd never believed it would progress any further.

But now he'd gone and kissed her and that kiss had turned everything on its head. Coming so soon after her quarrel with Kevin, she didn't know what to think. She'd dated Kevin for the better part of three years and she still enjoyed his company—well, most of the time. Occasionally he became tiresome, like when he sulked if he didn't get his own way. Like the week before when they'd gone to see a movie. That hadn't gone well. She grimaced at the memory.

Kevin had wanted to see the latest Jason Bourne action thriller, but he'd promised her they'd go and watch the new Harry Potter film. Kat loved all things Harry Potter. She'd read the books three times and seen all the movies. Kevin knew she was a fan. She'd even managed to secure tickets to the opening night. Then, out of the blue, he'd come home in a mood and had refused to go. In the end, she'd gone with her sister, Isobel. It was just lucky that Mason had been home that evening to look after her sister's kids.

Then there was last night. They were supposed to go out to dinner. It had been ages since they'd enjoyed some time out together, just the two of them. But first, Kevin had arrived late and then had proceeded to drink more than usual. At some point, he'd taken a phone call and soon after, they'd been joined by one of his friends. It was a man Kat hadn't met before, but he'd monopolized the conversation and had stayed until after their meal. On the way home, Kevin had been quiet and introspective while Kat drove.

Later, he'd turned to her in bed and demanded sex. She'd been surprised to feel his erection. After the amount of alcohol he'd consumed, she'd assumed he'd fall right to sleep. But it hadn't worked out like that and he'd taken her hard and fast from behind, his fingers digging into her hips.

Their sex had been rougher than usual and he'd slapped her on the butt several times. She'd told him to stop, but her words hadn't seemed to register. It was like he was in his own world, one that didn't include the real her. Eventually, he'd orgasmed and Kat had collapsed with relief. They hadn't spoken of it until that morning and she still wasn't satisfied the matter had been resolved. She could only hope that he'd be willing to listen properly the next time she brought it up.

With another sigh, she headed into the kitchen and began to prepare the evening meal. Setting a pan on the stove, she turned on the gas and waited for the pan to heat before adding a splash of oil. Next came some diced onions, garlic and salt. She had in mind to cook spaghetti bolognaise. It was simple and satisfying. No doubt Kevin had endured a difficult day, too. Dealing with the murder of his friend and colleague, answering questions from the police... It was a nightmare for all of them, but especially for Kevin...and Jake.

Jake.

What was she going to do about him? And what about his kiss? Should she tell Kevin? What if he took it the wrong way? They'd both known Jake had a soft spot for her. Kevin had only made reference to it earlier that day. But Jake had known her for three years and had never once made an inappropriate move. Kat was sure the kiss had been nothing more than him seeking solace after a traumatic event. His friend had just been found murdered. It was a reasonable enough response. Anyone could believe that, couldn't they?

Maybe not Kevin. He hadn't been himself lately and she wasn't exactly sure how he'd react. For months now, he'd been volatile and moody.

Sometimes distant, sometimes demanding. She'd begun to tiptoe around him without realizing it.

No doubt he was busy and stressed over work and she understood the pressure he was under as a doctor with not enough hours in the day, but it was still hard for her to accept the change in him and even more so when he refused to give her an explanation.

No. Kevin hadn't been himself at all for some time now and telling him about Jake's kiss was probably the last thing she should do. The way Kevin was acting, it might cause problems between the two friends and she certainly didn't want to do that when there was no real reason for concern, especially after what had happened to Shane...

Perhaps it would be better to say nothing? After all, it wasn't like Jake would ever kiss her again. He knew better than to mess up the friendship the three of them enjoyed and he'd never do anything to hurt Kevin. He loved him like a brother. They were family. All three of them. Four, including Shane. Except, now Shane was dead.

The sound of her phone ringing interrupted her thoughts. Reaching over, she picked it up from the counter. There was no caller ID on the screen. She frowned and debated for a few seconds about whether to answer it and then impatiently swiped the screen.

"Katrina West speaking, may I help you?"

"Doctor West. This is Detective Senior Sergeant Devlin Grayson from the City of Sydney Police Station. I was wondering if you would mind answering a few questions."

CHAPTER 4

Kat's heart skipped a beat and she blinked in surprise. *A detective? Why would he want to speak with her?* She'd known Shane, of course, but she knew nothing about his murder or the circumstances surrounding it. Still, she'd do whatever she could to help them solve the murder.

"Of course, Detective," she replied, giving the onion a stir.

"Good. I'm not sure if you've heard, but an ENT specialist by the name of Doctor Shane Cannington was murdered last evening."

Kat closed her eyes briefly against a surge of sadness. Hearing the news all over again brought the tragedy and pain rushing back. Still, the detective was waiting for her answer. She cleared her throat.

"Yes. I... I heard. My boyfriend called me and told me earlier."

"Your boyfriend. That would be Doctor Kevin Johnson, right?"

"Yes."

"Look, Doctor West, I appreciate it's after hours, but I'd like to conduct this interview in person. Are you able to come down to the station now?"

Kat eased her breath out on a sad sigh and turned off the stove. She wasn't sure how much use she could be to the investigation, but finding Shane's killer was a priority. Dinner would have to wait.

"I can be there in about fifteen minutes. Will I ask for you?"

"Yes. I'll meet you in the waiting area."

It was a little over twenty-five minutes later when Kat finally found a space in an underground parking lot and made her way to the police station. She smiled politely at the young constable who manned the front desk and asked for Detective Grayson. A short time later, a door at one end of the dreary gray waiting room opened and a tall, broad shouldered man with a weathered face that made him look older than he no doubt was, strode toward her.

"Doctor West, I'm Detective Devlin Grayson. We spoke on the phone."

Kat nodded in acknowledgement. "I'm sorry I'm a little late."

The detective merely inclined his head and she swallowed a rush of nerves. It was her first time inside a police station. There was something about the steel mesh and solid bars guarding the sparse windows that made her edgy. She was glad she was there only to answer questions and assist wherever she could and would then be free to leave.

The detective punched in numbers on a keypad

and opened the door he'd just come through. Kat followed him down a narrow corridor that was painted the same dismal gray as the reception area. Several desks covered in papers and files filled the smallish space. A handful of officers were also there—some in uniform and others in plain clothes. They sat behind the desks or lounged nearby, talking on the phone or to each other.

It was early evening and the phones were mostly silent. Kat could imagine how the room would be in the middle of the day, with the hustle and bustle of a busy office in full swing. Before she could ponder it further, the detective opened the door to an interview room and stood back for her to enter.

The room was sparsely furnished with a table and two chairs stained with years of human fear, anxiety and sweat. With her heart picking up its pace, she took a seat. The detective followed suit and dropped a blank legal pad on the desk in front of him. He went through the preliminaries, thanking her for coming in to answer a few questions, advising her the interview would be recorded and indicating a camera fixed to the wall, obtaining her personal details. Then he got straight to the point.

"Where were you last night, Doctor West?"

Kat started in surprise. "Am I...? Am I a suspect?" She laughed nervously.

The detective's expression remained grave. "Until we find out who did this, everyone's a suspect, Doctor. Now, can you tell me where you were last night?"

"Yes, of course, I was out to dinner with Kevin."

"That's Doctor Kevin Johnson, your boyfriend. Correct?"

"Correct."

The detective made a note on the pad in front of him and then looked back up at Kat. His gaze remained steady on hers. "Where did you go to dinner?"

"The Oyster Bar at Darling Harbour."

"What time did you get there?"

"I arrived about half-past eight. Kevin had called me earlier. He was running late. He asked me to go ahead and order for him. He joined me a bit after nine."

"So you arrived in separate cars?"

"Yes. No. That is, I drove to the restaurant. Kevin caught a cab."

"So, it was just the two of you?"

"For the first hour. Kevin took a phone call and we were joined by a friend of his. The man stayed for the duration of our dinner."

"What was his name?"

Kat frowned. "I can't recall his name."

"Was he a work colleague?"

"I don't think so. Kevin said he'd known the man in college. I understood they hadn't seen each other for quite a while."

The detective made more notes on the paper in front of him. Kat made a conscious effort to keep her hands still.

The detective looked up. "Did you all leave together?"

"Yes, although Kevin's friend went his own way as soon as we left the restaurant."

"What time was that?"

Kat frowned again, remembering back. "It was quite late. After eleven."

"Where did you go then?"

"We went home."

"You live together?"

"Yes."

Once again, the detective paused to scribble some notes. Kat counted the seconds until he was finished and did her best to keep calm. There was something about being interviewed in a police station that made her anxious.

"What time did you get home?" the detective asked.

Kat took a moment to recall the time. "It was going on for half-past eleven. I remember looking at the clock in the kitchen when I walked in."

"What did you do then?"

"We got ready for bed, Detective," she replied dryly. "It was late. I was tired. We both had to work the next morning."

"Did Kevin go anywhere after you arrived home?"

"No."

"Are you sure?" The detective's gaze narrowed on hers. His tone was insistent, as if he wanted to leave no room for speculation.

Kat thought back to the night before, to her and Kevin having sex. "Yes, Detective. I'm sure."

"Is it possible you fell asleep and Kevin went out again? As you said, it was late. You were tired. He might have left after you went to bed."

Kat gritted her teeth. *Did she have to spell it out*

for him? "What are you getting at, Detective? I've had a long and trying day. My boyfriend's business partner and friend has been murdered. I don't have time for games. Tell me what you want to know and let's get this over with."

If the detective was surprised by her outburst, he didn't show it. His expression remained grave, his tone remained steady and calm. She was sure they taught them in detective school how to maintain their self-control. She wished she'd had a few lessons. She drew in a surreptitious breath and eased it out between taut lips.

The detective continued to eye her steadily. "If you want me to be direct, Doctor West, I can be that. I can tell you this: The coroner's office has put Shane Cannington's time of death somewhere between nine and midnight last night. You say you got home at eleven-thirty. It's possible you went straight to bed and Kevin went out again. Your place isn't far from the hospital or the clinic where Shane was found. If he'd left shortly after your arrival home, it's possible he could have done it."

Kat's mouth gaped open in shock. She stared at the detective in disbelief. "You have to be kidding! You can't honestly believe Kevin would murder his best friend? He and Shane had known each other since high school. They went into business together. They were like brothers. There's no way Kevin could be responsible for this."

"I understand, Ms West. Nobody wants to believe someone they're close to could be capable of murder, but believe me, it happens more often than you think. I'm just doing my job, covering all the bases. Surely you understand that?"

Kat drew in a steadying breath and forced herself to calm down. The detective was only being thorough, like he said. He wasn't pointing fingers. At least, not yet.

"I appreciate your attention to detail, Detective," she replied in a much steadier voice. "But you can take Kevin Johnson off your list. We came home late and had sex. It was way past midnight before either of us fell asleep. Kevin fell asleep first. It took me much longer. There's no way he had the time, let alone the inclination, to do what you said."

The detective held her gaze for a long moment before lowering it to scrawl a few more notes. Kat sat in silence and did her best not to fidget. When he finally looked up, his gaze revealed nothing, but his voice was matter of fact.

"All right, Doctor. Thank you for your time. I appreciate you coming in. If I have any other questions, I'll be in touch. Enjoy the rest of your night."

Pushing back from the table, the detective strode over to the door and opened it. He moved to allow Kat to exit ahead of him. Once in the hallway, she dropped back and fell into step behind him, counting the minutes until she was once again outside the building. It was only then that she gave herself permission to relax.

Drawing in mouthfuls of air, she filled her lungs and forced herself to slow down her breathing. She stared down at her hands and noticed they were shaking. As if the reality of what had just happened had finally sunk in, she shook her head slowly back and forth, still filled with disbelief. Shane was dead and she'd just been interviewed by a detective in the bowels of a police station. It was like something out of a dream. Or a nightmare. She could only hope and pray they found the person responsible—and fast. That was the least Shane deserved.

———————

Devlin threw himself down in his chair and blew out his breath on a frustrated sigh.

"What's the matter?" Bryce asked.

Devlin looked up as his partner dropped a gym bag on the adjoining desk. Devlin's glance went to the windows that lined the wall on the far side of the room. Lights from nearby office buildings twinkled in the night. He sighed again. It was time to go home.

"I just interviewed Katrina West," he said.

"I take it she confirmed his alibi."

Devlin grimaced. "Yeah. They went to dinner. He got there about nine. They left at half-past eleven. Went home. Had sex. Slept the night through."

"What was the coroner's estimated time of death?"

"Somewhere between nine and midnight."

"So, provided she's telling the truth, Kevin Johnson's probably not our man," Bryce said.

Filled with a sudden surge of frustration, Devlin pushed away from his desk and strode to the whiteboard where he and Bryce had compiled the scant details they had of the investigation, including a very small list of possible suspects. He picked up the whiteboard eraser and scrubbed out Kevin Johnson's name, leaving a single name in blue marker.

Bryce stared at the board. He raised his eyebrows in silent query and nodded thoughtfully. "Jake Alexander it is."

Feeling grim, Devlin went back to his desk and picked up the phone. There would be no rest for him tonight.

––––––––––––

Jake looked around the four gray walls that surrounded him and did his best to shake off the sense of foreboding that had taken hold of him the moment he'd ended the call from Detective Grayson. Despite the fact the sun had set hours earlier and he'd come home after a long day in theater, he'd been summoned to the police station for further questioning and now sat alone in an interview room, waiting for the detective. Nothing about that scenario boded well.

If anything, the unwelcome invitation frustrated him. The police were wasting time. He couldn't believe they were seriously considering him a suspect. Meanwhile, the killer was free to cover his tracks and escape.

With a groan of impatience, Jake rested his elbows on the scarred and stained Formica desk and scrubbed his fingers through his hair. Up until that morning, his life had been traveling along just fine. His career was going strong; his business had been prospering. He had a nice place to live in a good part of town with enviable ocean views and friends he could count on to have his back. The only thing missing was a special someone to share his good fortune with.

Now it felt like his life was going off the rails. First with Shane's murder. It was obvious the police had no clue. They wouldn't have summoned him in for questioning if they had a better lead. Then there was the fact he'd kissed his best friend's girlfriend and didn't feel the slightest bit of remorse.

In fact, not only wasn't he sorry, he wanted to do it again, which was a bad idea—on so many levels. In the blink of an eye, his life had turned to shit and to think he'd actually been feeling good when he awoke that morning... *Had it really only been that morning?* It felt like a lifetime ago.

The door to the interview room opened, interrupting Jake's thoughts. The burly detective he'd spoken to at the clinic walked into the room, followed by another man Jake didn't recognize. He sat up straighter in his chair and braced himself for what was to come.

"This is Detective Bryce Sutcliffe," Grayson stated without fanfare. "He's assisting with the investigation."

Jake shot a half-smile of greeting in the stranger's direction in an effort to alleviate some of the tension. The newcomer remained stony faced. A fresh wave of nerves traveled up from Jake's gut. He was innocent and still his belly churned. He couldn't imagine what it would feel like to sit there, knowing he was guilty. Another surge of impatience went through him. He didn't have time for this crap. He cleared his throat.

"Ask your questions and be quick about it. I've had a long day. Shane Cannington was my friend and work colleague. We got on well. Business was thriving. I had no reason in the world to kill him and I'm telling you once again, it wasn't me. I didn't do this. Now, can you put this to rest and go about finding the person who *is* responsible?"

"That's not the way these thing work, Doctor Alexander," Grayson replied mildly. "We'll tell you when we've cleared you of suspicion. The sooner you answer our questions, the sooner we can determine who murdered Shane Cannington. Until then, everyone's a suspect. Got it?"

His gaze turned hard and bored into Jake's. The unspoken message was clear: Jake was on Grayson's turf and they were going to play by his rules. It was a game Jake couldn't win. Reluctantly, he lowered his gaze. Grayson pulled out a chair opposite and Sutcliffe did the same.

Grayson went through the preliminaries, including advising Jake that the interview was being recorded. The detective pointed to a camera that was fixed in the corner of one wall. Jake acknowledged it with a nod. After Jake stated his full name, address, date of birth and occupation, Grayson charged right in.

"Where were you last night, Doctor Alexander?"

"I worked at the hospital until ten. You can check with the staff."

"Oh, we will," Grayson assured him. "Where did you go after work?"

"I went home and went to bed."

"Straight away?" Sutcliffe asked.

"I heated up some leftovers. Watched some TV. Then went to bed."

"What time was that?"

Jake shrugged. "I didn't pay too much attention to the time, but I'm guessing it was around eleven, maybe half-past. Sometimes it takes me a little longer to unwind after a busy day saving lives." He narrowed his gaze on the two of them and waited for his veiled barb to hit its mark, but their expressions remained unchanged.

"Do you live alone?" Sutcliffe asked.

"Yes."

"In a complex?" Sutcliffe asked.

"Yes. I live on the seventh floor of a high rise."

"Did anyone see you arrive home?" Grayson asked.

"I don't know," Jake replied. "I drove into my parking space in the underground garage. I took the elevator up to my floor."

"Did you see anyone along the way?" Sutcliffe asked.

"No."

Grayson leaned forward with his elbows on the table that separated them. "So what you're saying is that we only have your word on this. Other than the staff at the hospital who can vouch for the fact you were there until ten, you have no one who can say where you were or who you were with from the hours between ten last night and when you arrived at the clinic this morning. Is that correct?"

Jake returned the man's hard gaze and forced himself to remain calm. He had nothing to hide. "Yes."

Grayson shot him a look of disbelief and shook his head. He scribbled something on the notepad in front of him. Jake clenched his fists in an effort to retain his composure. He was sure the detective was trying to rattle him. On a guilty man, it might have worked. Jake fixed his gaze on the table.

"How long have you been in business with Shane Cannington?"

The question came from Sutcliffe. Jake directed his attention to the other detective.

"Shane and I went into partnership two years ago, along with Kevin Johnson. I've known both men since college. We went through med school together."

Grayson stared at him. "Did you and Shane ever fight about the business?"

Jake's initial instinct was to issue a denial, but then he paused. Knowing how easily words could be misconstrued, he chose them with care.

"We had our disagreements from time to time. Who doesn't? But I wouldn't term it fighting."

Grayson's gaze turned feral. "That's interesting because early this morning, Holly Greenwood told me she heard the two of you doing just that. In fact, she was the one who used the term 'fighting.' What do you say to that, Doctor Alexander?"

Jake bit down hard on his lip and swallowed a curse. He remembered the argument Holly referred to. It had only happened a few days ago. He could see how the police might be interested in knowing more about it. Of all the times to get into a disagreement with his business partner…

"You do know Holly, don't you, Doctor?" Grayson asked, his tone pointed.

Jake held his gaze. "Yes of course. I was the one who employed her."

"So you can vouch for her character?" Grayson persisted.

"Yes."

Grayson's gaze narrowed. "So was she lying when she told me about a fight she witnessed between you and Shane Cannington?"

Jake compressed his lips and forced his anger down. "No, she wasn't lying. Shane and I… There was an argument."

"When?"

"Last week."

"What was it about, Doctor Alexander?" Sutcliffe asked, poised to take notes.

Jake drew in a deep breath and let it out slowly. He remembered the disagreement as clear as day. It seemed pointless now.

"Doctor, answer the question," Grayson barked.

"I wanted to expand the practice."

"I take it Shane was reluctant to go along with it," Sutcliffe replied.

Jake grimaced. "Yes."

Grayson leaned forward. "It must have made you angry when Shane refused to support your dreams."

Jake held his gaze, refusing to flinch. "Yes, of course it did, but that doesn't make me a murderer."

Grayson shot him a sly smile. "None of us know what we're capable of until we're put under pressure, Doctor. I'm sure you know that."

Once again, anger stirred in Jake's gut. "I didn't kill Shane, Detective," he managed through gritted teeth. "I'm willing to take a polygraph to prove it."

The detective taunted him with his eyes. "All in good time, Doctor, and for the record, I didn't say you did."

All of a sudden, Jake's control snapped. He glared at the officers who were seated across from him.

"In case you missed it, I'll say it again. I'm not a murderer and I didn't kill Shane Cannington. You're wasting precious time giving the idea even a moment's consideration. The real killer is making his getaway, covering his tracks, going about his business while you two sit there interrogating me into a confession. Well, just so you know, it's not going to work because I have the truth on my side."

Jake paused, his breath coming fast, but he wasn't finished. "This whole interview is bullshit and you know it. Okay, I had an argument with my work colleague. Big deal. It doesn't make me a murderer."

"No," Grayson replied coldly. "But it does give you a possible motive."

"If you really believe that, why would I stop at Shane? Kevin was against the idea of expansion, too. Having just one of them dead wasn't going to serve any purpose."

"Perhaps you got cold feet after the first one?" Grayson suggested, his tone deceptively mild. "Most people don't realize how difficult it is to take someone else's life in cold blood. It takes a certain kind of person to pull it off. Doing it twice is even more difficult. Then again, maybe you *are* that cold. Maybe you're just biding your time to bring about Doctor Kevin Johnson's end, too. Who knows? All I know is that the evidence points to the fact Shane Cannington was murdered by someone he knew, possibly even someone in his workplace. Your friend's murderer arrived at the clinic and he either let himself in with a key or Cannington unlocked the door. Doctor Johnson's alibi checks out. Right now, that just leaves you."

Jake gritted his teeth and silently counted to ten. He stared at Grayson. "I didn't do it."

Grayson scoffed and shook his head. Jake fought against the urge to wipe the smug expression off the man's face.

"Like I said, Doctor Alexander, all the evidence points to it being an inside job. There was no forced entry. Holly Greenwood confirmed she locked the door on her way out at six o'clock. She also told us Shane had been working back late, but you knew that, didn't you? You'd spoken to him earlier that evening."

Jake wondered how the detective had come by his information and then thought of Holly. She'd probably told the police he'd called. She'd answered the phone when he rang. He conceded the answer.

"Yes. I phoned Shane. So what? He's my business partner and a friend. We talk all the time."

"Yes, but this time it was on the same evening he wound up with two bullets in the back of his head," Grayson snarled.

Jake held his stare. "I'm not the only one with access to those rooms."

"All right, Doctor," Grayson replied, "who else has a key?"

"The cleaning service has a key and so does the owner of the building and of course, Holly. I think that's it. As a security measure, the three of us agreed not to give keys out to anyone unless they were employed by the clinic."

"Were the cleaning crew there last night?" Sutcliffe asked.

Jake shook his head. "No. They come Mondays and Thursdays."

"Have you ever had a problem with any of the cleaners?" Grayson asked.

"No. In fact, I've never met them. They usually come early in the morning, before any of us arrive. I'm not sure that Shane and Kevin would know them, either."

"What about the owner of the building?" Sutcliffe asked. "Does he have a beef with any of you?"

"Not that I know of. We've been there a couple of years. We always pay our rent on time. Shane made sure of that. I don't think we've seen the man since the day we signed the lease."

Grayson's frown darkened. He stared at Jake. "So you don't think it could be the cleaners or the owner. That leaves Kevin Johnson and your secretary. I've already told you Johnson has an alibi. Are you suggesting it's fake?"

Jake clenched his fists and fought to hold onto his temper. "Of course I'm not suggesting that and there's no way this was done by Kevin. He and Shane have been friends since high school. They knew each other years before I met either of them."

Grayson gaze narrowed. "Then perhaps you think your secretary should take the blame?"

It took all of Jake's self-control to hold onto his temper. He clenched his jaw tight and stared the detective down.

"Holly's a twenty-two-year-old dreamer," he said between gritted teeth. "You've seen her. She looks like a Barbie doll. But underneath those fake eyelashes and lip gloss, she has a keen intelligence and she has enough skill and competence to keep her job. She's been with us since we opened. I don't know much about her personal life, but I do know she's a sweet kid. There's no way she'd be capable of doing something like this. Besides, I was there not long after she found Shane. She was beyond distraught. You were there, too. You saw her. As soon as you were finished with her, I urged her to go home."

Grayson sat back. An insincere smile—almost a smirk—played around his lips. "So, that's it, then," he said, his voice deceptively casual. "You've just discounted everyone on our list. I guess it's a good thing we're the ones in charge of finding the person who did this." He leaned forward, his face inches from Jake's. "Make no mistake, Doctor. We're both extremely good at our jobs."

Jake refused to flinch. He met the Detective's stare head-on. "I'm very glad to hear it."

Chapter 5

Dear Diary,

I thought with Shane gone things would be different—I would be different. I thought I'd feel relieved my problem was solved. I could go forward, get on with my life. But it hasn't worked out that way. He was my friend. The only true friend I had. I miss him.

What have I done? I didn't think things could get worse, but right now, I feel so awful, it feels like I'll never be happy again. Oh, Shane! I'm sorry! So sorry! What have I done?

Kevin Johnson climbed the three flights of stairs that led from the foyer of his building to the apartment he shared with Kat. The paint had begun to peel off the walls in the stairwell and there was a distinct smell of mold in the air, but that didn't matter so much. Yes, the building was small and ancient when compared to the taller, glitzier, newer condos that had sprung up around it, but none of those could outdo the incredible view of the harbor he enjoyed from his living room window.

Almost unobstructed, he could stare at the majestic sweep of iron and steel that made up the Harbour Bridge and imagine the hundreds of men who'd toiled in the hot sun for more than eight years to build it. Sixteen lives had been lost, either on the job or from injuries sustained during the construction of what was colloquially known as "the coat hanger." Most of the deaths were caused by unsafe work practices. The work, health and safety laws weren't like they were these days. Interestingly, only two of the sixteen actually died as the result of falls.

It still surprised Kevin every time he thought about the vagaries of life. He'd been a doctor for more than five years and he'd seen his fair share of injury and death. Not so much now that he specialized in plastic surgery, but before then, during his training, he'd seen enough.

He saw people who suffered for a long time with terminal illnesses, as well as those who had been struck down by fate. Like the twenty-one-year-old student who'd been on her way to school when a brick wall collapsed on top of her, killing her instantly. One moment she'd been like everyone else, beginning her day, making the daily commute. The next, she was dead.

Just like Shane.

It had been a shit of a day.

Kevin hadn't told the police that he'd also been working late in the clinic the previous evening. He wasn't sure why he hadn't offered up the information, but so far, nobody had asked him. It was probably because of his preoccupation with Vlad and the Russian's increasing demands—and the need to alleviate any suspicion. He couldn't afford to have the police looking at him too closely.

But the truth was, he'd finished up with his last patient at the clinic, caught up on his paperwork and had then dropped by Shane's office for a chat. Little did he know that would be the last time he'd see his buddy alive. He'd left for dinner shortly before nine and had enjoyed a pleasant hour with Kat until Vlad had shown up.

Still, he'd managed to get through dinner without raising Kat's suspicions and had made it into bed before midnight. All that time Shane had been confronting his killer. It felt weird knowing Kevin had been fucking his girlfriend while his best mate was taking two bullets to the head.

Still, there was nothing he could do about it now. Shane was dead. All he could hope was that the cops caught the person responsible. Thank God he had an alibi. The last thing he needed was to take heat from over-zealous law enforcement officers.

Fitting the key to the lock on his front door, he pushed open the wooden panel with his shoulder and stepped inside. Tossing his keys on the hall table and setting his briefcase down nearby, he pulled off his jacket and loosened his tie before walking down the short corridor to the living room. It was empty.

He frowned. It was going on for nine. Kat should be home. He should have called her and told her he was going to be late. From the smell of fried onion and tomato wafting from the direction of the kitchen, she'd cooked. He hoped she wasn't pissed.

"Kat! I'm home!" he called and continued on into the kitchen.

He spied her standing by the stove and a burst of relief went through him. After their argument that morning and the subsequent awful events of the day, he wasn't sure what mood she'd be in. For a brief moment, the thought had flashed through his mind that she might have left for good. But no, she was here, in his kitchen, where she belonged. All was right with the world.

She looked up briefly at his entry and then returned her attention to the stove. His gaze wandered over the pale blue blouse and the short pencil skirt she'd been wearing that morning. She reached up for a packet of herbs in the cupboard overhead. The silky fabric of her blouse stretched tight across her breasts.

His gaze moved lower and he noticed how well the dark fabric of her skirt hugged the smooth curve of her ass. His gut tightened and blood rushed to his groin. *God, she was beautiful.*

Her long wavy hair was loose and messy, like she'd not long ago released it from its usual neat bun. He was reminded of the night before, when her hair had been spread across his pillow and then later, when it had hung low around her face while she moved back and forth in time with his thrusts. He couldn't wait to fuck her again, but not right now. Something was up. She hadn't looked at him for more than a few seconds since he'd arrived.

"Something smells good," he said and moved closer. He leaned in to kiss her, but she turned away and his lips fell on air. He frowned. "What's the matter?"

She shrugged and began to wash her hands in the sink. "Nothing. I-I was thinking about Shane. The whole thing is just terrible."

Her voice hitched. All at once, he understood. Of course she was upset about Shane. They all were. He was secretly relieved her evasiveness wasn't residual anger from their tiff that morning.

He reached for her. She resisted momentarily, but then relaxed against him. His arms went around her shoulders and he pulled her close.

"It's been a tough day," he murmured against the softness of her hair. "I'm as shocked as you. When Jake told me..." He shook his head. "I mean... Shane... It's unbelievable. I can't imagine who could have done such a thing."

"You're right," she replied, her voice muffled against his shirt. "I've been wondering about it all day. The police don't seem to have a clue."

Kevin stilled. Loosening his hold on her, he set her slightly away from him. "The police? Have you been talking to them?"

"Yes. They asked me to come down to the station. I gave a statement to a Detective

Grayson a little while ago. He said he was in charge of the investigation. They wanted to know where you'd been last night."

He stared down at her and his heart skipped a beat. He had no reason to suspect Kat wouldn't tell the truth, but still... His friend and work colleague had been murdered and though the police didn't yet know it, he'd been one of the last people to see Shane alive. His alibi needed to be watertight. Besides, Vlad had joined them for dinner. There was no way he wanted the police to access that information.

"What did you say?" he asked, keeping his voice casual.

"I told them the truth, of course," she said, pulling away slightly and frowning. "That we were out to dinner, came home and went to bed. What else would I say?"

He forced a smile and breathed a surreptitious sigh of relief. "Nothing. Of course you'd tell the truth. Neither of us have anything to hide."

"That's what I told the detective. Anyway, he gave me his number in case I think of anything else that might help with the investigation."

"Let's hope they find the culprit. Poor Shane! And poor you! I'm sorry you had to speak with the police. They also talked with me this morning, when I got to the clinic. I told them I was with you last night. I guess they were just following up. Did they ask you anything else?"

"Just where we went to dinner and if it was just the two of us. I told them about your friend who joined us half-way through, but of course, I couldn't recall his name. Did you even introduce us? I don't think so."

Kevin's heart skipped a beat and then thumped hard against the wall of his chest. Once again, he forced himself to remain calm and was relieved when his voice came out sounding normal.

"Of course I did!" he lied. "He's an old college friend. I haven't seen him for ages. When he called and told me he was in the neighborhood and asked if we could get together, I agreed. I didn't think you'd mind."

She gave him a tight smile and he could tell she was still upset. She wasn't the only one. He'd been livid when Vlad had called him and forced his way onto their table. Not that he could tell Kat that. But now she'd mentioned his unwelcome dinner guest to the police. He only hoped they didn't follow up on the unnamed friend.

Oblivious to his anxious thoughts, Kat tightened her arms about his waist and once again buried her face against his shirt. "I still can't believe he's gone!" she murmured. "Shane was the sweetest guy there was! And his poor mother! Who's going to care for her now?"

Kevin bit his lip. The thought of Shane's mother not only losing her son, but also her primary caregiver seemed like a double blow. He silently vowed to talk to Jake about providing the woman with some financial assistance.

"I'm sure she'll be fine," he said in an effort to reassure himself as much as Kat. "MS doesn't have to be a death sentence and Shane would have made sure she was under the care of the best neurologist." Another thought struck him. "Did Jake know?"

A blush stained the clear skin of Kat's cheeks. She dropped her gaze and turned her face away. Kevin stared at her in bemusement. *What the hell had he said to make her so uncomfortable?*

"Um… I think so," she muttered.

Her gaze remained firmly fixed on a point somewhere behind him. She dropped her arms to her sides and tried to wriggle out of his grasp. He tightened his hold. *What the hell was going on?*

"What's the matter, Kat? You're acting weird."

"No, I'm not."

She still wouldn't meet his gaze and made another attempt to escape him. He grasped her chin with his fingers and forced her head around to face him. "Yes, you are. I get that this has been a tough day on both of us, but there's something more going on. I can tell. Is this about that stupid argument we had this morning? I already told you, I'm sorry. Now, why don't you spit it out so we can deal with it?"

She remained silent a moment longer. Once again, she made an attempt to extricate herself from his grasp and this time, he let her. She stepped away, wrapping her arms across her chest as she did so.

His consternation grew and with it, a sense of foreboding. *Did she suspect something? Had she said more to the detective than what she'd told him?* He needed to know. He forced a casual tone.

"Talk to me, Kat. What's going on?"

"Jake kissed me."

The words hung in the air between them. Kat stared at him, her eyes huge, as if unsure how he might react. Kevin blinked. It was the last thing he'd expected her to say.

"What?"

Kat turned away, holding her head in her hands. "I'm sorry, Kevin. I didn't mean it. It just happened."

Relief that her anxiety had nothing to do with the police was quickly replaced by the knowledge that one of his close friends had kissed his girlfriend. Her words echoed in his mind. Like a flicker of a cigarette lighter, anger ignited in his gut. He leveled her with his gaze.

"Where?"

"At work. In my office."

"Did you kiss him back?"

"No. Yes. Oh, God. I don't know."

He stared at her in disbelief. "You're fucking kidding! You don't *know*? How does that work? You either kissed him, or you didn't."

Tears sparkled in Kat's eyes. At any other time, they might have moved him, but not this time.

"I'm sorry, Kevin!" she cried. "It's been a terrible day! It was a reaction to the shocking news. Jake came to me, upset. Like I said, it just happened."

Kevin's anger found its head. "Bullshit. That kind of thing doesn't just happen! He's had the hots for you ever since we met. Too bad for him, he lost the toss."

Kat frowned in confusion. "What are you talking about?"

Kevin cursed under his breath. He'd forgotten

she didn't know anything about what had gone on just before they met. Still, it hardly mattered now. She'd just kissed his best friend. All of a sudden he felt the urge to hurt her like she'd just hurt him.

"I can't believe I never mentioned it," he replied with a mocking smile. "The good old coin toss. Jake called heads and got the blonde. I can't even remember her name."

Kat stared at him, her face pale. The tears had dried on her cheeks. "Her name was Annaliese," she said coldly. "Do you mean to tell me, you and Jake tossed a coin over us?"

"Yeah," he goaded. "It was fun at the time."

Color stained Kat's cheeks and her eyes flashed with anger. Her hands went to her hips and her chin lifted. She stared at Kevin in defiance. "Is that what this has been for you? A *game*?"

"No, of course not," he replied, backpedaling. "We were young and stupid. We were just having a little fun."

Her steel-eyed gaze didn't soften. "It was three years ago, Kevin. Stupid, yes, but hardly young. In case you've forgotten, you're nearly thirty." She turned away, as if unable to stand the sight of him.

He stepped forward, now more than a little concerned. This was getting way off track. They were arguing about *her* and the fact she'd kissed his best friend. This wasn't about him and some childish prank. He opened his mouth to further his line of argument, but she spun on her heel and glared at him again.

"That's your problem, Kevin," she said, pointing

a finger at him accusingly. "Everything's a game to you. Well, guess what? We're adults. Life doesn't revolve around a coin toss." Her voice rose. "Your friend was *murdered* last night. Don't you even *care* about that?"

"Of course I care!" he exclaimed, feeling affronted. *Did she think she was the only one who was shocked and saddened over Shane's unexpected and violent death?* All of a sudden, the anger went out of him. Arguing was getting them nowhere. He drew in a deep breath and eased it out.

"Look, sugar. I'm sorry. It's been a tough day. I shouldn't have said anything. You just caught me off guard."

As if she stood on at a crossroads debating about which way to go, Kat said nothing for a long moment. Kevin held his breath. He didn't want to argue with her. Not after all that had happened. For months, his life had been going to shit. All he wanted was to kiss her and hold her close and tell her how much he loved her.

He watched her closely. He could almost pinpoint the moment she came to a decision. Some of the tension went out of her body. He breathed a silent sigh of relief.

"I'm sorry, too," she said quietly. "The kiss shouldn't have happened, but...the truth is..." She looked up at him, lifting her chin. The defiance was back in her eyes. He braced himself.

"The truth is," she repeated. "I'm not sorry it happened."

Just like that, his anger reignited. A fresh wave

of shock reverberated along his spine, followed quickly by panic. "What the hell are you talking about?" he shouted, unable to help himself.

"I think we should take a break, Kevin. It's probably not the best time to be having this discussion, but this has been building up for a while. It's not just Jake. It's lots of other things."

Her tone remained soft and controlled. The fact she could stay calm after dropping such a bombshell only served to infuriate him further. "Like what?" he yelled, the panic now surging through his veins.

"Like last night," she replied. "The rough sex. It scared me. It was like I wasn't even there, like I was just a warm body to be used and abused. And now I find out you won me in a coin toss. I assume if Jake had called tails, *you* would have been the one to go home with Annaliese."

Her tone had turned colder, but not as cold as the look of disgust in her eyes. His heart thudded. He was filled with desperation that bordered on fear. She couldn't break up with him. He wouldn't let her. He loved her.

"I'm sorry, Kat," he said, trying hard to get a hold on his emotions. "I don't know what you want me to say. Okay, Jake and I did a stupid coin toss, but that was only the way we met. As soon as I spoke with you, I knew you were the one for me. It's been that way for the past three years. We've been good together. You can't throw all that away."

She remained unmoved and his desperation increased.

"I'm sorry about the way I fu—" He cursed and

tried again. "I'm sorry about last night. I guess I wasn't thinking. It was late and I'd had too much to drink. I got a little carried away. It was my fault and I'm sorry. It won't happen again. As for Jake, I... I don't care that you kissed him, or that he kissed you, okay? I understand. It's been a rough day for all of us, finding out about Shane, being interviewed by the police. I get it. It happened, but it didn't mean anything and it won't happen again, right?"

She looked at him with something akin to pity and his temper once again flared to life. He clenched his jaw and gritted his teeth and forced the angry words back down. Kat stood her ground and her arms remained firmly crossed over her chest.

"I'm going to stay with my sister for a while, until I can think things through. Too much has happened today for me to think clearly about any of this." She turned away and he rushed over to her and took her by the arms.

"Please, Kat! Don't do this! Like you said, you're not thinking clearly. Let's go to bed. I promise I won't do anything." He shook her, trying to make her see.

"Let me go, Kevin. Don't make this any harder than it is."

He dropped his hands and stepped away, willing to do whatever she asked, if she'd only stay. He tried again. "Please, Kat. Don't leave me. I love you!"

Her expression remained closed. "And I love you, too, but I'm not sure it's enough anymore. I'm sorry, Kevin. I have to take some time to work things through."

Turning away, she headed for the bedroom. Stunned into silence, he tried hard to slow his breathing and get his pounding heartbeat under control. A few minutes later, she returned with a suitcase in her hand.

"I'll come back for the rest another time. See you round, Kevin," she said softly and then headed toward the front door. He took off after her.

"Kat! Please! Stay! Let's talk things through. You can't do this to me!" He heard the desperation in his voice and hated himself for it, but he was helpless to stop it. She couldn't leave him. She couldn't!

To his consternation, her steps didn't falter. She reached the door and turned the knob and then strode into the hallway. Without looking back, she pulled the door closed behind her. The click of the latch echoed in the silence and felt like a bullet lodging itself in his heart. He gasped from the pain of it and then once again succumbed to anger. Anger was good. Anger was safe. Anger would keep him from thinking about what had just happened.

She'd left him. He cursed long and viciously. With a howl of fury that was laced with hurt and disbelief, he spun on his heel. Bending at the waist and heedless of the neighbors, he screamed out his pain. With his anger filling every pore of his body, he stood and pulled back with his fist and then drove it through the wall.

The plasterboard splintered with a satisfying

crack. Blood oozed from a cut on his hand. He stared down at it and felt nothing.

Incredulous, he lifted his fist and drove it through the wall again. As he lifted his hand for a third time he pulled up short. The sound of his phone ringing broke through the fog of anger that clouded his mind. He gasped and sobbed and sucked in air in a desperate attempt to regain control. Tugging the phone out of his pocket, he checked the screen.

Vladimir.

His gut clenched. He was so tempted to ignore it, but Vlad knew he was home. They'd discussed his availability only the night before. Dragging in another calming breath, he answered the call.

"Vlad, now isn't a good time."

"It never is with you, Kevin," the rough, heavily accented voice replied.

Panic surged through him. There was no way he could deal with Vlad right now. His friend had been murdered. The love of his life had just walked out on him. Everything was going to shit. His life was falling apart before his very eyes. Vlad would have to wait.

"No, I mean it, Vlad. I'm having some…personal difficulties. I need more time."

"Yes, I gathered," came the dry reply. "The cops were crawling all over your office this morning. What the hell was that all about?"

Kevin frowned. *Why the hell had Vlad been in the vicinity of the clinic?* He pushed the question aside. There were far more important things to worry about—

"Where's my shipment?"

The abrupt question reverberated in Kevin's head. Once again, his gut clenched with fear. "It's coming, Vlad. Soon, I promise."

"You're a week late."

"I know. I'm sorry. You'll get it. It's just that—"

"What?" The single word was bitten off.

Kevin swallowed nervously. "The police. Like you said. They're everywhere. I... I need to lie low for a while. Just until everything settles down."

"I'll give you another week. No more. Don't fuck with me, Kevin. I'm warning you, be careful, or you might end up with a couple of bullets in the back of your head—just like your friend." The man's evil laughter echoed in Kevin's head. The phone went dead.

Kevin's feet went out from under him and he slowly slid down the wall. Unmindful of his expensive suit pants, he collapsed in a heap on the floor. He could barely remember what his life had been like before he'd succumbed to the call of the money his little side business offered. The irony was, he didn't need the money. Not really. The practice was going well. It would only continue to grow. The only reason he'd argued with Jake about expansion was because at the moment, he was too busy with his other sideline to give the proper attention to increasing his patient load. In the future, maybe, when that future didn't include Vlad.

At the reminder of the Russian heavyweight, Kevin shuddered. The man meant what he'd said. He wasn't to be fucked with. Kevin had seen firsthand how the man dealt with insubordinates who didn't come through with the goods. It had happened at their very first meeting.

If only Kevin's path hadn't crossed with Albina Petrov... But how was he to know the beautiful woman who'd come to see him about a boob job was connected to the Russian mafia? He'd been approached by her husband, Anatoly Petrov, right after the surgery was completed. The man paid the substantial medical fees with hundred dollar bills and then in an offhand manner raised the idea of Kevin supplying certain people in Petrov's circle with prescription drugs.

At first, Kevin had been shocked at the idea. He was an upstanding citizen. He always paid his taxes on time. He'd been raised to follow the rules and he lived his life accordingly. The closest he'd come to breaking the law was a traffic ticket three years earlier, when he'd been running late for an appointment and the only available spot had been in a disabled parking space.

He'd felt terrible about doing it and had willingly paid the fine. It was the least he deserved. The next thing, he found himself contemplating supplying prescription drugs illegally to a dug boss. It was unthinkable. And yet, after being given the weekend to think about it, he'd realized the money he could make with little or no risk and he could keep on doing what he loved—practicing medicine. *What could it hurt?*

It was Anatoly who then introduced Kevin to Vladimir Mikolaev. At the time, though he'd been decently intimidated by the burly Russian boss, he'd continued to reassure himself that he could cease his dealings with the man whenever he liked. He'd play the game long enough to acquire a handy, tax-free nest egg and then he'd bid the Russians a hasty farewell.

Only, it hadn't turned out that way. He'd been supplying codeine for the better part of six months and though he'd been paid well for his efforts, Vladimir's demands for more and more product in much shorter time frames had Kevin feeling increasingly anxious. Like now, when his usual source had let him down and he didn't have enough to fulfill the deal. The very thought of what Vlad might do to him if he didn't come through filled him with fear.

And it wasn't only him who was suffering. It had affected his relationship with Kat, too. He didn't deceive himself into thinking her call for time-out had come about purely because of what had happened the night before. Things hadn't been good between them for some time.

Vlad's strident demands had left Kevin irritable and short-tempered and he was ashamed enough to admit that it was Kat who'd borne the brunt of his bad moods. His decision to dip his toe into waters filled with teeth-gnashing drug dealers had not only fucked up his life, but it had also ruined his relationship with the woman he loved.

A fresh wave of apprehension surged through him and he bent his head low and rested it on his knees. The weight of what he'd gotten himself into was almost too much to bear. It was time to formulate an escape plan. He'd do everything he could to win Kat back and this time, he wouldn't fuck things up.

He'd be the Kevin of old, the man who went to work, played by the rules—the man Kat had fallen in love with. As soon as this delivery was finalized, he'd tell Vlad he was opting out. The man would have to find another sucker to supply him with what he needed.

Kevin was done.

CHAPTER 6

Kat lifted the cup of hot sweet tea her sister, Isobel Alexander, had pressed upon her and took a grateful sip. She'd arrived on Isobel and Mason's doorstep in a flurry of tears less than an hour earlier, still shocked at the sudden turn of events. Though that afternoon she'd been analyzing her relationship, she hadn't dreamed she'd bring it to an end like that. But as the conversation had progressed she discovered Kevin could just as easily have gone home with her friend that night they met. That, coupled with her other concerns… Enough was enough. It had been a day filled with shocks, and not the least, her kiss with Jake. She snuck a look at her sister's husband—Jake's cousin—and couldn't prevent a blush.

Isobel and Mason sat across from her on the matching two-seater, identical expressions of curiosity on their faces. Kat swallowed a sigh. The moment of reckoning had come. Isobel led the way.

"What's going on, Kat?"

"What do you mean?" she asked, trying to delay the inevitable.

"Kat..."

Kat heard the warning in her sister's voice. She compressed her lips on a grimace. "Okay, okay. I do owe you an explanation."

"You think?" her sister deadpanned. "You turn up here after eleven at night in tears and so far, you haven't told us why. I can only imagine it has something to do with Kevin. Am I right?"

Kat nodded. "Partly. But it's not just Kevin." She drew in a deep breath. "Shane Cannington was murdered in his office at the clinic last night."

"Oh, Kat!" Isobel gasped, holding her hand to her mouth. She glanced at her husband, who looked equally shocked. "We've both been on rostered days off. We hadn't heard." Both Isobel and Mason worked at the Sydney Harbour Hospital, too. They knew Shane through work and through his connection to Jake, Kat and Kevin.

"Yes, it's horrible," Kat agreed. "So far, the police don't have any suspects, but the detective I spoke to believes it was an inside job."

"No way!" Mason replied emphatically. "There's no way Jake would be capable of something like that."

Kat nodded. "I agree, and it's not Kevin, either," she said. "He was with me last night. We went to dinner and then went home together. I already told the police and it's the truth." She paused and then realized she might as well give them the rest of it. "There's something else. Kevin and I broke up today."

Mason opened his mouth and Kat hurriedly added, "The breakup had nothing to do with Shane's death. That's just the way things worked out. I might be upset with him, but I'm not going to make him out to be something he's not. For all his faults and failings, Kevin's not a murderer. He could never do something like that, and especially not to Shane. They've been best friends for decades!"

"What do you mean, you and Kevin *broke up*?" Isobel asked.

Kat sighed. She'd known they would ask sooner or later and she hoped to be able to stay with her sister and brother-in-law for a little while. At least until she sorted out what she was doing and where she was going to live.

"Like I said, Issy. We broke up."

"Who ended it?" Isobel asked.

"What does it matter?" Kat sighed and then added, "I did."

"Why?" Isobel asked.

"It doesn't matter," Kat replied, suddenly impatient with her sister's questions. "We needed to take a break. That's all. Like I said, it has nothing to do with Shane's murder. I'd been thinking on it for weeks. There were little things that had been building up for a while. Tonight, when things came to a head, I walked out."

"What kind of things?" Isobel persisted.

From the corner of her eye, Kat saw Mason stand and quietly leave the room. She breathed a sigh of relief. She got on well with her brother-in-law and was thrilled Isobel had found love again after her first husband, who'd been terribly violent. Mason was an angel and together, they were raising a beautiful family. It was so sweet to see how devoted they were to each other, but she didn't necessarily want to air her personal laundry in front of him.

"Talk to me, Kat," Isobel urged. "Tell me what happened."

Leaning forward, Kat picked up her cup from the coffee table that separated them. Before speaking, she took another sip and thought about how to tell her sister. She sighed again.

"It wasn't one thing in particular, Issy. He wasn't violent or anything like that," Kat added hurriedly, suddenly understanding her sister's insistent line of questioning.

"Oh, thank goodness!" Isobel breathed. "I wouldn't wish that on anyone."

Kat shot her a look of understanding. Her sister had been through hell and back before she managed to escape her ex-husband. With Mason's help, she'd found the courage to go to the police and Nigel Donnelly, her ex, was now warming his butt in jail. It couldn't have happened to a nicer guy.

Kat leaned back against the couch. "There wasn't any one thing that caused the break up. It was a number of little things. That sounds silly, but they were important at the time. The truth is, for a while now I've been feeling a little like a fifth wheel, like I'm there for Kevin when he needs me, but when he's otherwise occupied, as if I don't exist.

"For months, he's grown more and more distant. He's always working late and often forgets to call. I've lost count of the number of dinners I've wasted. He says he's doing it for us, for our future, but somehow that doesn't ring true. Last night, over dinner, he even told me he'd argued with Jake about expanding the business."

Isobel raised her eyebrows. "Do you mean they were looking for a bigger place? I can't understand why. They're in a prime position there, so close to the hospital."

Kat shook her head. "No, from what I gathered, they're not thinking about moving. Apparently, Jake wants to bring in a couple more partners— medical specialists to enhance the services they already provide—but Kevin wanted none of it. I found his attitude rather strange after all his reassurances that his long hours are all about securing our future and maximizing his ability to earn a living. Surely the addition of more specialist services would only increase their bottom line?"

Isobel looked thoughtful. "You'd think so. I guess it depends upon who Jake intended to approach. He'd have to make sure he had the right mix. Still, I'd think there's a market there for a one-stop medical specialist shop. The way parking is around the hospital, patients would be more than happy to access all the doctors they need in the same place."

Kat nodded in agreement. "Yes, that's exactly how I looked at it. When I questioned his opposition to the idea, Kevin just blew me off."

"To be honest, I'd think he was cheating on me,

except, when he does come home, he's always ravenous for sex." She chuckled without mirth. "He's out of control. It's like he can't get enough. Sometimes it feels like I'm not even there—like any woman would do."

"Oh, Kat!" Isobel cried and reached out for Kat's hand. "You poor thing! I had no idea! Well, you're more than welcome to stay here. You can have Lizzie's room. We'll get some bunk beds tomorrow and move her in with Ben and Sophie. She can sleep in our room tonight."

"I can't take Lizzie's room!" Kat protested. And then another thought struck her. She looked at her sister. "She isn't even six months old. Does she even sleep through?"

Isobel laughed. "Yes, most of the time. Don't worry. It'll be fine. Sophie and Ben sleep like the dead. Lizzie won't wake them."

Filled with indecision, Kat stared at her sister. She hated the thought of disrupting Isobel's household—forcing a baby out of her own room, no less—but right at that moment, she had nowhere else to go. She could always cough up for a hotel room, but after all she'd been through over the past few days, being completely on her own was the last thing she wanted.

"Kat, we want you to stay," Isobel urged softly. "The kids love having you around and it's no trouble to rearrange things a little. Please. Stay."

Kat offered a smile of surrender, grateful for her sister's kindness. Isobel was her only sibling and even though Kat was four years younger, they were still as close as they'd been while growing up.

"Okay, I'll stay, but it'll only be for a few days. In the morning, I'll make some calls. I'm sure I can find a friend with a spare room."

Isobel came over to Kat and sat beside her and then gave her a brief hug. "Do what you need to do, but remember, you're welcome to stay here for as long as you like. It might be a little more cramped and noisy than you're used to, but we'll make it work."

Kat smiled at her, filled with a surge of gratitude and love. "Thanks, Issy. I really appreciate it."

"Anytime, little sister. That's what family is for."

Kat nodded. "You're right. Speaking of family, have you heard from Mom recently? I've been so busy I haven't had a chance to call her."

"I spoke to her last week. She was doing okay."

"What about Daddy?"

Isobel shrugged. "Daddy's the same as usual. Poor Mom. I don't know how she copes."

Kat compressed her lips. They both knew how difficult it was to care for a person with symptoms of advanced dementia. Her father's illness had been caused by Alzheimer's and had been getting progressively worse. Her mom was becoming increasingly less capable of looking after him. Still, Elizabeth West wouldn't hear of putting her husband into a nursing home, despite the toll it took on her.

"She loves him and she promised to be there in sickness and in health," Kat said quietly.

Isobel nodded. "You're right and I admire her for her courage. She probably didn't ever imagine when she uttered those words that Daddy would get Alzheimer's. Nobody could predict that."

"Yes, and he hasn't made it easy on her. From what I've gathered, there are more and more days that he doesn't even recognize her," Kat replied.

"Poor Mom."

"Yes. Poor Mom."

"We should try and get a weekend off together and go up and visit them," Isobel suggested.

"You're right. Mom would love that and we could help her, give her a break from Daddy."

"And Daddy would love to see the kids," Isobel added, sitting forward. "It's been ages since we were there. He might not know who they are, but I'm sure he'd get a kick out of having them around. He's always loved kids."

"Yes," Kat replied, smiling fondly at long-ago memories of her father entertaining all the kids in their neighborhood with games of cricket, football and other antics. Their house had always been filled with laughter—a nice memory.

The phone in Kat's skirt pocket began to ring. She grimaced. If it was Kevin, she'd let it go through to voicemail. She'd had enough of talking to him tonight. Tugging it out, she glanced at the screen.

Mom.

"It's Mom," she said, smiling at her sister. "She must have ESP."

Isobel smiled back at her and Kat answered the call. "Mom, how are you? I'm over at Isobel's. We were just talking about you and Daddy. What are you up—?"

"Kat," her mother interrupted. "Thank God you're with Issy. I'm afraid... I'm afraid I have some bad news."

Her mother's voice hitched on a sob and Kat's heart skipped a beat. Right away, her thoughts turned to her father.

"Mom, what is it? Please, tell me it's not Daddy. Please, Mom."

"I'm sorry, Kat. He's been hit by a car."

Shock ricocheted through Kat's brain and bounced its way through to her chest. Her heart pounded. She reached out for Isobel, who'd gone still and pale beside her. Clasping her sister's hand tightly, Kat found the courage to ask the next question.

"Is he... Is he all right?"

"No, Kat. He isn't. I'm so sorry, honey. He... He didn't make it."

A sound of denial burst from her lips and a fresh wave of shock left her speechless. *Her father was dead.* Just like that. Isobel's forehead was creased with concern. She mouthed silent questions to Kat, but Kat was beyond answering. At last, Issy took the phone from her hands and stood.

From some distant part of her mind, Kat heard Isobel speaking quietly into the phone. *Her father was dead.* The words kept repeating themselves, echoing through the noise that filled her head. A car accident. No, her father hadn't held a license for years. Her father, who seldom left his room, and who was battling advanced Alzheimer's, had been outside for some reason and he'd been hit by a car. Somehow. Somewhere.

"How did it happen?" she cried, coming to stand near Isobel.

Her sister murmured into the phone and then listened for the response. At last, the conversation came to a close and Isobel ended the call. She handed the phone back to Kat and made her way to the couch again. Seating herself on the soft cushions, she swiped at a tear and let out a heavy sigh. Kat moved to join her.

"What happened?" she asked quietly, taking a seat beside her.

Isobel reached for Kat's hand. From the corner of her eye, she saw Mason enter the room. He leaned against the doorway with a somber expression on his face. She guessed he'd heard enough to know it was bad news.

"Daddy escaped from the house," Isobel started. "Mom doesn't know how. She's so careful about keeping the doors locked and making sure the keys are hidden. Somehow, he found one and went out the front door. He was more than two blocks away when they found him. The driver who hit Daddy said he stepped out onto the road, right into his path. Said Daddy didn't even look where he was going. It was dark. The driver had no time to brake. Daddy was flung over the hood and onto the roof and eventually onto the road. The paramedics were called, but there was nothing they could do."

Kat stared at the carpet, filled with shock. The whole situation was surreal. They'd just been talking about him, planning a visit... And now he was gone. A sob caught in her throat. She turned to Issy and saw the tears flowing silently down her cheeks. With a cry of anguish, she flung herself against her sister and together, they comforted each other through their pain.

———

Kat slept fitfully in the unfamiliar bed and woke to the sound of a baby crying. She wasn't sure what time she'd finally fallen asleep, but it felt like it had been only minutes since she'd closed her eyes. She and Isobel and Mason had discussed heading to her mother's place right away, but it was going on for midnight and the town where their parents lived was at least two hours' drive away. Kat had called her mother again and had received an assurance that Elizabeth would be fine until the morning. The girls promised to get there as soon as they could.

Now, Kat blinked and shook her head to clear it of the dazed feeling she'd been suffering ever since her mom had called. A new day had arrived and with it, the myriad of decisions to be made whenever a loved one died.

She needed to call her mother again and offer to help. No doubt there would be an autopsy to confirm the cause of death and funeral arrangements to be made. Her parents lived in the country. Kat would need to call the hospital and ask for some time off. She also needed to call Kevin.

As much as she didn't relish the idea of

speaking with him so soon after her abrupt departure, she needed to let him know about her dad's death. Kevin had known her father well enough. He'd want to know of her father's passing. Giving him the news was the proper thing to do. With a sigh, she reached for her phone that was still charging on the nightstand. He answered on the third ring.

"Kat! Thank goodness! I knew you'd come to your senses! Now that you've slept on it, you've realized how good we are for each other, right? Please, come home."

Kat bit her lip. It would be so easy to accept Kevin's offer, to return to the comfort and security of his arms, especially at a time like this. Then she remembered the reasons she'd left and knew she needed to give it more consideration, more time. She needed to think things through while she was calm and clearheaded. Now wasn't the time for rash decisions.

"I'm sorry, Kevin. I'm... I'm not calling about us. My mom called. My father died last night."

"Oh, Kat! That's terrible! Still, he's probably better off. Poor old thing. Last time I saw him, I remember thinking if I ever got like that, I'd want to be put out of my misery. There's something to be said for euthanasia."

While Kat understood where he was coming from, she was a little taken aback by his blithe commentary on her loss; his callous disregard for her feelings. Still, this was Kevin and though people found him easygoing, tact had never been his strongest suit.

"Dad was hit by a car and killed. It had nothing to do with his dementia."

"Oh, I'm sorry. I just assumed..."

"It's all right," she replied. "I understand. I'm not sure when the funeral will be, but I guess it will be later in the week. I'm driving up there today. I was hoping you might be able to come with me."

The moment the words were out of her mouth, she realized they were true. Despite their recent fallout, he'd been her boyfriend for three years. She needed his support.

"Oh, I... I wish I could," she heard him saying. "I'm sorry, Kat, I really am. It's just that I have patients backed up that I really need to see. With the police effectively shutting the clinic down yesterday morning, we're running well behind. The phone's been ringing off the hook. We should be able to get back to normal tomorrow or the next day if I work harder now. Holly's checking with the detectives about when they'll give us the all clear. As soon as they do, I'll have to be here."

Kat was flooded with disappointment and tears pricked the back of her eyes. "Oh. I see. I was hoping you might drive up with me, keep me company."

"What about Isobel? Won't she be heading up there, too?"

"Yes," Kat replied. "But she'll be going with Mason and the kids. They don't have room."

"Of course, I understand. I'm really sorry, Kat. I wish I could help. I really do."

Kat compressed her lips and forced back another surge of tears. She silently urged him to reconsider, to say of course he'd come with her and support her in her hour of need. He remained quiet.

She swallowed a heavy sigh. Kevin wasn't coming with her and that was that. She'd have to face whatever she needed to, alone.

Chapter 7

Devlin scanned the ballistics report in his hands. Shane Cannington had been shot twice in the back of the head with a .22 caliber pistol. Unfortunately, the bullets had passed through his skull and despite Devlin and Bryce combing the scene, the bullets and their casings were nowhere to be found. It meant that they couldn't identify the weapon used to commit the crime and the knowledge was frustrating.

He flipped open the file and pulled out the stack of colored 8 x 10 crime scene photos and flicked through them until he found the ones he wanted. He stared at the close-ups of the victim's head. The gunshot wounds were neat and accurate and had been shot from a reasonable distance. It was obvious the shooter was experienced. Coupled with the fact the perp had collected both the bullets and their casings, he couldn't help but wonder if one of their suspects could have hired a professional gunman to do the job. It was another angle to consider.

However he looked at it, Devlin's gut was telling him this was more than a casual crime of opportunity. The unforced entry was one factor, but there were other things that pointed to the murderer being someone who knew or was close to the deceased. The rooms of the clinic were undisturbed, including the one where the body had been found.

According to the doctors he'd interviewed, along with the receptionist, nothing appeared to have been taken. That seemed to rule out robbery as a motive and the neatness of the crime scene indicated it was unlikely there'd been a scuffle. At least, not one that left any evidence behind. Coupled with the fact Cannington had been shot in the back of the head, it led Devlin to think the murderer had come to the clinic with killing on his mind.

"What are you up to with the doctor-murder thing?"

Devlin looked up and spied Lachlan Coleridge heading toward him with a Styrofoam coffee cup in hand. "You could have bought one for me," he grumbled.

Lachlan glanced at the cup. "Sorry, mate. I didn't know you wanted one. Tough day?"

Devlin grimaced. "You could say that. It's been more than twenty-four hours since the murder and I have very little to go on. Jake Alexander looks good on paper. He's the one without the alibi, but he also has no motive. He admitted to having an argument with the victim a few days earlier, but was at pains to point out that getting rid of just one of his partners wouldn't have solved his problem."

"Which was?"

"Alexander wanted to expand the practice, bring in more specialist doctors. Cannington and Johnson were against it."

"Anyone back that up?"

"Yeah. Holly Greenwood. The receptionist. She heard them arguing."

"What did your suspects say?"

"I haven't put it to Johnson, yet, but Alexander admitted he and Cannington had an argument."

"Have Johnson and Alexander been let back in the clinic?"

"Yes. I called there a moment ago. Spoke to the receptionist. I told her Forensics was finished."

"I guess you'll have to see what else turns up."

Devlin rolled his shoulders in frustration. "Yeah. I guess I will." He dropped the photos and picked up another sheaf of papers. "I'm still waiting on the security company to get back to me with the CCTV footage of the building that evening and I've asked the receptionist for a copy of all the accounts. We know money is often a motivating factor. I've also been going over the phone records, both those of the clinic and the doctors' cell phones. One number keeps standing out. It's registered to a man by the name of Vladimir Mikolaev."

Lachlan frowned. "Mikolaev? Are you sure?"

"Yes. I checked with the telephone company myself. Why? Do you know him?" Devlin couldn't keep the hope from his voice.

"As a matter of fact, I do. If it's the same one. I'm investigating illegal meth labs in the inner west. Vladimir Mikolaev is at the top of my suspect list."

Surprise flooded through Devlin's veins. "You're shitting me."

"No, I'm not."

Lachlan came closer and perched on the corner of Devlin's desk. His expression reflected Devlin's growing excitement. "How's this for a scenario? Mikolaev cooks up meth. What does he need? Pounds of codeine. You're dealing with three doctors, all of them having easy access to prescription drugs."

"Including codeine," Devlin said.

Lachlan winked at him. "You just told me you have phone records that show a link between your doctors and a known drug dealer and now one of the three medicos has turned up dead." Lachlan shook his head. "It sounds like too much of a coincidence to me."

Devlin's heart picked up its pace. He could barely contain the adrenaline that surged through his body. It was always this way when he was on the brink of breaking open a case.

"Do you think that's it?" he asked. "Do you think this is drug related?" Another rush of adrenaline surged through him. He spoke quickly, barely able to keep up with his thoughts. "Maybe Cannington didn't know about the arrangement and found out about it by mistake? Or maybe he was involved from the beginning and wanted out? Maybe that's why one, or both of them, had him killed."

Lachlan shrugged. "Either scenario is possible. Your victim could have wanted a bigger cut. It could have been any number of things, and yes, my gut's betting on a connection to the drug thing. Whether it's one or two or all three of them involved, it makes sense this connection to Vladimir Mikolaev had something to do with the doctor's death. There's no other reason to have Mikolaev on speed dial." He paused and then added, "Which one has the alibi?"

"Kevin Johnson."

"And which one's phone records are linked?"

Devlin flipped through the papers in his hand. "It's Johnson's cell, but Mikolaev's name shows up on the office number, too. There are several lines out of the clinic. I can't tell who made those calls."

Lachlan frowned. "I thought you said Johnson had an alibi?"

"Yes, I did and it checks out, so if Johnson and Alexander are in it together...?" He let the words drift off.

Lachlan shook his head. "You'd think the other one would have been smart enough to have an alibi."

"Yeah," Devlin replied, "but you know as well as I do it wouldn't be the first time a seemingly intelligent man has been brought down by a simple act of carelessness." He pulled Jake Alexander's file toward him. "Johnson's alibi checks out. I'll ask him about the calls on his cell phone, but I'm also going to take a closer look at Alexander. Let's hope we get lucky. Perhaps his carelessness will be his downfall."

Lachlan nodded and pushed away from Devlin's desk. "Best of luck. I'll see what I can find out on my end as far as Mikolaev goes. I'm hoping the boss will give me approval for surveillance. It's always possible this could be about a drug deal gone bad. The doctors might not be involved at all. If Cannington knew Mikolaev, he might have let him in, even at that time of the night. If I hear anything, I'll let you know."

––––––––––

Kevin strode along the corridor, intent on making it to the ward before morning rounds commenced. After his night of drama and introspection, it had been the early hours of the morning before he'd dragged himself to bed. He'd tossed and turned, not used to sleeping alone. His alarm had gone off at the usual time, but he'd overslept and now he was late. He hated being late.

"Hey, Kevin! Wait up."

He turned and spied Jake heading toward him and reluctantly slowed his steps. Not only was he going to be late, now he had to speak with Jake. "What's up?" he asked as Jake reached him.

"I just got off the phone from Holly. The detective who attended the scene phoned the clinic. They're finished there. We can go back in."

Kevin nodded. "That's great. Any word on Shane's funeral?"

"No. I meant to call you yesterday about the two of us breaking the news to his mother, but Holly beat me to it. The police offered, but she wanted to do it. She went around there after she left the clinic. I didn't realize she knew her."

Kevin ignored the silent question in Jake's eyes. The last thing he felt like doing was filling Jake in on Holly's extracurricular activities. "That was good of her," he said instead.

"Yeah. She's also offered to help with the funeral arrangements once the morgue releases Shane's body."

Kevin hid his astonishment. Little Holly was full of surprises. He hadn't realized she cared so deeply about Shane.

"I've told her the business will cover the costs," Jake added.

Kevin quickly agreed. "Of course we'll pay. I wouldn't have it any other way. Shane wasn't only our business partner. He was our mate." He paused and then added, "Speaking of funerals, Kat's father died last night."

Jake's expression filled with surprise. "Shit. That's not good. Was it expected?"

"No. Well, sort of. He's been suffering from Alzheimer's for years and it was only a matter of time, but last night he was hit by a car and was killed."

Jake shook his head. "Hell. Poor Kat. How's she taking it?"

Kevin shrugged. "About as well as you'd expect."

"Is her mother still alive?"

"Yes. She's been caring for the old man. They live in Maitland."

Jake nodded. "I assume you'll be heading up there with her. I'll cover your patients, if you like. It's bad timing with the police just allowing us back into the clinic, but I'm sure your patients will understand. It's been a rough twenty-four hours for everyone."

Kevin shot him a look of reassurance. "Oh, you don't have to worry about that. I already told Kat I'm not going. I can't get away."

Jake frowned. "Not going? What do you mean?"

"Like I said, I have patients who are wondering what the hell is going on. They need to be seen. I can't do that from Maitland."

Jake's frown deepened. "Look, I understand. It's tough on your patients coming so soon after Holly told them about Shane, but Kat will need you. I can cover your patients. I was supposed to have surgery this week, but they've closed a couple of the theaters and my list has been scrapped. I'm happy to see whoever needs to be seen this week."

Kevin hid his irritation and instead, shot his friend a look of gratitude. "Thanks, Jake. I appreciate the offer, but I have a few things to do here that can't wait. My patients are the least of it." That was an understatement. He couldn't take off for the country, even for Kat. He had Vladimir breathing down his neck. He had to get his hands on another shipment of tablets and quickly.

Unaware of Kevin's thoughts, Jake stared at

him, confusion flooding his face. "What the hell are you talking about? What's more important than being there for Kat? She's your girlfriend. She'll want you close at a time like this."

Kevin shrugged. He hadn't planned to say anything to Jake about Kat calling time out on their relationship, but his friend had given him no choice. He decided to have it out.

"Look, Jake. Kat and I are going through a rough patch. She told me about the kiss."

Jake's eyes flared with emotion and a blush stole across his cheeks. He squirmed and lowered his gaze. "I'm sorry, Kevin. It shouldn't have happened. I don't know what to say."

Kevin grimaced. "It's fine. I understand. You were upset about Shane. I get it. We were all upset. When Kat told me you kissed her, I was mad as hell, but now that I've had a chance to cool down, and consider the circumstances, I'm fine. It wasn't the only reason we decided to take a break. There were...other things."

He could see the curiosity in Jake's eyes, but refused to embellish. It wasn't anybody else's business. He and Kat would get through this. He was sure of it. As soon as he got rid of the problem of Vlad, he'd fight to win her back. He just hoped she hadn't moved on with someone else.

Only that morning, as he made his way to work, he'd caught up with two of the nurses who worked on his ward. They offered him their sympathy over his break-up and then commiserated with him over the fact his girlfriend had moved on with his best friend. At the time, he'd brushed off their words with a forced smile, but now he couldn't help but wonder if there was any truth to the rumors. The nurses were probably referring to that kiss. Somehow, someone had seen it. It didn't take long for any kind of mischief to circulate around the hospital. He hoped that's all it was.

The beeper clipped to the belt on his hip went off. He pulled it out and checked the screen.

Vlad.

Kevin's gut clenched, but he was filled with a sudden surge of cold determination. This wasn't the time or place to question Jake over whether or not he'd made a move on Kevin's girlfriend. Right now, he had more important things to focus on. Hurriedly stowing the beeper back where it came from, he slapped Jake on the back.

"Look, mate. I have to go. Something's come up. Don't worry about me and Kat. We'll sort things out." He suddenly eyeballed Jake. "I'm sure of it." And with that, he left.

Jake stared after his friend and frowned. *What the hell was that all about?* Kat's father was dead. Her mother lived hours away. Her sister, Isobel, lived in Sydney's eastern suburbs, but she was married to Jake's cousin. She, at least had her husband to help her through the death of a close family member. Kat had no one.

He tried not to think about what Kevin had told

him—that he and Kat were on a break—but he couldn't help it. The woman he loved was single once again. His heart leaped in his chest.

He didn't know why she'd told Kevin about their kiss but the fact she had must mean something. If it had merely been a spontaneous, never-to-be-repeated kiss between good friends, surely she wouldn't have felt the need to say anything to her boyfriend. *Would she?* It frustrated him that he didn't know.

Still, he had to make sure Kat had some kind of support while she went through the ordeal of burying her dad. It was bad enough that his death had come so close on the heels of Shane's. One funeral was tough enough. Now she was facing the reality of attending two services and probably in the same week. It was a lot to ask of anyone. Doing it alone was beyond reasonable.

With his mind made up, he pulled out his phone and dialed Kat's number. There was no way he was letting her go through this on her own. She might not be his girlfriend, but that didn't mean he didn't care.

That was the problem. He *did* care. Way too much.

CHAPTER 8

The funeral arrangements have been set in motion. It will happen toward the end of the week. I was sitting there in that dark, quiet room with death all around me and the reality of what I did hit me. I might have been furious enough to pull the trigger, but that didn't mean I didn't care. Now he'll never know how I truly felt, how much I enjoyed the time we had together. Time we'll never have again...

———————

Kat glanced across at Jake where he sat in the driver's seat of his Audi and was filled with gratitude. He wove in and out of the mid-morning traffic with confidence, his hands firm and sure on the wheel. She'd been surprised and touched when he'd called her and offered to drive her home to Maitland.

Home. She hadn't been back since Easter and that was more than eight months ago. She'd been so busy at work and on her rostered days off she was usually caught up with a myriad of other things, or catching up on lost sleep and spending time with Kevin. Now she was returning to attend her father's funeral. She couldn't believe she'd never see him again. It still seemed surreal.

"Thank you for doing this for me, Jake," she said quietly. "I really appreciate it."

He glanced across at her and then returned his attention to the road. "It's fine. I'm happy to do it. I didn't want you driving up here alone."

She nodded and turned to stare out the window. The busy lanes of metropolitan traffic had given way to the less-crowded freeway. It was the middle of the week and they were heading north, away from the city. It made for pleasant driving and as the city gave way to wide open spaces and lush green countryside, she began to relax.

Without intending them to, her thoughts turned to Kevin and she immediately tensed. She'd been right to break things off with him. Even with everything else, *he* should have been the one beside her, accompanying her to face whatever she needed to face, helping her, offering her comfort. Until recently, he'd been her boyfriend. They'd dated for the best part of three years. That should have counted for something. Instead, it was Jake beside her—Jake offering comfort, doing the driving, distracting her from her sober thoughts.

She moved her head and once again took in

the sight of him behind the wheel. His black hair brushed the back of his collar and curled over his ears. It was longer than he usually wore it and she found that she liked it. It suited him. It gave him a boyish air that was missing most of the time when he was in serious doctor mode. Though he had a wonderful reputation, he was an oncologist who often came face to face with death in his patients. She understood the serious visage he frequently showed the world. She wasn't sure she could ever work in such a demanding field and she admired his dedication.

He'd offered to take them in his car. Given that he had a brand new, sleek silver A4 Audi and she drove a modest secondhand Corolla with unreliable air conditioning, it hadn't taken much to convince her to go along with his suggestion. She couldn't imagine making the two-hour trip alone, with nothing more to occupy her thoughts than sad memories and the radio or the music on her iPod. Once again she thought of Kevin and frowned.

"There's no need to look so tense. It'll be all right, Kat."

She gave him a wan smile. Once again, he was looking out for her. "Thanks," she said. "I was actually thinking about Kevin."

Jake's expression turned grim. His gaze remained fixed on the road. Kat hurried to explain.

"I'm not sure what you're thinking, but you're probably way off track. Kevin and I are... We're over."

Jake shot her a quick look. "That's not what he told me."

Kat frowned in confusion. "What do you mean? You know about us?"

"Kevin told me you were taking a break. He didn't think it was permanent. He also told me you told him I kissed you."

Kat stared at him surprise. The only time she and Kevin had discussed the kiss, he'd been furious. It was one of the reasons she'd eventually carried through on her threat to leave. She couldn't believe he'd spoken of it to Jake.

"W-what did he tell you?" she asked.

Jake shrugged. "Just that you'd told him and he was okay with it. He understood it was a simple reaction to the situation we were in and he was confident it wouldn't happen again. He said there were other reasons why you were having some time apart."

Jake shot her a searching glance and Kat squirmed with discomfort. She'd called things off with Kevin and she was almost certain they were over for good, but she was also aware of Jake and the way he felt about her—had always felt about her. She needed to take things slowly, clear her mind; choose her words with care. She owed it to herself and to Jake to take the time to think—*really* think—about her future and what direction she wanted things to take.

She was also conscious of the friendship Jake shared with her ex. Despite Kevin's recent unsavory behavior toward her, she knew he still loved her. At least, that's what he said. He'd be hurt to discover she'd moved on so quickly—and with his best friend, no less. She needed to do all she could to keep everyone's feelings intact, including doing whatever she could not to jeopardize the friendship between the two men.

Was Jake part of her future? It was possible because she and Kevin were no longer together. Did she *want* something to happen between her and Jake?

The memory of their scorching kiss hit her full force. She almost reached up to touch her lips and then caught herself in time, blushing with embarrassment. At first, she'd been so surprised, she hadn't been able to think, but within milliseconds of his lips touching hers, she'd been filled with white hot passion and need.

What did it mean? Did she like Jake more than she'd realized? He was smart, sweet and undeniably good-looking. It was Jake who'd offered to drive her to Maitland; Jake who was there to support her through the ordeal ahead. Kevin, her *boyfriend*, had been otherwise engaged.

Kevin wasn't the only one whose friend had been murdered, whose patients were backing up. Jake was just as affected and had just as many patients demanding his time, and yet he'd rearranged his schedule so that he could accompany her. He'd done that for *her*, when her boyfriend hadn't.

Though she was disappointed in Kevin, knowing Jake was there beside her sent a shaft of warmth and gratitude surging through her. She glanced at him again. He was so good and kind and generous. He was solid and dependable. He was a true friend and had been from the moment they'd met.

So, where did that leave her? Had Jake already become more than a friend? She definitely hadn't been thinking in terms of friends throughout the kiss, fleeting though it had been. *Was it possible she harbored feelings for him that went beyond the friendship thing?* Did friends feel hot and needy when they shared a kiss in a moment of grief? She didn't think so, but she didn't know for sure. She'd never kissed a friend like that before. What she did know was that she wanted to do it again.

"Talk to me, Kat. What's going on?"

Kat forced herself to look at him, her thoughts in turmoil. She shook her head and offered him a helpless shrug.

"I don't know, Jake. Things are complicated. Yes, Kevin and I are over, but it's not as easy as that."

"You know how I feel about you," Jake said quietly.

"Yes. And I... I care for you, too. And that kiss... I'm not going to pretend it wasn't amazing, but you're one of Kevin's closest friends. He's just lost Shane in the most horrible way and now he's...lost me. He might even lose you as a friend, too. I'm not sure he's strong enough to accept that I've moved on from him with you. Not that I have," she added hurriedly, unable to stem another blush.

"I understand," Jake replied, his voice pitched low. "And like you said, it's complicated. But I'm glad you thought our kiss was amazing. I thought it was pretty amazing, too."

He smiled softly and Kat's heart skipped a beat. Once again, she marveled that she'd been blind to his beauty—beauty that was more than skin deep. Unable to help herself, she reached out and squeezed his hand where it lay near the gear shift. He looked at her, his green eyes dark and turbulent with emotion.

Kat swallowed the lump that clogged her throat. Nerves of excitement and anticipation fluttered low in her belly. She could so easily fall in love with this man, but there was Kevin to consider. She didn't want to hurt him more than she already had, and she didn't want to be the reason his friendship with Jake was damaged, or worse, destroyed. She told Jake as much.

"I get it, Kat. I do. But if you're really certain you and Kevin are over, I don't think it's fair that he's the reason we can't get together and try and make it work—if that's what you want."

"I understand, but—"

"Would it make you feel any better if your first romance post-breakup is with someone other than me? Would that make it more palatable for you, and for Kevin?"

Kat made a sound of frustration deep in her throat and pressed her knuckles against her mouth. She turned to Jake.

"What do you want me to say? I like you, Jake. In other circumstances, it wouldn't be an issue. We'd date for a while, probably fall in love and live happily ever after, but these aren't normal circumstances, and you know it."

"What I know is that you and Kevin are over.

You're single and free to date who you like. Kevin's a big boy. I think you're underestimating him. We've been friends for a long time. He'll get over the fact we're dating. And who knows? It might not last between us, either."

Kat sighed heavily and turned to stare out the window. Jake was right. They might not last. And Kevin might not be so distraught about her leaving him for his best friend. It seemed almost ridiculous to be thinking about possible difficult scenarios when she and Jake weren't even together.

Caught up in her thoughts, it seemed no time at all before she directed Jake to turn into the driveway of her childhood home. The old weatherboard siding was just as she remembered. The sky-blue paint that had been applied more than a decade ago had faded and the white trim dulled, but the lawn was green and freshly mown and the Agapanthus that filled the garden beds on either side of the path leading to the front door were in full bloom, their soft lilac color, vibrant against the noon sky.

Jake brought the Audi to a halt and switched off the ignition. He turned to her. "Are you ready, or do you need a minute?"

She drew in a deep breath and nodded. "I'm ready."

He reached over and squeezed her hand. She felt the contact all the way to her toes. Steadfastly, she kept her gaze fixed on the console.

When had Jake Alexander become so attractive? Was it because he'd kissed her and she could still feel his touch on her lips? Was it because she was newly single and dating other guys was possible? Or was it because she was sad on so many levels and he was such a nice guy, going out of his way to help her in her moment of need—like now, when she had to walk inside and offer comfort to her mother, a woman grieving the loss of her spouse.

Kat didn't know the answer and right now she was through with trying to analyze the situation. No doubt her mother was wondering about the strange vehicle in her drive. It was time to go inside. Pulling her hand gently from his, she fumbled for her door latch then stepped out into the hot, bright sunshine.

Jake hung back to collect their luggage from the car. She walked ahead, her heart heavy. She dreaded entering the home where her father's absence would be felt acutely. Home would never feel the same again. Stepping up onto the porch, she gave a perfunctory knock on the front door, turned the handle and opened it.

"Mom? It's Katrina. Are you home?"

The sound of footsteps could be heard coming toward her on the polished timber floorboards and a moment later, Elizabeth West appeared in the hallway. At the sight of her daughter, her face lit up with a smile and tears glistened in her eyes. She hurried forward, her arms outstretched.

"Katrina! Oh, honey! It's so good to see you!"

Kat hugged her mom close and breathed in the familiar smell of her gardenia-scented perfume. Her mother had worn it all of Kat's life.

After a little while, Kat drew back. She noticed Jake had come up behind her.

"Mom, this is Jake Alexander, a...friend of mine. You might remember him from Isobel's wedding. He's Mason's cousin."

Elizabeth West looked Jake up and down. "Hello, Jake. I'm not sure that we met at the wedding, but welcome and thank you for bringing my daughter home. I wish you were here under more pleasant circumstances."

Jake stepped forward and shook Elizabeth's hand. "It's nice to meet you, Mrs West and I'm so sorry for your loss."

Her mother compressed her lips and nodded, lowering her gaze to the floor. Kat caught a glimpse of unshed tears in her mother's pale blue eyes and her heart clenched with pain.

"Momma, how are you holding up?" she asked quietly.

"It's... It's been tough, Katrina, but I'm getting there. Now, why don't you come inside and bring your bags?" she said, glancing at the luggage at Jake's feet. "I take it you're staying here, Jake?" She looked from one to the other. Kat hurried to reassure her.

"Of course, Mom. If that's all right. I'm not sure how long Jake's staying. He's a doctor and runs a very busy practice with Kevin. I don't—"

"I've cleared my schedule for the next few days," Jake interrupted. "I'm here for as long as you need me."

Kat shot him a grateful smile. Her mother watched the exchange with interest.

"That's fine," Elizabeth said. "We have plenty of room." She looked back at Kat. "When's Kevin arriving?"

Heat crept up Kat's neck. She refused to meet her mother's gaze. "Kevin had to stay in the city, Mom. He's crazy busy at work. He... He's not going to be able to make it."

Her mother nodded. Her expression remained filled with curiosity, but to Kat's relief, she let the matter go.

"Isobel called a little while ago," her mother said instead. "They've just left Sydney. She's hoping to get right through without a stop, but that will depend upon Lizzie. She's not the best of travelers."

Kat smiled, remembering a weekend away with the Alexanders a few months earlier. Lizzie cried the whole way. It had been a long trip.

"Anyway, come in, come in," Elizabeth urged, stepping back and allowing them to enter.

Kat headed down the hallway toward the kitchen, past the row of family portraits that lined the walls. From the corner of her eye, she saw Jake pause at the one where she and Isobel and their parents had posed for a formal portrait. Her mother had arranged for a professional photographer to take the picture. Kat had been sixteen.

"I always wondered if that red hair of yours was natural," he murmured.

She stopped and turned to face him, filled with indignation. She caught sight of his teasing smile and the words of outrage died in her mouth.

Instead, she said, "Haven't you seen my sister? We're both as red as carrots. Have been all our lives." She softened the words with a smile.

He laughed softly. "I like it. It suits you."

His voice had dipped to a husky drawl. His gaze lingered on hers. Her heart skipped a beat and then took flight. There it was again. That damnable attraction. *Had it always been there, under the surface? Why had she never noticed it? Perhaps she'd never allowed herself to appreciate how attractive he was, how much he appealed to her. Was she willing to pay attention to it now?* She had a sneaking suspicion the answer was yes. After her quandary regarding Kevin, the thought was both alarming and exhilarating.

"Would you like a cup of tea, or a cold drink?"

Her mother's benign question broke the spell that seemed to surround them. Kat blinked and continued toward the kitchen. "Thanks Mom, I think I'll have some lemonade. It's gotten warm out there."

"Well," her mother replied, "it *is* summer, although some days it's easy to forget. It's been so mild, really, although I guess we have to expect some warm days now and then. How about you, Jake?" Elizabeth added, turning to him. "Would you like some lemonade?"

"Thank you, Mrs West. That sounds delicious."

"Please," she replied, waving his words away. "Call me Elizabeth."

Jake inclined his head, acknowledging her offer, and together they entered the comfortable farmhouse kitchen. Kat looked around her and noted the shiny new appliances that had recently replaced the ones that had been there while she grew up. It had taken some convincing for her parents to agree to spend the money, but Kat and Isobel had eventually gotten them to come on board with their daughters' suggestion to update and renovate.

The result was comfortable and stylish with natural butcher block countertops and rich, cream-colored cupboard profiles that complemented the wood. Kat glanced across at the pine dining room table visible in the open concept kitchen, living and dining room and noticed the vases of flowers that lined every available surface. With a start, she was reminded of the reason for their visit. As if sensing the change in her mood, her mother moved closer and touched her arm.

"Flowers have been coming from everywhere. Some of the bouquets have come from old neighbors I haven't seen for years and old Mr Edwards from three houses down stopped by earlier and mowed the lawn. People have been so kind."

Kat nodded, once again overwhelmed by memories of her dad. "He was much loved by everyone, Mom. He always had a kind word. Though he was often busy with his accounting business, we always felt he had time for us. He had a special gift for making everyone feel they were the most important person in the world."

Her mother nodded sadly. "He was a wonderful man. When he was diagnosed with Alzheimer's, I was so angry at God. To reduce such an amazing, special person to the man he became... It was so unfair. He became someone I didn't even recognize. He looked like my Jim, but as the disease took hold, he turned into a monster. He was rude and belligerent. He shouted all the time. A few times, he even hit me."

Kat gasped in shock. "Oh, Momma! I had no idea. Isobel and I knew you were doing it tough and that Daddy could be unusually demanding, but we didn't know he'd become violent. Was he that way often?"

"Not very often, thankfully, but more and more he was angry. He didn't know who I was most of the time. He kept demanding I take him back home to his wife." Her voice hitched with emotion and Kat pulled her in close for a hug. Her mother's shoulders shook with her sobs.

"I'm sorry, Kat, but when the police came to tell me what happened, on some level, I was actually relieved. Not that he'd died such a horrible death, but that he was finally at peace." Her mother raised her face and stared at Kat. Tears ran down her wrinkled cheeks.

"I'm such a terrible person for feeling like that, Kat," she sobbed. "I'm so ashamed. But I was so tired, so heartsick, so depressed over the man he'd become. It wasn't his fault. It was never his fault, but it was harder and harder to believe who he was in my life. He looked like your father, he sounded the same. But what was coming out of his mouth was totally foreign. We used to love each other so dearly. Before his illness took hold, he used to tell me almost daily how special I was, how much he adored me. His change of attitude and hostility toward me was the hardest to take."

Kat hugged her mother again and did her best to comfort her with quiet words of reassurance. She glanced over her shoulder to where Jake stood on the other side of the room, giving them privacy. He looked as sad as she felt. Alzheimer's was such a cruel disease. There were never any winners. Kat understood how her mother felt and she could tell Jake did, too.

The knowledge warmed her through. She looked at him again and this time, tears clouded her vision. She mouthed *thank you*.

He acknowledged it with the tiniest movement of his head, but it was enough. He understood.

CHAPTER 9

It was hours later, after Kat and her sister and their mother had met with the funeral director and confirmed the arrangements that Kat found time to sit for a moment in the rocking chair that was still in one corner of her old room. Echoes of her father remained everywhere, making it even more difficult to come to terms with the fact he was truly dead. Though he'd been slipping away from them little by little as the disease ravaged his brain, he'd still been there physically. Now, all of him was gone.

She looked around her. Though much of the main part of the house had been updated, the bedrooms remained the same. The pale pink wallpaper had faded and was peeling here and there. The double bed with the pink-and-white floral comforter she'd loved so much as a teenager, still covered the bed. The posters of James Blunt, Mariah Carey and The Black Eyed Peas had long since been discarded, but their music echoed in Kat's ears. She thought about the hours she'd spent lying on her bed, listening to her stereo and dreaming of her future.

Even then, she'd wanted to do something in the health profession. At first, she'd set her sights on becoming a surgeon, but after fainting at the sight of the gash Isobel sustained when she cut her leg falling off her bike, Kat had let that one slide. It was when she was fourteen and had broken her arm while swinging from a rope into the river, and had to have X-rays, that she decided she'd go into radiology. Though she still had to go to med school and suffer through the cadavers and other queasy stuff, she'd kept her sights set on being a radiologist, helping people in a different way, and that had been the best decision of her life.

A movement by the doorway caught her eye and she turned to see her mother standing in the opening.

"Can I come in?" her mother asked quietly.

Kat straightened in her chair. "Of course."

Elizabeth walked in slowly and perched on the end of Kat's bed. She sighed softly. "What a day."

"It hasn't been easy. How are you holding up, Mom?"

Her mother shot her a look of gratitude. "As well as can be expected. Thank you for being here, for helping me. I'm not sure I could have made all the arrangements on my own."

"You're welcome, Mom, but you're wrong. You're the strongest woman I know. There's nothing you can't do. Look what you did for Daddy! Caring for him all these years, even when he didn't know you and when he hit out at you for your trouble. I don't know how you did it." Kat shook her head. "Why didn't you say something to us?"

Elizabeth drew in a deep breath and her shoulders slumped on another sigh. "I didn't want to worry you. The first time it happened, Isobel had just given birth to Lizzie. She had enough on her plate. Besides, I didn't want you to think differently about him, and pressure me into putting him into a home. I loved him. I'll always love him. I wanted to look after him. I wanted to keep him home."

Fresh tears crowded Kat's eyes. She stood and went to her mother. Sitting beside her. She put her arms around her and pulled her close. They'd both been the same height, before her mother had shrunk a little with age. The past few years since her father's diagnosis had been tough. Kat couldn't help but feel guilty she hadn't known the truth; hadn't visited more often. Now it was too late, at least for her father.

"Will Jake stay for the funeral?" her mother asked quietly, after the two of them had collected themselves.

"I think so," Kat replied.

"He's very nice," her mother said. "It was good of him to come with you and to chauffeur us around all day."

"Yes, it was."

Her mother turned to look at her. "What's happening with Kevin? I know you said he had to work, but there's more to it, isn't there? Did you break up? Is that why he isn't here with you?"

Kat compressed her lips and shrugged. Her

mother was far too shrewd to be put off with lies and half-truths. Besides, Kat had nothing to hide. She wouldn't be the first person to call a halt to a relationship. It wasn't like they'd been married.

"Yes, Mom. We broke up. I needed some time apart."

Her mother nodded. "Does it have anything to do with Jake? Anyone can see he cares for you. Is that why he's here?"

Kat shook her head. "No, Mom. The breakup had nothing to do with Jake, but...I'm glad he's here. You're right. He's a nice guy and a very good friend. I... I probably don't deserve him."

Her mother frowned and shook her head. "What kind of nonsense is that? Katrina West, you ought to be ashamed of yourself. You're a kind, generous, beautiful girl with a heart of gold. You deserve the very best. If not Kevin, then someone else. I'm not sure how you feel about Jake, but honey, I've seen the way he looks at you, the way he hovers, making sure you're all right. A man only does that when he cares deeply and I'm not talking about how it is with friends. He's well on the way to falling in love with you."

Kat stared at her mother in confusion. "Jake? In love with me?" She laughed. "No, I don't think so."

Her mother's jaw jutted out at an angle Kat knew well. "Believe what you want to, honey. I know what I saw. Maybe you're just not ready to accept it and that's perfectly all right. Time has a way of working these things out, one way or another."

With that, her mother stood and leaned over to

kiss her on the cheek. Kat watched her depart in silence and pull the door closed behind her. Flopping backwards on the bed, Kat stared up at the ceiling.

Jake's things had been put into the spare room. She wondered where he was. Probably helping Mason keep the kids occupied. She'd heard them playing a game out in the backyard awhile ago. He was so good with them. He'd make a great father one day. He was so different from Kevin...

Right from the earliest days of their relationship, Kevin had made it clear he wasn't the marrying kind. His parents had divorced when he was seven. It had been a messy battle over property and the kids. As for having kids of his own, she still remembered the look of horror that had filled his eyes when she'd raised the possibility.

Three years ago, it hadn't seemed that important. She wasn't thinking long term about anything and she certainly wasn't thinking about kids, but eventually, she wanted to get married and raise a family. For her, it was a natural progression, the way things were meant to be. She'd always thought Kevin would change his mind when the time came, but the more she came to know him, the more she realized he'd meant what he said and there was little likelihood of it happening. He'd never want to marry and children were not in the cards. If she were to go back to him and try to make their relationship work, she had to accept that.

Unbidden, her thoughts circled back to Jake. He was everything Kevin was and more. A successful, kindhearted doctor who cared deeply for his patients, but he also made time for her. He'd set aside his busy schedule to be there when she needed him, which was more than she could say for Kevin. The truth was, she was tired of Kevin taking her for granted. It was just another reason why she'd reconsidered their relationship and brought it to an end.

On the other hand, Jake made her feel special, important. *But hadn't Kevin made her feel that way at first?* Was it because Jake was in love with her, like her mother said? And if so, how could that be? Until recently, she'd been with Kevin and had been for the entire time she and Jake had known each other. She'd always known he liked her more than as a friend, but she was someone else's girlfriend. *Was it possible his feelings had truly morphed into love, even so?*

She remembered the way he'd kissed her, the firm softness of his mouth. The way heat had traveled from her lips, all the way deep down inside. The tenderness and passion in his touch, like she was a most treasured thing, to be loved and cherished and valued. She'd never felt that way with Kevin.

Now that she'd put some distance between them—literally and figuratively—she could view their relationship more objectively. All of a sudden, it felt like she'd been accepting second best, like with Kevin she'd won the consolation prize. She thought about the coin toss. The fact Jake had also been a party to it wasn't endearing, but she couldn't help but wonder what would have happened if things had turned out differently—if Jake had lost the toss and Kevin had chosen Annaliese—and Jake had won her, instead?

Would she now be happily involved with him, maybe even married to him and would Kevin merely be her husband's friend? She didn't know and looking at it like that was weird. The whole situation was confusing as hell and she was no closer to a resolution.

A gentle knock on the door interrupted her tumultuous thoughts. She sat up. "Come in."

Expecting to see her sister, she was surprised and filled with a rush of nerves when the door opened and Jake filled the doorway.

"Do you want some company?" he asked.

His voice was low and washed over her the way single malt whisky slid down her throat. She wasn't a big drinker, but she had a weakness for fine scotch. Ignoring the silent warning in her head, Kat patted the spot beside her. Here at home, she could be footloose and fancy-free. If she wanted to sit in her bedroom with a man, then so be it.

Jake closed the door behind him and took a seat on the bed. Despite her cavalier attitude, Kat's nerves ratcheted up another notch. *What was she thinking?* He liked her. He liked her a lot. Her mom thought he might even be in love with her. And she liked him, too. But was it wise to be seated in such close proximity? Alone, in her bedroom, no less.

Despite her frantic thoughts, she realized she didn't want him to leave. Ever since their kiss, she'd seen him in a different light. For the first time, she didn't see Kevin's friend and business colleague. She saw Jake, the man, in all his Technicolor glory.

Once again, she noticed his midnight dark hair and the way it curled just above his collar. She saw his green eyes filled with kindness and compassion. She noticed the keen intelligence, the humor and the caring that filled his expression and when he spoke she heard how that caring colored his every word. She saw the strong jaw, the broad chest, the way he filled out his polo shirt and jeans. In fact, she noticed everything about him and it was like a revelation. He was smart, sexy and caring. *What more could she want?*

Something of her thoughts must have shown in her face. Without a word, Jake's gaze turned dark with emotion. As if in slow motion, he reached up and brushed the hair out of her eyes. His touch was warm and tender, like the light that now filled his eyes.

Her lips parted on an indrawn breath and his hand moved to cup her cheek. He drew her toward him. Slowly, slowly, his head descended until his mouth touched hers.

Like tinder had been lit and tossed into the hayshed, heat scorched a path to her core. Her hands came up to cradle his head. Her lips moved under his. Their kiss seemed to go on forever until at last, they came up for breath. Gasping, they stared at each other. An instant later, they kissed again.

This time, his lips tasted the skin at her earlobes

and nuzzled the side of her neck. He kissed his way across her jawline before finding her mouth again. His lips claimed hers and she reveled in his possession. He tasted of lemonade mixed faintly with the coffee they'd enjoyed over lunch.

She turned to face him fully and her arms came up around his neck. She drew him toward her and it seemed natural to keep going until they were both lying on the bed. Chest to chest, they kissed and touched and through fabric, they explored every nook and cranny. Finally frustrated by barriers, Jake loosened the buttons on her blouse. Moments later, it hung open, exposing her to his gaze. He spread the fabric wide, his gaze filling with wonder.

"You're so beautiful," he uttered hoarsely. "Even more beautiful than I imagined."

She flushed with pleasure. Reaching over, she ran her hand across his chest. The muscles were firm beneath the soft fabric of his shirt. All of a sudden, it wasn't enough. Tugging the shirt out of his jeans, she bunched it up around his shoulders. Loosening a few of the top buttons, Jake crossed his arms and pulled his shirt over his head.

His chest was broad and well-muscled, just like she imagined it would be. His pecs were well defined and covered in a sprinkling of black hair that drifted lower in a thin line that disappeared into his waistband. A black-and-white tattoo of the head of a border collie was emblazoned across his right shoulder. She traced the outline with her finger, wondering about its significance.

"Her name was Sadie. My parents gave her to

me when I turned five. She died three years later, trying to save my life."

Kat started in surprise. "What happened?" she asked.

Jake blew out his breath on a sigh. "Like you, I grew up in the country. I grew up outside the small township of Moree, a few hours west of here."

She nodded. "I've heard of Moree. It gets pretty hot out there. Hotter than Maitland."

"It sure does. It's nothing for the mercury to rise well above one hundred and four over summer. Anyway, that year, my brother and I were swimming in the river, like we did most weekends during the hotter months. Water had been released from the storage dam upstream to assist the farmers to irrigate their fields. The river was flowing faster than normal. My mother warned us to stay close to the edge and to watch out for hidden logs, but of course, we didn't pay much attention."

He shrugged. "I got caught up in the current and was carried off downstream. My brother—Hugh's his name—was a couple of years older, but he was no match for the force of the water. I was certain I would drown."

Kat stared at him, her heart thumping. "What happened?"

I yelled at Hugh to go for help. We weren't that far from home. He didn't want to leave me, but there was nothing else he could do. Going for help was the only option. So, he took off, shouting for anyone who might come by. It was then Sadie jumped into the water. She could see I was in trouble."

He shook his head slowly and Kat could see he was lost in his memories. His tone softened as he remembered.

"She was such a brave little dog. She swam out to me, barely keeping her head above the water. My swimming shorts had snagged on a log. Although it held me in one place, it also made it impossible for me to make it to a shallower part of the river where I could stand.

"Sadie somehow knew there was a problem. She kept ducking her head beneath the water, pulling at my clothes. Eventually, she tore my shorts and I was able to get free. I held on to her collar and she swam back toward the shore. We were nearly there when she faltered. It had been too much for her."

His voice drifted off. Kat leaned over and pressed a kiss against the tattoo. "She was a special dog," she whispered.

Jake reached for Kat's hand and squeezed it. "Yes, she was. She died in my arms, on the muddy bank of that river. I found out later she'd had a heart attack. The strain of the rescue had been too much for her."

Jake's voice had turned husky with emotion. Kat reached over and once again traced the outline of the tattoo. "It's a beautiful story and I'm sure she'd be proud that you've remembered her that way. When did you get it?"

Jake shot her a small smile. "The day I turned eighteen. I didn't say a word about it to anyone, but when my parents found out, they understood. We all knew if it hadn't been for Sadie, I'd have died."

Still lying on her side facing him, Kat reached over and pulled his head toward hers. Their lips met and fused in a kiss so sweet, it brought tears to her eyes. There was so much they hadn't talked about, so much they had to work out, but right here, right now, there was nothing she wanted more than to have Jake naked by her side.

As if sensing the need that burned inside her, Jake pulled her into his arms. Pressed close against him, she felt his erection through his jeans. Knowing that he wanted her as much as she wanted him filled her with a thrill of desire.

How could she have been blind to him all this time? This man, who was perfection. This man who was good and kind and thoughtful, who loved his dog and had honored her memory by emblazoning her image on his arm, there for all time. Compared to Jake and his selfless goodness, Kevin could never measure up. She couldn't believe it had taken her three years and one kiss to see the truth.

Pressing herself against Jake, she threaded her arms around his neck and kissed him with all the passion and hope she felt inside. She wondered what he was thinking as he kissed her back. When they pulled apart, both were breathing hard.

Jake stared at her, his emerald eyes dark with desire…and confusion.

"Kat… What are we doing?"

Chapter 10

Jake drew in a breath and did his best to get his breathing under control. The feel of Kat in his arms, against his lips was driving him wild, but he couldn't help but wonder what had caused the change in her. They'd kissed once before, in her office and at the time, she'd given him no indication she wanted to repeat it.

And then there was their discussion in the car about Kevin and how their bourgeoning relationship might affect him. That discussion hadn't been resolved. And yet, now it was like she'd dismissed all those reservations and couldn't get enough.

As much as he wanted to take all that she so freely offered, he couldn't. The truth was, he was as confused as hell. And now she stared at him with those big blue eyes looking as uncertain as he was.

"W-what do you mean?" she stammered, keeping her gaze directed somewhere in the vicinity of his navel.

"Kat, look at me."

Reluctantly, she lifted her gaze.

"What's going on here?" he asked gently.

Embarrassment bloomed across her cheeks and he hurried to reassure her. "Don't get me wrong. I'm enjoying every second of it, but you've only just come out of a long-term relationship and a few hours ago you were making arrangements for your father's funeral. As much as I want to make love to you, I've wanted you far too long to settle for anything less than your full awareness and commitment. Do you know what I'm saying?"

She squirmed against him, her discomfort obvious, but he merely tightened his hold. He wasn't going to let her get away with a blithe explanation that they'd merely let their hormones get out of control. He'd loved her for so long, he refused to accept anything but a full and frank explanation. He wanted to believe her actions pointed to feelings long since denied, but he wouldn't read more into this than there was until she set him straight with the truth, whatever that might be.

"I... I don't know what you're talking about."

"Bullshit," he said quietly.

She had the grace to look embarrassed and he was glad. He was through playing games.

"Talk to me, Kat. You know how I feel about you, how I've always felt about you. I need to know how you feel, where your head is and why we're lying half-naked beside me, on this bed, in your room. Is it merely a reaction to the trauma of the day? A way to forget the sadness for a while?"

He spread his arms wide and did his best to keep the hurt and frustration from his voice. "Is that what this is?"

She was shaking her head even before he'd finished, but he refused to acknowledge the tiny spark of hope her action ignited in his gut. Okay, so it might not be a mercy fuck she wanted, but that didn't mean she felt any more for him than she had yesterday or the day before that.

"It's not any of those things, Jake," she said quietly. She looked up at him then and he saw the sincerity in her eyes.

"I've known you for as long as I've known Kevin and yet, it's like I'd never really seen you until you kissed me."

He frowned and she hurriedly continued. "Please, try and understand. Kevin was my boyfriend. From the moment we all met, he and I were together. You were his friend and colleague, much like Shane. As much as I liked Shane, I never knew him. Don't you see? It wasn't anything personal. It's like, when you've met friends of mine from time to time. You have no special interest in them because they're just people to you—acquaintances."

He stared at her, doing his best to understand. She looked down and drew her blouse closed, as if only then becoming aware it was open. When it was re-buttoned, she looked up at him again.

"I'm not explaining myself very well, am I? The thing is, I like you, Jake. I've always liked you—but until now, only as a friend. I'm a one-person girl and I was all in with Kevin and the man I thought he was. But lately I've had my doubts and I haven't been happy. It's kind of like I've removed the rose-colored glasses and finally seen what's been in front of me all along. I'd pretty much decided there was no happy-ever-after future with Kevin. Then, when you kissed me and it felt so good, I couldn't help but think about you in a different way. It was like I was seeing you—*really* seeing you—for the first time. I was confused. I didn't know what to think. I kept coming back to your kiss. Then things came to a head with Kevin and I did what I had to do. I broke up with him."

Kevin had assured him the breakup had nothing to do with the kiss, but now Jake wasn't so sure. He opened his mouth to speak but before he could, Kat held up her hand to silence him.

"Please, let me finish. I know what you're thinking, but our kiss that time in my office had nothing to do with Kevin and I calling it quits. Things had been building up for a while. I was unhappy with a lot of things. For a long time I was in denial."

"Things... Like what?" Jake asked, wondering what could have happened between Kat and his mate to cause her to feel that way.

She sighed. "Kevin doesn't want to get married or have kids. He told me that right from the start and yet, I ignored it. I was twenty-one. Marriage and kids seemed a long way off. Now I realize those dreams are important to me and I've also had to accept Kevin's never going to feel the same way." She shrugged. "It was just another bone of contention, or at least, it would be one day."

Jake stared at her nonplussed. "Kevin doesn't want kids? Why the hell not? Who doesn't want kids?"

Kat nodded sagely. "Exactly. Except, for Kevin, it was a big deal. He lived through his parents' messy divorce. It scarred him for life. He's never going to change his outlook, even for me. I can see that now. It's just another reason why I can't see us going the distance."

Jake pursed his lips, still not convinced. "I still don't get how you went from that to getting up close and personal with me. Don't get me wrong," he added hurriedly, "I'm not complaining, but I don't want to be anyone's pity party, or worse, a rebound fling or convenient sperm donor."

She sat up and drew her legs up to her chest. Wrapping her arms around her knees, she looked at him.

"You could never be that, Jake. It's hard to believe, but it feels like I've finally opened my eyes after three years with shutters on. I won't lie. I believed I was in love with Kevin. For almost three of those years, there was nothing and no one but him. But people change. He's not the man I once knew, or if he is the same, I wasn't open to seeing any flaws. Or maybe it's me who's changed? It doesn't matter. What matters is the way I feel. I don't love Kevin anymore. I want more from life and the man I'm sharing it with. And now I believe Kevin will be happier with a woman who wants the same things and the same life he does."

Jake stared at her, still trying to reconcile this

conversation with their discussion in the car. "What about all that stuff you talked about on the way up here? About not wanting to hurt him by going out with me? Have you changed your mind?"

Kat sighed and looked away. "I'm not sure it's a change of mind or whether I've come to accept what you said. Kevin's an adult. I'm sure it won't be the first time he's had a relationship come to an end. People drift apart, move on. Okay, it's not often with someone you know or worse, someone you call a friend, but like you say, the two of you have been good mates for a long time. I'm hoping your friendship will endure, despite the fact we might start a new relationship." She looked at him. "What do you think?"

Hope warred with uncertainty deep in his gut. He wanted to believe she cared for him and that their coming together had nothing to do with Kevin or her father's death. He loved her with everything that he was. From those very early first moments, he'd been drawn to her. He was in this for the long haul. He needed to be sure she felt the same. He told her as much.

"It's like I said," she replied quietly. "This—us—has nothing to do with anyone or anything else. It's just one of those things. It could have happened at any time. For me, it was when you kissed me. For the first time, I *saw* you. I *really* saw you." She ran a hand through her hair, wincing in frustration. "I don't know how else to explain it."

She sounded so sincere. He stared at her, probing her gaze, looking for signs of deceit and found none. His heart leaped with hope. *Was it possible she did feel something for him; something more than a fleeting attraction; more than wanting a temporary distraction?*

As if sensing his capitulation, she reached out for him. As one, they moved until once again they were back in each other's arms. He groaned at the feel of her soft breasts crushed against his chest. His hands roamed over her back, feeling the soft warmth of her through her blouse. When their lips met and fused, the kiss was even sweeter than before.

And then, like gasoline poured over a fire, sudden need overtook them. Frantic, they tore at their clothes and rushed to feel skin against skin. At last, they were naked and pressed together from head to toe. Jake did his best to slow his breathing. It was their first time together. Despite the need burning inside him, he didn't want to rush it, to disappoint.

With his finger, he traced the delicate whorls of her ear and then tiptoed his fingers down her neck. "You're so beautiful," he murmured. He caressed the smooth skin of her chest before moving lower to palm her breast.

Soft and full, it filled his hand and was crowned with a dusky pink nipple. He lowered his mouth and suckled. She gasped and arched against him.

"Jake!"

Moving from one breast to the other, he rewarded her with more of the same.

She groaned and her fingers tangled in his

hair, holding him in place. He kissed his way across her stomach, taking his time, tasting, discovering; enjoying the sweet taste of her skin. At last, he moved lower and buried his face between legs.

"Oh, Jake!" she groaned again and the words seemed to have been torn from her on a gasp laced heavily with desire.

Her eyes were closed, her hands fisted. The sight and sound of her need filled him with satisfaction while at the same time, he was overwhelmed with the desire to do everything in his power to please her. This was Kat. Smart, gorgeous, funny Kat. The woman who'd stolen his heart.

His tongue slid along her soft folds slowly, rhythmically, lovingly. She tasted sweet and warm and musky. He delved deeper, probing her, loving the feel of her. His cock was rock-hard and throbbing, but he ignored it and concentrated his attention on the woman spread before him. He wanted her to forget everything and everyone but him. For this infinitesimal moment in time, he was hers and she was his.

Her breathing came faster, hitching on little gasps of pleasure. She moved, lifting her hips, turning her head from side to side, twisting in restless murmurs of invitation. He continued his onslaught, intent only on driving her wild.

"Please, Jake. I need you. I want to feel you inside me."

She half-sat and reached for him. He slid slowly up her body, loving the feel of her soft curves pressing against his hard cock. He wanted nothing more but to plunge inside her, to surround himself with her heat.

"Please," she murmured again and he captured her plea in his mouth.

His lips moved over hers, kissing her again and again. His tongue stole inside, tasting her warmth and sweetness. She clung to him, her hands tightening on his shoulders. He knew what she wanted and he wanted it too. Breaking off the kiss, he positioned himself between her legs and pressed at her opening.

"What about protection?" she gasped.

He clenched his jaw and gritted his teeth in an effort to regain control. As quickly as he could, he retrieved his wallet from his pants and pulled out a condom. Tearing open the packet, he sheathed himself and returned to the promise that beckoned to him between her thighs.

Once again, his cock stroked her entrance. Leaning forward, he threaded his fingers through hers, pressing them back, alongside her head. His gaze locked on hers.

Slowly, slowly, he eased into her warmth. His breath halted. She felt so snug around him, so good, so right. So *his*.

He slid forward, all the way inside and it was like nothing he'd ever felt before. She held his gaze, her eyes wide. A smile of wonder played around her lips. And then he moved, withdrawing almost all the way before plunging in again. Over and over, he thrust into her wetness and each time was better than the last.

Her smile faded and was replaced by a look of

fierce concentration. She shook her hands free and reached for him. With her arms tight around his neck, she wound her legs around his hips and pulled him hard against her. His breath came fast, matching hers. He wanted the moment to last forever.

All too soon, she arched against him and cried out her release. The feel of her muscles pulsing around him almost sent him over the edge. He rode out the waves of her orgasm and it was the hardest thing he'd ever done, but the feel of her clenching around his cock was also the sweetest thing he'd ever experienced.

When she was done, her body relaxed against him. She smiled up at him in contentment and more than a little awe.

"That was…amazing," she whispered.

"Yes," he replied. With his body still taut with need, that was all he could manage.

As if sensing how close he was to losing control, Kat once again reached for him. He came down upon her and groaned at the feel of her breasts; the smell of her perfume; the touch of her skin; the sight of her satisfaction… She moved against him and it was the end of him.

With a growl of need, he thrust into her, his only thought finding the relief his body craved. The pressure built inside him, centered in his balls. Over and over, he plunged inside her, desperate for release. And then he was there, at the pinnacle and she was right back there with him. Together, and with a cry, they climaxed and catapulted over the other side. With his breath coming fast, he collapsed against her, momentarily exhausted.

It seemed like a long time later when he stirred and moved his weight off her. Disposing of the condom, he returned to the bed and gathered her against his side. He was just about to drift off to sleep when he was startled by a knock at the door. Kat tensed beside him.

"Wh-who is it?" she asked.

"It's Isobel. I just put the kettle on. Would you like a cup of tea?"

Kat glanced at him and he smiled and shook his head. They'd eaten an hour earlier. He was all for an early night.

"Thanks, Issy, but I'm fine. In fact, I'm going to call it a day. I'll... I'll see you in the morning."

"Oh, all right," came the slightly amused reply. "Well, goodnight. And goodnight to you too, Jake."

Heat rushed up Jake's face. It wasn't like he and Kat weren't consenting adults, but still... They were in her parents' house. Her father was to be buried the day after next...

"Goodnight, Isobel," he managed and breathed a sigh of relief when she made no further comment. A moment later, he heard her footsteps fade away.

Kat giggled. "Busted."

Jake looked across at her and his heart swelled with love. His embarrassment faded away. "Big time."

He followed the words with a smile. He refused to let anything ruin the magic of their first time together. Reaching for the sheet, he pulled it up around them and drew her close. With his arms around her, he pressed a kiss on her hair and drifted off to sleep.

The day of Kat's father's funeral dawned bright and sunny. Jake woke to the feel of Kat's naked body pressed against him. It was the second morning he'd woken with her beside him and he couldn't help but think how wonderful it would be to have her permanently in his life and in his bed. He hoped she felt the same.

Like he had the previous morning, he kissed her awake and made sweet and tender love to her. Though she hadn't said the words, he could tell she cared for him. He was quietly confident that over time, her feelings would deepen. For now, this was enough.

Replete from their lovemaking, she stared up at him and sighed. "I could get used to this."

His heart soared, but he kept himself in check. He didn't want to scare her off by coming on too fast, too soon. She'd just come out of a relationship. He didn't want to hurry her into another and she probably didn't want that, either. Pulling her into his arms, he kissed her.

"Move in with me."

The words fell out of his mouth. He flushed and turned his face away, mortified. *What the hell was he doing? Hadn't he just given himself a lecture about rushing things?* He snuck a peek at Kat and was even more embarrassed to see the frown that marred her forehead.

"Wh-what did you say?"

He stared at the sheet. "I'm sorry, Kat. I get it. It's too soon. You've only just broken things off with Kevin. You're not looking to get into a relationship with me. You—"

"Love that you want me to move in with you, Jake, but you're right. It's too soon," she interrupted, her voice gentle.

He compressed his lips and nodded. "Forgive me. I shouldn't have said anything. I guess I just thought, with you staying with Mason and Isobel and the kids, it's probably crowded. I thought you might be more comfortable at my place. I have a spare room and..."

His voice drifted off. There was no need to prolong his embarrassment. She didn't want to move in with him and that was that. And then she surprised him. She reached over and cupped her hand against his cheek.

"You're a special man, Jake Alexander and I could very easily fall in love with you. I think we owe it to each other to take things slow." She looked down at them, naked beneath the sheet and a wry grin tugged at her lips. "Okay, maybe I should have said something before we ravished each other's bodies over and over again, but I guess I've had other things on my mind."

He frowned, suddenly stricken with the thought that the past couple of days of bliss had been nothing more than a distraction from the reality of attending her father's funeral, like he'd first thought. He opened his mouth to ask the question, but she shushed him and pressed her fingers against his lips.

"I know what you're thinking," she said, "and you're wrong. I've already told you, what happened between us has nothing to do with my father's death or Kevin or Shane or anything else. It's about us, two people coming together with a mutual caring and respect. The fact that we fancy the hell out of each other is a bonus."

He nodded, relieved, but forced himself to ask. "Why can I hear a 'but' coming?"

Her gaze remained steady on his. "Already you know me so well," she murmured, smiling.

He wanted to smile back, but his heart was beating so hard, he could barely breathe. The next few words she uttered would make or break them. His gut knotted.

"You're right about Isobel and Mason's place. Their condo is bursting at the seams. I was going to call some friends upon my return to Sydney and ask if anyone had a spare room." Her expression became earnest. "Moving in with you is an answer to my prayers, but I don't want to rush things. You're a very special person. You're someone I could fall in love with. I don't want to jump into another relationship on the rebound. You deserve better than that."

"Then move in as a roommate," he blurted out, desperate to have her on any terms.

Her eyes widened in surprise. "A roommate? Would you be all right with that?"

"Yes, of course. Like I told you, I have plenty of space. You can pay your share of the expenses and then come and go as you please, like any roommate would and it might help soften the blow for Kevin. We could keep things low key until he has time to get used to the idea of us together."

A tiny smile played around her mouth. "You're right. A roommate. Yes, I like the sound of that."

"It's the perfect solution," he added and wondered how the hell he'd gotten into this situation.

It wasn't the solution he wanted. He wanted Kat beside him, as his partner, in his bed, every night. Roommates shared periphery details of their lives but they most certainly didn't share body fluids. Still, if this was the only way she'd agree to live under his roof, he'd take it and use the opportunity of having her in such close proximity, to win her over.

Satisfied that he could make it happen, he pulled her in for a hug.

"Thank you, Jake," she murmured against his shoulder.

"Hey, it's no big deal. Like I said, I have plenty of room."

"I mean, thank you for everything. For driving up here with me, helping me and Mom, coming to the funeral... It means a lot to me."

His heart swelled with love and tenderness. He tightened his arms about her. He'd been in love with Katrina West for almost as long as he'd known her. There was nothing he wouldn't do for her.

CHAPTER 11

Dear Diary,

The funeral service was uninspiring. Apart from me and my work colleagues, there were only a handful of family and friends. Who knew Shane had such a small circle of acquaintances? Not that it would have mattered to me. I've always had fewer friends than most.

I reintroduced myself to his mother, reminded her who I was. She remembered me, of course. We'd met earlier in the week, when I came to give her the sad news and later, at the funeral home. She thanked me for caring enough to come to Shane's funeral and then surprised me by telling me how her son often spoke of me. For a moment, I was paralyzed with shock and then the horror set in. I was the reason he was lying there, still and pale in his coffin. All the time I knew him, he never gave me any indication that my name had passed his lips.

Whenever we spoke, it was about his mother and how she needed him; how much he loved her and why he couldn't be with me. It was my daddy and mom all over again. Once again, I was the outsider, the interloper standing on the outside looking in.

I looked at that old woman in her wheelchair, squinting at me through her almost-blind eyes and all I felt was hatred. I made the wrong decision! All this time, I was convinced it was Shane who had to die. How did I not see what was right before my eyes?

It was her, this old, worn-out woman, this woman who life had used up, spat out, forgotten. It was her I should have sent on her way. It would have been so easy and yet, the thought never occurred to me.

Stupid! Stupid! Stupid! I want to scream and thrash with rage. I killed the only man I've ever loved while the reason he couldn't be with me is still alive and well. Okay, maybe not well, but alive and that's what matters.

She tells me how Shane spoke of me with such fondness and I want to smile at the sheer pleasure of knowing I meant something to him; that, despite everything, I was more than he led me to believe...

And then I remember: He's gone. He'll never speak of me or to me again.

I still can't believe how fucking stupid I've been!

———————————

Kevin cast a furtive glance over his shoulder, despite the fact he'd twice checked the clinic for occupants. The office was closed for Shane's funeral. Everyone would be there. Kevin was expected too, but he knew any minute Vlad could call, reminding him his week was up.

Stealthily entering the storeroom, he opened

the built-in cupboard that stood in the far corner of the room. Reaching in, he pressed against the fake back wall he'd had installed for just this purpose. Pulling the board out of the way, he felt in the cavity behind. His hands closed around the packets of codeine and he couldn't help but sigh. His tension eased.

Working quickly, he counted the packets and for the second time confirmed they were all there. Almost lightheaded with relief, he returned them to their hidey-hole. His pharmaceutical friend had come through for him just in time. He replaced the back panel and closed the cupboard. It was going to be fine. He'd managed to procure enough to fulfil Vlad's order. The pressure was off him. For now.

He cursed under his breath at the thought. *What the hell was he doing?* Only a week earlier, desperate and defeated, sitting on the floor of his apartment, he'd vowed to put an end to this. It wasn't like he needed the money. The practice was doing well. It was more the adrenaline rush of knowing he was doing something illegal. He liked the feeling of living on the edge. All his life, he'd played by the rules and always done as he was told.

'You're such a good boy, Kevin,' his mother would say, even when he wanted to rant and rave about the injustice of the divorce that had torn their family apart. His brother went to stay with their father and Kevin got to live with their mom. They were never a real family again; just people related to each other on paper, passing in the night.

He studied hard, made the debating team, was prefect in his final year of school. He went to college, finished medical school—all because he wanted to make his mother proud. 'I've sacrificed a lot for you, son,' she'd told him. 'You owe it to me to achieve great things. Don't let me down, now, will you?'

And so Kevin had kept playing by the rules right up until earlier that year, when he'd crossed paths with Anatoly Petrov's wife. After his initial shock had worn off, he'd given the man's proposition due thought and had finally agreed to the terms. The deal was quite precipitous, especially for Petrov and Vlad. The sale of codeine had long since been restricted in drug stores. Customers purchasing it had to leave their details so law enforcement could keep a record of who was buying and in what quantities.

Then there was talk the purchase of codeine products would soon require a prescription. No longer would folks be able to walk into the drug store and buy it over the counter. Obtaining it by legal means would become so much more difficult.

At first, he'd been shocked and ecstatic when he considered what he'd agreed to do. But gradually, a few transactions later, the reality of dealing with the fringes of society took their toll, not the least being how he'd managed to get himself tied up with the likes of Vladimir Mikolaev. And now, though he was filled with a burning determination to bring their association to an end, once and for all, he didn't have a clue how to go about it without risking a beating, or worse. All he wanted was to return to his old life, to once again become the law-abiding Kevin Johnson who worked hard, played hard and abided by the rules.

"Kevin? Are you in here?"

Jake.

Fuck.

Kevin's depressing thoughts dissolved like instant coffee grains in hot water. *What the hell was Jake doing here?* He was meant to be at Shane's funeral. Dragging in a breath and forcing himself to remain calm, Kevin strode across the storeroom and opened the door. Jake stood with his back to him, just inside Kevin's office.

"Jake," he said.

Jake spun around. "What the hell are you still doing here? We're meant to be at the church. Shane's service is about to begin."

Kevin compressed his lips. Even now, the thought of Shane's death filled him with sadness. "Yeah. I'm sorry. I thought I left my...wallet here. I couldn't find it at home."

"And did you?"

"Yeah." Kevin slapped Jake on the back. "Come on, let's go."

———————

Devlin and Bryce stood unobtrusively off to one side and scanned the small crowd of funeral goers, looking for something out of place. It was a normal part of any murder investigation to attend the funeral of the deceased. The attendees were scrutinized and sometimes photographed, and later, the photos were analyzed and discussed. It was always interesting to know who showed up to the funeral of a murder victim, and even more interesting, who stayed away.

"Isn't that Vladimir Mikolaev over there?" Bryce murmured, his lips barely moving.

Devlin looked in the direction Bryce had indicated and noted the short, heavyset man dressed in a dark, ill-fitting suit who stood on the periphery of the crowd in the shade of a tall eucalypt.

"That's him," Devlin replied.

"Now, why do you think a man like that would be at the funeral of the well-respected Doctor Shane Cannington, Devlin?" Bryce mused.

Devlin compressed his lips. The fact that one of the prime suspects involved in illegal meth labs was there told them everything. There had been far more going on in that medical practice than anybody realized and Devlin was determined to get to the bottom of it.

"I ran a firearms check on the doctors and their secretary," he said, pitching his voice low.

Bryce looked at him. "What did you find?"

"It's pretty interesting reading. Both Kevin Johnson and Holly Greenwood hold licenses. Holly Greenwood leans toward handguns. She owns an M9 .22 caliber Beretta and a .22 caliber semi-auto Buckmark Browning."

Bryce's eyes widened in surprise. "Nice."

"Yeah, and they just happen to be the same caliber gun that killed our victim." His lips twisted in a humorless smile. "Like I said, it was interesting reading."

"What kind of gun is Johnson licensed to carry?" Bryce asked.

"It appears he favors rifles over handguns. According to the firearms registry, he owns a Remington 700 BDL bolt action rifle and a Winchester Safari Express. Not without funds, our doctor. The Winchester was purchased a month ago. I made some enquires. Apparently he likes to go hunting."

Bryce looked dubious. "In Sydney?"

"He owns a small farm out near Richmond."

"What about Holly Greenwood? What's her story?"

The small gathering of people began to move toward the front door of the church. Devlin hung back and answered Bryce's question.

"She's into target shooting. According to Joe at the St Mary's Pistol Club, she's quite good at it, too."

"So, Holly Greenwood has a gun the same caliber our perp used on the victim. Kevin Johnson is also familiar with firearms and he has a suspected methamphetamine manufacturer on speed dial."

Devlin nodded. "You've summed it up well, except Johnson has an alibi."

"Right. The girlfriend."

"Ex-girlfriend, apparently."

Bryce raised an eyebrow. "Really?"

"Yes. My sources tell me the happy couple went their separate ways not long after the murder. Interesting timing, don't you think?"

"Very interesting. Still doesn't prove anything.

People break up all the time. A good lawyer would convince a jury of that in an instant."

Devlin stared toward the church and noted the funeral goers had now disappeared inside. "You're right. We need more." He glanced at his partner. "Let's talk to Lachlan and see what else he's got on Mikolaev."

"Did the secretary send those accounts over yet?"

"Yes. They appear in order although there are a few entries that have a cross next to them, like someone was drawing attention to them. The initials KJ were also written beside them."

Bryce's expression registered the significance of the letters. "As in Kevin Johnson."

Devlin shrugged non-committedly. "Perhaps. Or it could mean Kevin and Jake."

"What do the entries relate to?"

"I'm no bookkeeper, but they seem to be random withdrawals and deposits, often of large sums each time. It all balances, though. What came out eventually went back in."

Bryce frowned in thought. "What do you think it means?"

"I don't know, but I sure as hell intend to find out."

Jake glanced across at Kat and then returned his attention to the road. The funeral was over. Shane had been laid to rest. Jake had offered his condolences to Shane's wheelchair-bound mother and made small talk with relatives he'd never met and would likely never meet again. Kat looked pensive and he could only guess her thoughts were still on the sad events of the day. Coming so close on the heels of her father's funeral, he could only imagine her somber state of mind. Still, they were on their way home. Together. Despite everything that had happened, Jake couldn't help the spurt of excitement that traveled through his veins.

Kat was coming home with him. She was moving into the spare room. A few yards from his bedroom. They would share the bathroom and pass in the hall. They'd be bumping into each other in the modest kitchen. Maybe even sit across from each other at the breakfast table, drinking coffee and eating bagels.

The fantasies became intimate and then even more lurid and it wasn't until someone blasted a horn behind him, reminding him the light had turned green, that he dragged his thoughts back to reality. The fact was, she was moving in as his roommate. He'd been the one to suggest the terms and now he had to live with them.

He gritted his teeth and prayed for the strength to see it through. Having Kat in his home, sitting on his couch, sleeping down the hall was better than nothing. It was a start and right now, that would have to do.

Kat pushed away thoughts of Shane and her

father and followed Jake into the foyer of an ultra-modern, cement-rendered apartment complex situated in the beachside suburb of Maroubra. His new lodgings were at least an hour further away from the place they'd all shared in the city and meant the commute to work would also be much longer, but unlike their old place, this building was sleek and new and with its off-white exterior and navy-blue trim, it looked sufficiently maritime to complement the ocean backdrop she spied not far away.

"You have a nice place," she said as they waited a little awkwardly for the elevator to arrive.

Jake glanced at her. He held a suitcase in either hand. "Thanks. It's not as convenient as the place we had in the city, but it comes with all the mod cons and I still get an ocean view."

Kat remained silent. She was the reason Jake had moved out of the older style apartment he'd once shared with Kevin. She was sure Jake bore her no ill will, but the reminder made her slightly uncomfortable, just the same. As if sensing her discomfort, Jake reached out and touched her arm.

"Hey, it's okay. Everything happens for a reason. I didn't mind moving out. I wouldn't have found this place, if I'd stayed. It might not be as close to the city or to work, but it beats the four-storey walk-up I left behind."

She gave him a small smile, appreciating his effort to lighten the mood. "You're right. Lugging shopping bags up all those stairs is one thing I'm definitely not going to miss. You can't beat the convenience of an elevator."

As if on cue, the elevator announced its arrival with a *ding*. The doors slid open and she and Jake stepped inside. Within moments, they were transported to his condo on the seventh floor. After a quick tour of the place, Jake left Kat to get settled with the promise that as this was her first night, he'd cook dinner.

Kat heard the door close softly behind him as he headed to the shops. She went to the window of the spare bedroom he'd shown her and pulled back the drapes. The view wasn't quite as good as the one she'd left behind in the city, but they were above all the rooftops and she saw the blue of the ocean in the distance. The beach was probably half a dozen blocks away.

Turning away, she picked up one of her suitcases and set it down on the bed. She'd only packed the bare necessities. She'd go back later for the rest of her stuff when Kevin was at work and on a day he hadn't just buried his friend.

Coming so soon after her father's funeral, Shane's service had reduced her to tears. She and Shane had never been close, but it saddened her to think how his life had been cut short so tragically. He'd been a talented surgeon and would be sorely missed, both in the medical community and by his friends.

Kat had offered her condolences to his mother and wondered how the woman would cope now that her son was gone. It was obvious her illness had developed to the point where she was quite debilitated. Wheelchair bound, almost blind and unable to stand without assistance, she'd need live-in help. Either that or she'd be faced with the prospect of selling her house and going into a nursing home. Kat was sure neither option filled the woman with joy.

It had surprised Kat to discover only a small number of friends and colleagues were at the service. Shane had been well liked and respected and yet Kat knew most of the people there. Holly had sobbed uncontrollably throughout most of it to the point where Kat was concerned the woman might need something to calm her down. Kat had tried to convey her concern to Jake through eye movements and shakes of her head and she'd been relieved when he'd gone over to the girl and offered her comfort.

Pulling clothes out of her suitcase, Kat turned and opened the closet door. Apart from a couple of winter coats, the hangers were bare. With quiet efficiency, she unpacked her belongings and steadfastly kept her mind off the fact she was now living in Jake's home.

Ever since she'd returned from Maitland, he'd been on her mind. Despite their agreement to keep things low-key for Kevin's sake, it was going to be harder for her to do that than she'd thought. It wasn't just that she and Jake had enjoyed mind-blowing sex, although that was enough to disrupt any warm-blooded female's equilibrium.

No, it was Jake himself. The more time she spent with him, the more she liked him and the more time she wanted to spend with him. She wanted to know everything about him, right down to his favorite color. She still found it hard to believe how she'd been blind to his appeal. It just went to show how besotted she'd been with Kevin. She hadn't noticed what was right before her eyes.

Kevin.

He'd been at the funeral, of course, and she'd greeted him with a polite hug and a kiss. They were burying his friend. It was the least she could do. But when he'd cornered her at the wake and had asked her to move back in, she'd quietly told him she'd meant it when she'd said they were over and they wouldn't be getting back together.

Like they'd talked about at her mom's place, she and Jake had kept their distance from each other. Neither wanted to inflict upon Kevin any unnecessary pain. There would be time enough to tell him she'd moved into Jake's spare room.

The sound of the front door opening caught her attention. It must be Jake returning from the shops. She heard him call out to her, followed by the rustle of bags. Finishing up her unpacking, she put the last things on the shelf and closed the door to the closet. Her toiletries remained in their bag on the bed. Jake had warned her there was only one bathroom.

She didn't mind. She'd shared with a man before. But Kevin had been a man she was sleeping with. She wasn't sure how it would be, sharing with Jake. Waiting for him to finish in the shower, knowing he was naked and wet. The thought sent a shiver of desire coursing down her spine. Heat centered in her core. It had been three days since they'd returned to Sydney. Three days since he'd held her in his arms, kissed her, loved her, touched her every way she could ever want.

Had she made the right decision? Before they'd left Maitland, Isobel had pulled her aside and impressed upon her there was always room at her place. Her sister was concerned that Kat was jumping into another relationship way too fast. That it wasn't healthy. Said Kat needed a break. Needed time to sort out who she was and what she wanted out of life before deciding who she wanted to share that with.

Kat had been grateful for her sister's concern and her offer of a bed, but she wanted to spend time with Jake. She'd vowed to herself and her sister to take things slow, to maintain the friendship she'd had with him for years. But knowing he was right down the hall and even now, preparing their dinner, she wondered how long she could keep her promise.

Jake stared at Kat where she sat opposite him at the dinner table. The steak and jacket potatoes had been eaten, along with the green salad, the store-bought apple pie and ice cream enjoyed with coffee and liqueurs. Kat confessed she had a weakness for butterscotch schnapps and Jake just happened to have a bottle.

Together, they ate and drank and talked about everything from Shane and his funeral to the current state of political affairs. They chuckled over a cartoon they'd both seen in the newspaper a fortnight earlier and they discovered a mutual love of mystery authors. By the end of it, the sadness he'd seen in her eyes earlier had all but disappeared. It was all Jake could have dreamed of and more. He never wanted the evening to end.

But end it did, after clearing the table and stacking the dishwasher. Kat declined his offer of coffee and bid him a quiet goodnight. She reached up and pecked him on the cheek and it was all he could do not to take her in his arms. Her sweet perfume wafted toward him. His heart took off double time.

"Thank you for dinner, Jake. It was lovely."

He struggled to speak. "You're welcome. It's nice to cook for someone other than myself."

She smiled. "You like to cook?"

"Yes. I don't do it as frequently as I'd like and of course, it's not the same when you're only cooking for yourself. What about you? Do you cook?"

She laughed and the sound of it worked its way down to his soul. "I'm not sure that you'd call me a cook. I have a few tried and true recipes I call on when I have to, but Kevin and I spent a lot of time eating out."

Jake nodded and tried not to let the mention of Kevin dampen the mood. She'd broken things off with Kevin. She'd assured Jake it was for good and said it was time to look forward, to the future. A future he hoped would include him.

Kat smothered a yawn. Jake shot her a grin, his

heart turning over with tenderness. It had been a long week, for both of them. He was weary, too.

"I'm sorry, I guess I'm more tired than I thought," she said. A faint blush stained her cheeks.

Jake moved closer and gave her a brief hug and then forced himself to step away. "Go to bed, Kat. I'll see you in the morning. I don't have to leave for work until eight."

"Thanks, Jake. I appreciate everything you've done."

He waved her thanks away. It wasn't her gratitude he wanted. "There are clean towels in the linen cupboard in the hall. Help yourself."

With a nod and another smile, she turned and walked away.

CHAPTER 12

Holly made sure the way was clear before heading stealthily down the corridor to Kevin's office. Jake was still at the hospital and Kevin was in between patients. He looked up when she entered and then frowned when she closed the door.

"Not now, Holly. I'm busy. Whatever it is, it will have to wait."

Ignoring him, she stepped closer until she reached his wide desk. Leaning over, she smiled at him, taking care to give him a good view of her generous cleavage. Appearing unaffected, Kevin stared back at her, his expression blank.

She swallowed her irritation and pouted. "I'm lonely, Kevin and it's all your fault."

His expression remained unchanged. "How is it my fault?"

"You know Shane and I were seeing each other and now...he's gone. You and I always got along well together. We've helped each other in the past." She looked at him from beneath her thick lashes, her voice full of innuendo. "We could always do that again."

Kevin sighed and shook his head. "I'm sorry, Holly. I'm not interested."

She bit down on her irritation and tried harder. Shooting him a calculating smile, she twirled a stray piece of hair around the end of her finger. "That's not what you said last time."

"I was trying to be nice. Now it doesn't matter."

His words stung. She pulled back and glared at him. "Don't give me that bullshit. You were the one who came on to me and you enjoyed every minute of it."

He shrugged and his casual disregard infuriated her.

"Let's not pretend we both didn't benefit from it, Holly. You were trying to make Shane jealous and I was looking for a fuck. For a while, we enjoyed what each of us had to offer. But guess what? Shane's dead and I couldn't care less about the fact that you're feeling lonely. We're done. Got it?"

Her anger hit the boiling point. Without thinking, she reached out and slapped his handsome face. He stared at her in shock. In seconds, an angry red handprint was visible on his cheek.

"You little bitch!" he swore, pushing away from his desk.

She stepped back in alarm. He towered over her and outweighed her by more than a hundred pounds. She was no contest for him and he knew it. Thankfully, she'd brought along just the thing to set him in his place. Diving into the deep pocket of her dress, she pulled out her shiny Beretta and pointed it right at his head.

"Touch me and I'll tell the police everything," she said in a rush, trying hard to conceal her panic. It wouldn't do to let him know she feared him. It was never a good idea to let the enemy see your weakness.

Her fingers itched to pull the trigger, but she resisted the urge. Killing someone took planning. A failure to think things through properly resulted in errors and she prided herself on never making mistakes. Besides, from the look of shock and anger that warred with fear on Kevin's face, she didn't need to do more than threaten.

Then anger appeared to get the upper hand. His face turned a mottled red and his lips twisted on a snarl.

"Careful, Holly. You might want to watch yourself or you could end up like Shane. We wouldn't want that to happen."

She laughed without humor. His threats meant nothing to her. "You haven't got the balls to do something like that."

His eyes narrowed. "How do you know?"

Holly shivered at the menace in his voice, but her trigger hand didn't move. She kept her expression carefully blank. Shane was dead. Kevin was right: There was no longer any point in sleeping with Shane's colleague. The man she'd hoped to make jealous by her actions was now buried beneath the ground. But Holly had another ace up her sleeve. There was something else she could get off Kevin Johnson and it didn't involve sex.

She lowered the gun. "I want money," she said boldly, pleased at her fearless tone.

Kevin merely smiled and shook his head. "Poor little Holly," he said, his gaze raking over her in a condescending way. "You just don't get it, do you?"

A sudden surge of anger pushed her forward. Once again, she raised the pistol in Kevin's direction and glared at him.

"No, Kevin. You're the one who doesn't get it!" she hissed. "Have you forgotten what I know? One word and I can ruin you. How do you think Kat would feel if she knew you've been fucking me for the past six months?"

Kevin merely laughed, surprising her. "Ha! It appears you haven't heard. I guess you were too busy weeping over Shane to notice. Kat and I broke up. She won't care what you say."

Holly blinked back her astonishment. The hand that held the gun went slack. Kat and Kevin had been together for years. They'd been a couple for as long as Holly had known them. To tell the truth, she'd been envious of their closeness. It was the reason she'd tried so hard to make things work with Shane, even to the point where she slept with Kevin. It was maddening to know that her efforts had come to nothing and now Shane was dead...

"What is it, Holly? Nothing to say?" Kevin goaded.

Holly clenched her fists at her sides. The hard metal butt of the pistol dug into her fingers. She wanted nothing more than to wipe the smug expression off his face and she could do it so easily. Raising her hand, taking aim, pulling the trigger... It could be all over in less than three seconds. He'd never know what hit him. Unfortunately, Jake could arrive any minute. He usually checked in with them at some point in the day. And then there were the patients due in shortly...

Swallowing a sigh of resignation, she glared at the man who stood across from her. "Okay, you have me. Kat might not care about your infidelities. She's always been a rather understanding girl, but I wonder if Jake will be so understanding when I tell him about the drugs."

That barb struck home. Kevin's face lost most of its color. A moment later, he seemed to regain control of himself though anger still glittered in the depths of his blue eyes.

"You wouldn't dare," he snarled, but he couldn't hold her gaze.

She smiled and moved closer, sensing victory. She caressed the barrel of the gun like it was the firm, toned skin of a lover. "Just watch me."

––––––––––––

Devlin headed back to his desk with a cup of coffee in tow and saw Lachlan there, waiting for him. "To what do I owe this pleasure?" he asked, pulling out his chair.

Lachlan tossed a USB stick on Devlin's desk.

Devlin picked it up. "What's this?"

"Surveillance taken four nights ago."

"Who were you watching?"

"We've been tailing Vladimir Mikolaev. Guess where he showed up?"

Devlin shrugged, but his heart had picked up its pace. Lachlan wouldn't be here if he didn't have something Devlin could use. "Tell me."

"Your boys' medical center."

Excitement surged through Devlin, but he forced it back in check. "Is that so?" he said casually.

"Yep. We caught him driving past the building twice before he eventually pulled up and went inside. We can't prove which floor he visited, but it was late. The building was locked up tight."

"Someone let him in," Devlin guessed.

Lachlan nodded, his expression grim. "Yeah. The question is, who? No lights inside to indicate where he went or who he met. There were two cars in the nearby parking lot. One belonged to Kevin Johnson."

Devlin grimaced. "Let me guess. The other one belonged to Alexander."

Lachlan winked. "Go straight to the top of the class, Detective."

"Shit." Devlin hit the desk with the flat of his palm. He welcomed the sting. It distracted him momentarily from the frustration that had been building inside him ever since the murder had been reported.

"So, it could have been either of them Mikolaev was meeting," Devlin stated.

"Or both," Lachlan replied.

Devlin let out a heavy sigh. For every step

forward, it felt like they took two back. Still, any progress was better than none. It was the second time they'd found a connection to Mikolaev. Lachlan's theory that the doctors were involved in illegal drug trafficking had just been given a boost. The only thing they had to do was prove it.

"Have you looked at the CCTV footage from the night of the murder?" Lachlan asked.

"The security company still hasn't handed it over. Apparently they need consent from the building's owner."

"You could always get a warrant."

"Yeah. I was hoping to do it the easy way. I'll give them a call and chase it up. Hopefully they'll be ready to hand it over." He took a sip from his coffee cup and set it back down on the desk. He drew his keyboard toward him. "In the meantime, I'm going to dig a little deeper into our suspects, starting with the reputable Doctor Alexander."

Lachlan pushed away from Devlin's desk and made to leave. Devlin looked up at him.

"Thanks for that, Lachie. Appreciate it."

Lachlan nodded. "No problem. Always happy to help get another criminal off the streets."

He disappeared in the direction of the staff restrooms and Devlin returned his attention to the screen in front of him. He'd left a message for Jake Alexander to call him, but as yet, hadn't heard back from the man. Logging onto the police database, he entered Jake's details. Several hits filled the page. He slowly scrolled through them, eliminating the first ones based on age. Finally, he narrowed it down to two. Clicking on one of them, he scanned the bio. His heart skipped a beat.

"Well, what do you know," he murmured. Jake Alexander had a criminal record.

Devlin scanned the meager details, taking notes. The case involved an ex-girlfriend, but had never gone to trial. According to the police records, the charges had been dropped. In Devlin's experience, the main reason charges were dropped in cases of domestic abuse was because the victim was too terrified to testify.

The information on the screen didn't give him any further details, but that wouldn't stop him from finding out. He already wanted to speak to Alexander about the strange deposits and withdrawals. This was something else that warranted a closer look and it was another strike against the man.

Not only had Jake Alexander had an argument with the victim just days before his murder, the good doctor was the only suspect without an alibi. And though he might not own a firearm, they were easy enough to come by illegally if someone had enough money and knew where to look.

Clearing the search screen, Devlin entered Kevin Johnson's details. Though several Kevin Johnsons came up, none of them were a match. Apart from a couple of minor traffic offenses, Shane Cannington also came up clean.

With a sigh, Devlin pushed the keyboard away and contemplated what he'd found. A criminal record for a domestic assault didn't necessarily make someone a murderer, but coupled with the other evidence, things weren't looking good for Jake Alexander. Forget about waiting for the man to return his call. It was time to pay him another visit.

Kat padded to the kitchen to pour herself another cup of coffee. She'd been enjoying her day off, kicking back on Jake's balcony with the latest Nora Roberts novel. A knock on the door caught her attention and she frowned. She'd been living in Jake's condo for less than twenty-four hours and there weren't many people who knew she was there. She hadn't even told her boss. Whoever it was would more likely be looking for Jake and he was at work.

The knock came again, followed by a voice. "Doctor Alexander, it's Detective Grayson. Are you in there?"

Kat's heart skipped a beat and then her pulse took off at a gallop. It was the detective. The same one she'd spoken to at the station the day Shane's body had been discovered. She hurried to the door, hoping he had good news.

"Oh, I'm sorry. I'm looking for Doctor Alexander."

Kat noted the confusion on the detective's face and held out her hand. "Hello, Detective. It's nice to see you again."

The detective frowned. "I thought you lived with Kevin Johnson?"

Heat crept up Kat's neck, but she resolutely ignored it. *So what if she'd broken up with her boyfriend?* People broke up all the time. She'd done nothing to be ashamed of. She cleared her throat and set the detective straight. "We broke up."

"Really? It didn't have anything to do with the fact he nominated you as his alibi witness, did it? You didn't suddenly get cold feet, did you?"

Kat stared at him, not sure how to respond. *Did he really think she'd lie about something like that, even for her boyfriend?*

The detective shot her an inscrutable look and kept speaking. "So, you broke up with Kevin and moved in with his business partner and best friend… Is that right?"

Kat bristled at the detective's insinuation, but forced her anger back under control. "Yes, Detective. That's exactly what happened. Is there a problem?"

The detective shrugged. "No, no problem. It just seems a little hasty. How's Kevin taking it?"

Once again, Kat held on to her temper. "Not that it's any of your business, Detective, but I don't think Kevin knows yet. I moved in to Jake's spare room yesterday afternoon. I haven't had a chance to tell anyone. We're roommates. That's all."

The detective shot her a knowing look and Kat was filled with a surge of irritation. He didn't believe her. She crossed her arms over her chest and glared at him, already done with the conversation.

"Look, Detective, you didn't come here to speak with me. Jake's not at home. He won't finish work until late tonight, so there's no point wasting any more of your time. Give me your card again. I think I lost the last one. I'll let him know you were here and tell him to give you a call."

The detective shot her a smile that failed to reach his eyes. "That's all good, Doctor West, but you know, my trip over here hasn't been a waste of time. It turns out I have a few more questions for you, too."

Kat tensed. "For me?"

"Yes. Do you mind if I come in?"

Kat stared at him. She was tempted to refuse him entrance. After all, what more could she tell him? She had hardly known Shane Cannington and she definitely didn't know anything about who might have murdered him. Still, there was no point antagonizing the detective unnecessarily. Without his help, they might never find Shane's killer.

Stepping back, Kat released the security latch and pulled open the door. The detective followed her down the short corridor and into the open concept kitchen and living room.

"This is a nice place you have here," he commented, taking in the tastefully furnished room that was dominated by the ocean view.

"Thank you. Like I said, it belongs to Jake."

"Yes, he's done well for himself, hasn't he?" the detective mused. "Who would have thought a man with a criminal record could set himself up with something like this?"

Kat frowned, not sure that she'd heard him right. "What are you talking about? What criminal record?"

The detective turned to face her, his hands in his pockets. "Seriously? He didn't tell you?"

A sense of foreboding trickled through Kat's veins, but she forced herself to reply. "Tell me what?"

"That a few years ago, he was charged with a serious assault. It related to a claim of domestic abuse. The victim was his ex-girlfriend. A woman by the name of Joanna-Marie Penberthy."

Kat stared at the detective. She saw his lips moving, but the noise in her ears blocked out any further sound. *Jake on assault charges? Domestic abuse?* That couldn't be right.

"There must be some mistake," she blurted out and heard the desperation in her voice.

The detective merely shook his head. "No. There's no mistake. I saw the record."

Filled with shock, Kat felt her legs give out. Stumbling toward the couch, she collapsed on the leather seat. The detective continued speaking and she saw him hold out a card. Blindly, she reached for it. The next time she looked up, he was gone.

Devlin returned to the station deep in thought. He'd known Kevin Johnson's girlfriend had ended their relationship, but he'd been surprised to discover she'd moved on so quickly, and with her ex-boyfriend's best friend. It was an interesting development and right now, he didn't know how it all fit together. Katrina West was Kevin's alibi. He was with her the night of the murder. Or so she said.

Was it possible she'd lied for him and was now having second thoughts? He wished he knew.

Putting his shoulder to the door of the squad room, he made a beeline for his desk. Bryce sat behind the desk opposite. He acknowledged Devlin with a nod. "You're back. How did things go with Alexander?"

"He wasn't home. I left a message with Katrina West for him to call me ASAP."

Bryce looked at him quizzically. "Katrina West? You mean, Doctor Johnson's old girlfriend?"

"Yes, it appears she's gotten over him already. She's moved in with none other than Jake Alexander. She tried to give me some bullshit story that they were only roommates, but I'm not sure if I believe it. All I need to figure out is what it means and how it affects our investigation."

"So, what are you waiting for?" Bryce joked.

Devlin gave him the finger. Bryce chuckled. "How did things go with Holly Greenwood?" Devlin asked.

"I have a meeting with her this afternoon at the clinic. She offered to stay back late so I can speak to her after the last patient leaves."

Devlin raised an eyebrow. "That's mighty accommodating of her. Did you tell her you were prepared to make a house call?"

"Yes, but she said she lived way out at St Mary's and offered to save me the time it would take to travel there and back. As she's already at the clinic, it makes sense for me to see her there. Don't worry, I'm not complaining. The clinic is a hell of a lot closer than St Mary's and with peak hour traffic about to kick off any minute..."

Devlin nodded. "I get it. Don't forget to ask her about those guns. See if she will hand them over for testing."

"I'll try, but if she knows anything about the law, she'll know that without a warrant, she doesn't have to hand over anything. Besides, without the bullets, we can't match them to a specific weapon. The best we can do is prove her guns were fired recently. Given that you told me she attends the rifle range on a regular basis, any defense lawyer worth his pay packet would blow that one out of the water."

Devlin cursed quietly, his frustration getting the better of him. They were going around in circles. There were circumstantial links to a suspected drug supplier, but no evidence that the connection had anything to do with the murder; one of the doctors had no alibi and admitted to a disagreement with the victim in the days before his death, but once again, they had nothing linking the man to the murder; the other partner was familiar with firearms, but didn't own the same caliber gun that was used to kill his colleague. What was more, *that* doctor had an alibi and no motive.

Then there was the receptionist. Even in the

midst of the trauma of discovering her boss dead in his office, she'd remained helpful and compliant. She'd answered their questions, provided information, was available to take their calls. She'd done everything she could to assist the investigation and though she owned the type of gun that could have been used in the murder, as far as they knew, she was also without a motive.

"Does Holly Greenwood have an alibi?"

Bryce frowned. "Apart from the fact she said she left work around six the evening of the murder, I'm not sure. She's a long way down the suspect list. I haven't asked her to give an account of her movements after she left the building that evening."

"We need to ask her, just to make sure. After all, of all the suspects, she's the one who actually owns a .22 caliber weapon and she had access to the building."

"You're right. I'll add that question to my list."

"Good. Let me know what you find out."

The phone in Devlin's pocket vibrated. He drew it out and looked at the screen: a number with no Caller ID. It could be anyone. With a sigh, he answered it.

"Detective Grayson."

"Detective, it's Doctor Jake Alexander. I'm sorry, I've been caught up at work and haven't had a chance to return your call. What can I do for you?"

"Where are you, Doctor?"

"I'm at work, Detective. I'm calling from the hospital."

That explained the lack of a Caller ID. "I see. Have you spoken to your girlfriend?"

"If you're referring to Katrina West, she's not my girlfriend, and no, I haven't spoken to her today. Like I told you, I've been busy at work. Should I have?"

"Forget about it," Devlin said hurriedly. He had more pressing things to discuss with Alexander than the status of his relationships or whether his bombshell had hit its mark. "I want to talk to you about the financial books of the partnership. Are you able to come down to the station again?"

There was a beat of silence and then Alexander sighed. "Sure. I'll be there in twenty minutes."

True to his word, twenty minutes later, the constable who manned the reception desk buzzed Devlin and announced the arrival of Doctor Jake Alexander. With a surge of anticipation, Devlin pushed away from his desk and hurried out to the waiting room. He offered the doctor his hand.

"Doctor Alexander, thanks for coming in at such short notice. I appreciate it."

The doctor nodded grimly. Devlin took his cue and led the way to an empty interview room. In short order, the interview began.

"Like I said on the phone, Doctor, I've been looking into the financials of the partnership. I understand Shane Cannington was the partner who did the books?"

"You mean, the accounting records? Yes, Shane took care of all those. He loved dealing with numbers. It was his thing. Kevin and I were only too happy to have him look after them."

"There are a handful of deposits and withdrawals going back over the last four or five months that have me puzzled," Devlin said, keeping his tone deliberately casual.

"Oh?"

"Yes. Withdrawals of quite large sums of money, followed a few weeks later by deposits of the same amount. Do you know anything about them?"

Devlin closely watched the man who sat across from him. Alexander's tone remained even and his expression didn't change.

"No, why would I?"

"Well, you are one of the partners. I would expect you to cast your eyes over the accounts every now and then. Isn't that what everyone in business does?"

"I guess, but I've been busier than usual these past few months. I haven't had time to check. Besides, Shane was great at doing the books. I trusted him implicitly."

Devlin chuckled, hoping to put the other man on edge. "See, that's the thing about trust. You seldom know when it's been broken until it's too late."

"What's your point, Detective?" The words came out clipped.

Devlin noticed the slightest tic near Alexander's lip. So, he'd gotten under the doctor's skin. It was time to press home his advantage. "The thing is, those entries I was talking about, the ones that caught my attention... They've been referenced along with the letters KJ—presumably by Shane Cannington. Now, the letters could be initials—Kevin Johnson, for example, or they could stand for two first names—Kevin and J—"

"Jake."

"You see where I'm coming from, Doctor?"

Alexander remained silent, staring at his hands where they lay folded on the desk in front of him. Devlin pressed on. "And another thing. What can you tell me about Vladimir Mikolaev?"

The doctor looked up briefly and frowned. "Never heard of him."

"Really?" Devlin goaded. "And yet, he was at your colleague's funeral yesterday and again at your building on Friday night. Your car was in the parking lot nearby, so I know you were there, along with Kevin Johnson."

"I don't know who you're talking about and I left my car there overnight because I'd returned from a trip to Maitland and caught up with some friends. I had a few too many drinks and it wasn't safe for me to drive. I caught a cab home and came back for my car in the morning."

"How responsible of you, Doctor. But let me tell you why I ask. Vladimir Mikolaev is a suspect in a huge methamphetamine racket. We believe he has meth labs set up across the city. We haven't been able to get enough on him to make an arrest, yet. But we're getting closer every day. You might pretend not to know him, but his number shows up on your phone records."

"That's a lie!" Alexander cried, his eyes wide

with surprise. "I've never even heard of the man."

Devlin reached over and picked up the stack of phone records. Several hundred calls had been highlighted, going back over five or six months. He tossed them toward his suspect. "Believe what you want, Doctor," he said mildly. "But I have the proof right here."

Some of the bravado left Alexander's voice. He shook his head slowly back and forth. "I... I don't understand."

"To be fair, many of those calls were made from your office. There's no indication who actually placed the call."

"So why are you breaking my balls over this, Detective? You just said you had no proof."

"What I said was I had no proof you made the calls. I suspect it was your colleague, given that there are also several calls made to this scumbag from Johnson's cell phone."

Devlin's announcement was met with shocked silence. The man who sat across from him paled, but a part of Devlin remained skeptical. He couldn't help but wonder if Alexander was truly surprised by the information.

"So, Doctor, what I want to know is, are you going to come clean and admit you and your partner are in this together, or is Johnson solely the one to blame?"

CHAPTER 13

As Jake left the police station, the tension that had held him taut throughout the interview with Detective Grayson began to ease, but a hard knot of dread remained in his gut. He'd called Kat as soon as he could, but the call had gone through to voicemail. Reaching his car, he unlocked it and slid in behind the wheel. Switching on the ignition, he wiped the sweat from his brow and leaned over to turn up the AC. The day had been unseasonably warm. According to the news, a heat wave was on its way. He found no humor in the fact the weatherman had gotten it wrong: The heat wave had well and truly arrived.

Backing out of the parking space, he headed down the ramp and exited the lot. With a glance over his shoulder, he changed lanes and merged with the heavy late afternoon traffic. He cursed under his breath. It would be a long trip home. If the detective hadn't called, he would have been there by now. Home with Kat, putting one of the worst days of his life behind him.

His conversation in the police station kept circling around in his head. It had been that way since he'd stepped outside of the dark gray concrete building. Shane and Kevin and Kat and back to Kevin again. *What did it all mean?*

A drug dealer's number found in Kevin's phone records? The very thought was ludicrous. Kevin didn't do drugs. Not even in college. There was no way he was caught up in something so shady. Nothing about that idea made sense.

And what about Kat and the detective's earlier oblique reference to whether Jake had called her, or not? What did *that* mean? Seeing as she wasn't answering her phone, he supposed that little mystery would have to wait until he got home. Cursing once again, he did his best to curb his impatience as the Audi inched forward.

The light ahead changed to red and Jake brought the car to a halt. He reached for his phone and noticed he'd missed a call from an unidentified number. He hadn't even heard it ring. Then he checked the phone and realized he still had it set to silent.

He dialed into his voicemail and listened to another message left by Detective Grayson. This one had been received only minutes earlier. Grayson obviously had more pointless questions. The knowledge that the detective was wasting everyone's time infuriated him.

And then Jake heard the rest of the message and all thoughts of Shane and his murder disappeared...

An hour later, with dread weighing down his

every footstep, Jake dragged himself to his front door. He wasn't surprised to discover the condo bare of every last trace of Kat. Apart from the faintest scent of her perfume, it was like she'd never been there. And he knew exactly why and who was to blame.

"Fuck you, Detective Grayson!" he shouted. He swiped at the tears that burned behind his eyes and then shouted it once again.

———————

Bryce strode into the elevator of the building that housed the consulting rooms of Doctors Alexander, Johnson and Cannington, and pressed the button for the fifth floor. The elevator arrived and he wasn't surprised to discover it was empty. It was past the time most people left for home and the last patient appointments would be over. With a bit of luck, he'd have Holly Greenwood to himself. The thought filled him with anticipation. She'd been on the periphery of their investigation, but the truth was, she had as many strikes against her as the two doctors.

She owned and was familiar with firearms and not just any firearms, but ones that could have been the murder weapon. She had access to the building after hours. Her presence wouldn't have caused alarm. Surprise, maybe, but not alarm.

There was no motive that they knew of, but Kevin Johnson didn't appear to have a motive either, and as Jake Alexander had pointed out, his argument over expanding the medical practice had been with both partners. Jake gained nothing by getting rid of just one.

The door to the clinic was unlocked, like it had been the first time he and Devlin had attended the crime scene. Holly sat behind a low counter. She smiled when she saw him.

"Good evening, Detective Sutcliffe."

Bryce inclined his head in greeting. "Ms Greenwood, thank you for staying back late to meet with me."

"It's no trouble. I was here anyway. In fact, you did me a favor. The train home will be much less crowded later in the day."

She laughed. It was a light, tinkling sound that suited her. She wasn't a tall woman and weighed less than one hundred pounds. Her thick blond hair was piled up on top of her head and probably comprised at least half of her body weight. Her wide blue eyes were expertly made up with dark blue eye shadow. Black mascara added to the dramatic effect.

She was dressed from head to toe in pale pink and the smart jacket and skirt fitted her well, like it had been custom made. He wondered idly how a secretary could afford such an expensive outfit. Perhaps she came from money or maybe she had a rich boyfriend... Or perhaps she saved hard, lived simply and spent all of her wages on clothes. She wouldn't be the first twenty-something woman to do that.

"How about we sit over there?" she suggested,

indicating the row of straight-backed chairs that lined the wall of the waiting room.

Bryce nodded and took a seat. While Holly followed, he pulled out a pen and his notebook.

"I hope you don't mind, Ms Greenwood, but I have a few more questions."

"Of course not, Detective. I'm happy to help. I want to find the person responsible for this as much as anyone."

"I'm glad you feel that way. It always makes our job easier when people cooperate."

Holly lifted her shoulders in a pretty shrug. "What do you want to know?"

"You're a target shooter, right?" Bryce asked.

"Yes. I've been shooting most of my life. My daddy used to take me with him to the rifle range whenever he needed to practice. He used to compete in amateur competitions. I guess I caught the bug, too."

"You shoot competitively?"

"Yes. I specialize in handguns. I own an M9 .22 caliber Beretta and a .22 caliber semi-automatic Buckmark Browning."

"Nice. You know, Shane was shot with a .22 caliber gun. Would you mind giving me yours for the purposes of testing and comparison?"

She smiled in response and shook her head. "I'm sorry, Detective. I wish I could, but they're locked up in a safe at home and I have an important shoot at my local club coming up in a couple of days. I need them." Her tone was soft and pleasant, but a keen intelligence brightened her gaze.

So, there was more to the pretty Barbie doll than he'd suspected. Still, there was nothing he could do about the guns. Without a warrant, she was under no obligation to hand them over. He put his next question to her. "Where were you on the night Shane was killed?"

"I was at work until six, like I told your colleague the first time. I caught the train home to St Mary's, like I usually do. I wandered around the shops for a while, picked up a few things for dinner and arrived home a little after eight."

"Is there anybody who can verify your whereabouts and timeline?"

Holly shook her head and gave a resigned sigh. "No, there isn't, apart from all the strangers on the train. Most times, I catch the same train home every night and I'm sure many of them do, too. You could talk to some of them and see if they remember me."

"What about at home? Do you share a house with anyone?"

"Unfortunately, no. I live in a tiny cottage on my own, unless you count my cat, Chocolate. He knew I was there. He always knows when I'm at home. If I'm half a minute late, he scolds me." She laughed her tinkling laugh. "Really, Detective, he's quite a handful at times. But I do recall curling up on the sofa in front of the television and watching an old episode of *Law & Order*. It ran until half-past nine. I had a cup of hot cocoa and then curled up with Chocolate on my bed. The next thing I knew it was morning."

Bryce jotted down some notes on the pad and

then slipped the pen back in his pocket. As far as he was concerned, Holly Greenwood remained on the bottom of the suspect list. She'd been exceedingly pleasant and helpful and if she happened to be an expert marksman, well, she'd already told him she'd been shooting since she was a child. It was no wonder she was good at it.

Pushing away from the chair, he stood and thanked her for her time. It wasn't the outcome Devlin had been hoping for, but there was nothing further Bryce could do without a warrant.

The moment he returned to the station, Devlin pounced.

"How did you do with Holly Greenwood? Was she prepared to hand over her firearms?"

"No. She might look like Barbie, but she's no dummy. I'm guessing she knew I had no right to take them without a warrant. She told me she had an important shoot to attend and she needed them." Bryce shrugged. "I believed her. Besides, why would Holly kill her employer with her own gun? That would be plain stupid and like I said, she doesn't strike me as dumb."

Devlin slumped in his chair, his expression grim. "So you think we should take her off the list?"

Bryce paused and thought for a moment. "I wouldn't take her off the list. She's a bit of an oddball—there's no doubt about it. She fires a gun like a sharpshooter, dresses in pink, looks like a Barbie doll, but obviously has a mind that's quicker than you'd think. I believe she's the type most people underestimate and a person who is frequently underestimated can often surprise us the most."

Devlin groaned in frustration. "I thought you just told me you believed her?"

"I do. I'm just saying. Don't take her off the list."

———————

With the TV turned low and Chocolate purring contentedly in her lap, Holly ran the emery board back and forth over her nails, frowning in concentration. It didn't do to let them grow too long. It interfered with the way her finger felt on the trigger and that interfered with her accuracy.

She might have lied when she'd told the detective she didn't have her pistols on her—after all, she'd taken the Beretta in with her that morning for the sole purpose of scaring Kevin and it had been tucked up in her handbag at the very moment the detective posed his question—but she hadn't lied when she told him she had an upcoming shoot. It was something he could easily verify and it would be stupid to be caught out on such a trivial lie.

Still, that wasn't the real reason she'd declined to hand over her guns. Whilst she'd been careful to collect the bullet casings and the lead that had passed through Shane's brain, there were advances being made in technology every day. She didn't want to discover some new and improved method of bullet matching was the cause of her downfall. No sense handing over evidence when she didn't have to. She wasn't dumb. It was obvious the detective hadn't come armed with a warrant. He'd have taken the guns otherwise. As it was, he had no choice but to accept her explanation.

The detective had made notes as she spoke. He asked intermittent questions. He appeared to accept her story, but even still, it might be time to tell the police about Kevin. It couldn't hurt to create a diversion, or to have a little extra insurance. Of course, she wouldn't say anything until she could make it worth her while...

The thought made her feel a little uncomfortable. Shane wouldn't have been pleased she was going to use Kevin's secret to her advantage. But, guess what? Shane was gone and he wasn't coming back. He wasn't around to see. Besides, someone had to look out for her. After all, nobody else was going to do it...

A surge of loss went through her and she almost gasped aloud at the pain. *Oh, Shane!* How she missed him! Why did he have to die? It was all his fault. He shouldn't have laughed at her. Why couldn't he at least pretend to care? It wasn't fair! It wasn't fair! It wasn't fair! First her mom and daddy and now him.

When would it end?

———————

Kevin poured himself two fingers of scotch and went back to sit on the couch. The view of the harbor from his living room window usually calmed him, but tonight, nothing seemed to be able to alleviate his growing feeling of unease, including the excellent scotch.

The phone in his pocket rang loudly in the stillness, startling him. He checked the screen, but the Caller ID was blocked. Sometimes that happened when staff used certain hospital phone lines. He hoped it wasn't an emergency. He'd had a shit of a day. He was looking forward to kicking back at home.

The phone continued to peal. With a sigh, he set the glass down on the coffee table and answered the call.

"Doctor Johnson."

"Kevin, how good of you to answer. I was beginning to think you wouldn't."

Holly's sugar-coated tone sounded in his ear. He swore quietly under his breath. She'd spent most of the past week harassing him in one way or the other. Everywhere he turned, she was there, smiling her knowing smile. It was irritating the hell out of him and to be frank, he was running a little scared. For Pete's sake, she'd actually pulled a gun on him that morning and they both knew she was trained in the use of it. Now, she was calling him after hours. This had to stop.

"Holly, this is bullshit," he snarled as his anger stirred low in his gut.

"Ha! Look who's found his balls!" she crowed. "You're much braver when there isn't a gun pointed at your head. Not that it matters."

"What are you talking about?" he demanded.

"I've been thinking about our little chat. The one we had a few months ago. You know, the one where you confessed to dealing in drugs? Remember?"

Kevin gritted his teeth and waited her out.

"See, I was thinking that you must be making a heap of money and that little secret must be worth quite a bit for me to remain silent."

His anger grew, but this time, it was tinged with dread. "What do you want?"

"Oh, I think I could keep quiet with one hundred thousand dollars of untraceable bills deposited into my account."

Kevin sat up with a jerk. "Are you insane? I don't have that kind of money!"

"Well, you'd better find it because that's what my silence will cost."

Kevin thought fast. "What about a new boob job? I could bump a couple of patients further down the list. I could schedule you in next week."

"I don't want another boob job, Kevin. I'm perfectly content with the one I had. I want one hundred thousand dollars. Find it, or else."

The call disconnected in his ear. He hung up the phone with a hand that trembled from fear, or fury—maybe both. He was just glad Kat hadn't been around to witness the conversation. At least something good had come of her moving out. He still missed her like hell and he hadn't given up on the possibility of winning her back, but first he had to deal with Vlad and the problems the crime boss represented. And now Holly.

It was unfortunate she'd discovered his secret. All these months later, he still kicked himself over that. He'd been under the impression everyone had left for the day, but Holly had been in the bathroom. She'd caught him red-handed, elbow deep in codeine packets. She'd been too smart to fob off with a feeble excuse. Right away, she'd cottoned on to what he was up to.

He'd panicked when he realized he'd been busted, but at the time, she'd brushed off his concerns with a tinkling laugh. Said she didn't care that he was dealing in prescription drugs; that he was taking advantage of an opportunity. She told him she admired him for it.

Like the arrogant asshole he was, he'd basked in her praise, believing her every word. He charmed her into sleeping with him as added insurance—surely she wouldn't turn her lover in to the police? They'd enjoyed a mutually satisfying affair. It had worked for Holly, too.

From the moment she'd started as their receptionist, Kevin could tell she had a thing for Shane. She'd made endless excuses to speak with him, over the phone and in his office. She flipped her hair over her shoulder every time he walked by and followed his every move. The few times Kevin saw Shane pay her any attention, she'd blushed all the way to her roots.

It was Holly who'd told him she wanted to tell Shane about their affair in an effort to make him jealous. Kevin didn't think Shane would care one way or the other, but he agreed to it just the same. He never asked Holly if it worked the way she wanted. Now Shane was dead and Holly was proving extremely difficult.

And not only difficult, her threats were

becoming more and more explicit. Arriving with a pistol at work that day was a prime example. He knew she was a target shooter, of course. It was something they had in common, although he tended to favor rifles, but this was different. If he were completely honest, she'd begun to frighten him, which was plain ridiculous. A petite, young woman weighing less than a hundred pounds, she was no match for him physically. In fact, up until recently, she'd enjoyed her fair share of time in his bed. Albeit, at the clinic on the less than comfortable examination table and once or twice on his desk, but she'd never voiced any complaints.

He thought he could sweet talk his way out of this latest predicament the same way he'd charmed her in the past, but so far, she'd thwarted his attempts. Okay, maybe he hadn't given it his best effort, but he really thought she'd go for it. Unfortunately, that morning when he'd tried, she'd laughed in his face, right before she'd pulled out the handgun.

As familiar as he was with firearms, he'd nearly shit his pants. It wasn't every day his receptionist threatened him with a gun. The fact she was competent in its use was what frightened him.

He remembered how Shane had been shot twice in the back of the head. At the time, he'd thought it was a coward's shot. Now, he couldn't help but think of Holly and whether she'd had something to do with it.

The thought came from nowhere and hit him hard up the side of the head. He bent forward, gasping for breath. It was like he'd been sucker punched. Nausea swirled in his gut and he pushed away from the couch. Stumbling down the corridor, he ran into the bathroom and barely made it to the stall.

Could it have been Holly? Was she capable of such a thing? The very thought was repugnant and yet the more he thought about it, the more it made a horrible kind of sense. Until this week he'd never have thought Holly was capable.

Ever since Shane's death, he'd seen a change in her that was disturbing. She vacillated between bouts of hysteria over the fact Shane was no longer there, to prancing around the office with what could only be described as a swagger. It was like she knew something no one else did and he couldn't help but wonder if it had something to do with Shane.

A knock on the front door permeated his frantic thoughts. He frowned and struggled to his feet. A moment later, it came again. Loud and forceful, whoever it was sounded determined to be seen. He moved over to the sink and bent low and rinsed. The insistent knock came a third time and this time, he called out to whoever it was.

"Okay, hold your horses. I'm coming!" Without checking the peephole, he undid the security lock.

CHAPTER 14

Vladimir Mikolaev shouldered his way past and all Kevin could do was gasp in shock. Never before had the man come to his home. By unspoken agreement, their deals had always been done after hours at the clinic. And yet, here he was, solid and dark and threatening, although for the life of him, Kevin couldn't think why he was there. Kevin had fulfilled their last deal and had received his money. As far as he was concerned, they were square.

"What's this I hear about you quitting?" the drug boss snarled.

Kevin backed up the hallway until he came to the open concept living room and kitchen, needing more space. He cursed under his breath. He'd mentioned to Petrov when the man had stopped by on Vlad's behalf to collect the latest cache of codeine that he was getting out of the business and that Vlad would have to look elsewhere for his supply.

At the time, Petrov had barely reacted. He'd

shrugged as if it didn't matter to him one way or the other and after stowing the box of codeine under his arm and handing Kevin the money, he'd left as abruptly as he'd arrived.

Kevin now realized he should have been suspicious of the man right away. Though, at the time, Petrov appeared unmoved by Kevin's announcement, it was obvious the lackey hadn't wasted time reporting their conversation back to his boss and now the man was here, in his living room, glaring at him with enough malevolence to flood Kevin's heart with fear.

"I... I've had enough," he stammered. "The death of my colleague's hit me hard. I've been thinking things over, contemplating my life and the direction it's taken of late. I want to go back to the way I was before. I'm done with the drugs."

Mikolaev's gaze narrowed. With measured footsteps, he advanced on Kevin, every pore exuding menace. Kevin backed up as far as he could go. When he came up hard against the wall of the living room, his gut clenched in panic.

For one frantic moment, his thoughts went to the rifles that were locked up in his bedroom safe. The guns had been stored away unloaded, but there was ammunition there as well... Almost immediately, he dismissed the possibility. He'd never get to them in time. No, far better to bluster his way out of this and hope like hell Vlad accepted his explanation.

He forced a smile and spread his arms wide. "Come on, Vlad. We can keep this friendly. Our arrangement has worked well, but like all good things, sooner or later, they must come to an end and that's just the way it has to be. No hard feelings. I wish you well."

"You talk pretty, Doctor," Mikolaev replied with a humorless smile. "I've been contemplating my life...thinking about my dead friend... No hard feelings..." the drug boss crooned. "Well, good for you, but listen hard and listen well because I'm not going to repeat myself."

Once again, Mikolaev advanced upon him and didn't pull up until his face was inches from Kevin's. "*I'll* be the one to tell you when this arrangement has come to an end. It's up to me to tell you when you can quit and get back to your old life, you hear me? No one quits on Vladimir Mikolaev without his say so. *No one.*"

The man's fetid breath, along with a fresh wave of fear, nearly had Kevin's stomach turning inside itself again. His only thought at that point was to pacify the drug boss in whatever way he could and get the man the hell out of his apartment. Brushing away the curls that had fallen across his eyes, once again, he held his hands up in a sign of surrender.

"All right, Vlad. There's no need to get so upset. You call the shots. I get it. I'm sorry. I was out of line. Now, if you wouldn't mind, it's way past late and I have to be at work early in the morning."

Vlad shot him a final narrow-eyed glare before turning and lumbering away down the hall. A moment later, the front door opened and closed. Kevin collapsed against the living room wall in relief. It was a long time later that he made his way into the bathroom to wash the smell of sweat and fear off his face. Switching on the light, he went to the sink.

Staring at his reflection in the mirror, he was shocked at what he saw. The man who looked back at him was pale and disheveled and looked like he'd aged a decade. The stress of having to keep up with Mikolaev's endless demand for codeine, coupled with Shane's shocking and unexpected death and Kat's abrupt departure, was taking its toll. And now, there was also Holly to worry about. Not only were there her ridiculous demands for money, she was still threatening to tell Jake about the drugs.

His life was falling apart right before his eyes and there was nothing he could do about it. He felt like he was on a train that was hurtling along the edge of a crevasse out of control. Any moment, it would derail. The worst of it was, he had no one but himself to blame.

He needed to come clean, to purge his tortured soul. Only then could he start the process of clawing his life back. After wiping his hands dry with some paper towel, he balled it up and tossed it in the trash. It was time to man up and do what needed to be done.

———

Jake stared blankly at the far wall of his living room. It was late and he was tired, but the thought of going to bed knowing that Kat had left him was more than he could bear. The bottle of scotch on the coffee table was half empty, but the pain of Grayson's betrayal still hadn't gone away.

Why had the detective told Kat about his record? That past had nothing to do with Shane and his murder, or Kat. There was only one possible explanation: The man had done it solely out of spite. Perhaps the detective was frustrated with the lack of progress with his investigation. He seemed hell-bent on blaming Kevin or Jake, or both. It seemed he wanted to take out his frustration on someone and Jake was in the firing line. Getting to him through Kat was an easy way to do it and the detective probably hadn't given two seconds' thought to the fallout.

The buzz of Jake's doorbell broke into his tumultuous thoughts. He glanced at his watch. It was way past late. *Who the hell was calling here at this time of the night?* And then his mind hit on Kat. Was it possible she'd come back? Had she doubted the detective's revelation? Was she going to give him the chance to explain? Did she care enough about him for that?

Getting to his feet, he stumbled down the hall. Looking through the peephole, he frowned at the sight of Kevin. Removing the security latch, he opened the door and stood back to let his friend enter.

"Kevin! What the hell are you doing here? This isn't a good time."

Kevin pushed past him and walked into the living room and threw himself down on the couch.

For the first time, Jake noticed his mate's appearance and through the foggy depths of the alcohol, he felt a twinge of concern.

"Is everything all right?" he asked.

Kevin covered his eyes with the back of his hand and shook his head. "No. Everything's gone to shit."

For the second time, Jake felt a sense of foreboding. He barely dared to ask the question. "What is it? What happened? Does it have anything to do with Shane?"

Kevin leaned forward and buried his face in his hands. Jake's apprehension increased and he turned away and poured both of them a scotch. In silence, he handed a tumbler to his friend.

"Talk to me, Kev. Tell me what's going on."

In stilted sentences and with much anguish, Kevin did.

It was more than an hour later when Kevin fell silent. Jake did his best to hide his shock. He couldn't believe his friend and colleague was involved in illegally supplying prescription drugs to a thug. On top of that, Jake was left to contemplate the possibility that their meek and mild receptionist might be anything but... It was too much to comprehend and right at that moment, it was more than his scotch-clogged brain could absorb.

He stood shakily and went into the kitchen. He filled the jug and set it to boil and then forgot about it. He stared off into space, trying to come to terms with what he'd heard. Finally, he turned back to Kevin.

"Why are you telling me this now?"

Kevin heaved himself off the couch and walked over to where Jake stood. He threw his arms up in a sign of surrender. "My life's gone down the toilet. My stress levels are through the roof. I'm drinking to get to sleep. I'm always looking over my shoulder. I dread the sound of the phone ringing. Kat left me. Holly's shaking me down for money. She also threatened to tell you about my extra-curricular activities."

Jake nodded grimly. Kevin's spontaneous confession suddenly made sense. "I get it now. Holly was going to spill your little secret. That's the reason you came to me, isn't it? It has nothing to do with feeling guilty or wanting to make things right."

"No! Jake! Please, you have to believe me! It wasn't like that. All right, I'm feeling the pressure. Holly's gone psycho. Vlad's refusing to let me out. I don't know what to do. But I made the decision to come clean, regardless. I wanted you to know about all this, from me."

Anger stirred in Jake's gut. He narrowed his gaze at Kevin. "Why? So you can pass off your guilt onto me? Now I know your dirty little secret, you want me to share the responsibility. Is that right?"

"No, Jake! I swear!" Kevin ran a hand through his curls, leaving them awry. "I came to you because I didn't know what else to do, where to turn. You're my mate, my best friend. We've been through so much together." He drew in a breath and let it out on a shudder. When he looked back at Jake, his expression was bleak.

"I fucked up, Jake. I fucked up so bad. And I'm sorry."

Jake stared at his friend and his anger found its head. "You're *sorry*? This isn't some college prank that can be laughed off in the morning. You broke the law! And you did it in my office! Who's to know I wasn't also involved? Have you thought of that? No wonder the detective's still hounding me about Shane. He probably already knows something's off." Jake rounded the counter and stopped just short of where Kevin stood. "Did you think about that while you were dealing with your supplier? Did you give any thought to how it would affect the rest of us? Shane's probably thanking his lucky stars that he got out of this one."

The words were no sooner out of Jake's mouth when another thought occurred to him. "Fuck. Shane. He knew, didn't he? He was in on it with you. The pair of you!"

Kevin didn't deny it. Jake shook his head, disgusted by his own gullibility. "You must have had a right royal laugh about me behind my back. Stupid Jake. Too trusting for his own good. Oblivious to what was going on right under his nose! Ha! Ha! Ha!"

"No! Jake, it wasn't like that! I swear!" Kevin cried. "Shane had nothing to do with it. He didn't know what was going on, either. Not until..."

Jake glared at his friend. "Not until when?" His voice was rough with barely concealed rage. His tone brooked no argument.

Kevin blew out his breath on a heavy sigh. His

shoulders slumped in defeat. Suddenly, he looked far older than his twenty-nine years.

"The night of Shane's death, we were both working late. Holly came in and said goodnight. She left at her usual time."

Jake frowned. "I thought you told me a little while ago that you were worried she might have had something to do with Shane's death?"

Kevin grimaced. "Yeah, that's what I said, but I forgot she left way before I did. Despite the fact she came in to my office today and threatened me with a gun, she couldn't have had anything to do with it."

Jake digested the information. He was still shocked at the thought of Holly doing what she did with the gun. He nodded for Kevin to continue.

"I was finishing up some paperwork. Shane was in his office. He came in, concerned about some discrepancies he'd found in the books."

Jake stared at Kevin and was once again filled with a sense of foreboding. Knowing what he now did about Kevin's illegal activities, he could nearly guess what his friend was about to say.

"You took money, didn't you?" His voice was flat as he considered the consequences for the clinic.

Kevin flushed and stared at the floor. "Yes."

Jake's heart dropped and his anger ignited. The fact the detectives were already onto it only further infuriated him. He slammed his hand against the counter. "For fuck's sake, Kevin! You stole from us! Your partners!"

"Hey, I'm not proud of it and I paid back every

cent. It was just that, there were times when I was short of cash. My pharmaceuticals guy wouldn't wait. So every now and then I borrowed from the partnership and then I paid it back."

Jake shook his head in disbelief. He barely recognized the man who stood before him, confessing to crimes Jake would never have thought him capable of.

He stared at Kevin. "Shane found out about it, didn't he?"

"Yes. He did. He came into my office that evening and asked me about the strange withdrawals that matched up a few weeks later with equally strange deposits." Kevin shrugged. "There was nothing else I could tell him. So I told him the truth."

"You told him you were dealing in pharmaceuticals."

"Yes."

Jake stared at him, flooded with a fresh wave of disbelief. "What did he say?" he managed.

"He was shocked and angry. Like you. He yelled at me, demanding to be told how I could be so stupid and jeopardize everything we'd worked for. I apologized. I told him I didn't know what to do. I'd gotten into bed with some nasty people. One, in particular: Vladimir Mikolaev. He's one mean Russian."

Another rush of surprise filled Jake's veins. He shook his head. "Mikolaev. That's the name of the criminal Detective Grayson told me about. He thought *I* was the one in bed with the scumbag. All along, it was you. I denied knowing anything about him and I assured the detective you wouldn't know the guy, either."

"I'm sorry, Jake. I really am. Vlad's threatened to kill me on more than one occasion if I fail to come through for him and I know he'd follow through. He turned up at the restaurant where Kat and I were having dinner. I had to sit across from that prick and lie to Kat about who he was and smile and pretend we were friends. And then there was the visit he made to my apartment a few hours ago. He as good as threatened me with dire consequences if I even thought about wanting to quit. But I have to, Jake. I can't take this anymore. I want it to stop! I want it to all go away! What do I do? How can I fix it?"

Jake dragged his hands through his hair, taxed beyond his limit. Kevin had been living such a charmed life—had a great job, good friends, a nice girl. *How had he gone so far off course?* What was even more alarming—how had Jake been so oblivious?

"You could always go to the police and confess," Jake said tiredly. "From what you've said, they'll be more than interested to hear what you have to say about this Russian."

"Yeah, right before they slap the handcuffs on me. They'll have me on a string of charges before I even finish the interview."

"Maybe they'd be willing to cut a deal? Your testimony against the Russian drug lord and his cohorts in return for your release? Grayson seemed pretty interested in the guy when he spoke to me."

Kevin rolled his eyes. "This isn't some TV show, Jake. It doesn't work like that in real life."

The comment stung, as did Kevin's unusually condescending attitude. Jake clenched his jaw.

"All I'm trying to do is suggest ways you might get out of this fix before it affects everyone connected with you," he said through gritted teeth.

To his credit, Kevin refrained from offering another smart-mouthed reply. Jake sucked in his breath and did his best to get his temper back under control. What was done, was done. Now it was time to come up with a solution.

He looked across at Kevin. "Who else knows?"

"No one."

"Did you tell Kat?"

"No! I've told no one. The only people who found out were Shane and Holly. I don't know who Vlad has chosen to share our arrangement with. It's not beyond reason that his drug cronies know."

Great. Just great. One wrong move and they could have the entire Russian mafia breathing down their necks. All because of Kevin's stupidity and greed. Once again, Jake's anger stirred. He eyeballed his friend.

"We're not going to muck around with this, Kevin. I refuse to have this shit hanging over my head. First thing in the morning, you're going to the police. You're going to tell them everything and if that means they lock your sorry ass in jail, then so be it. After all you've done, it's the least you deserve."

A look of panic spread across Kevin's face. "No! Jake! You can't be serious. Haven't you listened to a word I've said? You don't know Vlad. He means business. I go to the police and I'm as good as dead."

CHAPTER 15

Jake stared at Kevin and wanted to scream out his frustration. "I don't believe it!" he cried. "How could you get involved in something like this? What the hell were you thinking? And doing it out of the clinic means you've dragged me into this, too. You're an asshole, Kevin. I can't believe I ever looked upon you as a friend and not only a friend, but someone I had respect for and trusted!"

"Ha! You want to talk about trust? What about Kat? She'd barely left my bed and she was warming yours. You think I don't know about that? Your little tryst in the country? The nurses on the surgical ward can be very accommodating with the information they choose to share."

Jake saw red. He didn't know which staff members had given Kevin his information, but Jake refused to feel guilty about what had happened between him and Kat. She'd been a free agent when they got together. There was no way Kevin could accuse her of cheating.

"You don't know what the hell you're talking about," he growled low in his throat.

"Ha! Tell me I'm wrong? Tell me she hasn't moved in here and is setting up house with you a week after she walked out on me."

Jake opened his mouth to deny it, but then closed it again without speaking. The truth was, he and Kat had been intimate very shortly after she'd called it quits with Kevin. The fact that Jake had been in love with her for years, or that she'd moved in as his roommate didn't matter. He wanted to call her his. He wanted her to *be* his. And nothing was ever going to change that.

Kevin's lip turned up into a sneer. "Nothing to say, Doctor?"

Clenching his jaw against any further comment, Jake turned away. It was late. He was tired. He didn't want to think about anything for a while. Not Kevin, not Holly, not Kat. As if sensing his surrender, Kevin moved back to sit on the couch and threw himself down with a heavy sigh.

"Fuck, Jake. What are we doing?"

Jake merely stared at him and shrugged.

"I'm sorry." Kevin's expression was filled with remorse.

Jake stared at him a moment longer and then let his anger slide. There was no point staying angry. They needed to work together to find a solution, not tear each other apart. He made his way around the counter to sit on the couch opposite Kevin.

The two of them sat in silence, alone with their

thoughts. Jake looked at the scotch bottle. It was now only a quarter full. He was tempted to pour them both another drink, but then decided against it. More alcohol wasn't going to fix anything. They needed clear heads in the morning to sort out what needed to be done.

It was a long moment later that Kevin looked over toward him. "When I first got here, you said this wasn't a good time. Why? What happened? Did something go wrong at work?"

Jake compressed his lips and deliberated his answer. *What the heck, Kevin already knew there was something going on with him and Kat. What did it matter if he told his mate the reason he'd already finished half a bottle of scotch before Kevin arrived?*

He looked back at Kevin and cleared his throat. "You're right about Kat and I—well, about some of it. You know how I feel about her, how I've always felt about her. I did the honorable thing while you were together. I kept my distance. I never said a word. But when she confirmed the two of you had called it quits, I couldn't help but feel I finally might have a chance."

He risked another glance at Kevin, but his friend's features remained unreadable in the shadows. He drew in another breath and continued.

"You know I took time off and drove Kat up to Maitland. We attended her father's funeral. One thing led to another..."

He saw Kevin tense and hurried on.

"It wasn't planned, but I won't deny that I was

thrilled that it had happened. She'd been staying with her sister in their cramped apartment and I offered her a room in mine. Of course, I wanted her to move in with me as my girlfriend, but she wanted to take things slow. I agreed. I'd have taken her on any terms."

"Then where is she?" Kevin muttered, looking around.

"She's not here. That's why I told you it wasn't a good time."

"What happened?" Kevin asked.

Jake balled his fists and rubbed them against his eyes. He didn't have the energy to recount what had happened, the reason why Kat had fled his home. But Kevin had posed the question and Jake knew from experience his mate wouldn't let it slide.

"She was here when Detective Grayson came calling earlier in the day. He was looking for me. I was at work. He caught Kat here alone."

"So? We all know you had nothing to do with Shane's murder. What could Grayson have said to get her to leave?"

"He ran my name through the police database. He discovered I have a criminal record."

"Don't tell me that shit Joanna-Marie put you through is still on the system?"

Jake compressed his lips and nodded. "Yeah."

"But that happened years ago and those charges were thrown out! That stupid bitch cooked it all up to get back at you for—"

"I know, Kevin. I was there, remember? I was the one whose name was dragged through the mud; the one who had to front the judge and explain myself."

Kevin rested his head on the back of the couch and stared up at the ceiling. "So what did the detective say to Kat to make her run away?"

"Who knows?" Jake replied grimly. "But you can bet your sweet ass he didn't tell her the truth."

Kevin shook his head. "Why would he do something like that? To try to rattle you? He must know you had nothing to do with Shane's murder."

"I think he came around here to stir up trouble. I wasn't around, so he tossed a few pieces of bait Kat's way. He knew Kat was your girlfriend. She's your alibi. Now he probably also knows you broke up. Even though we both know your breakup had nothing to do with Shane, the police probably find the timing of it more than coincidental. They don't like coincidences."

Kevin nodded. "No, they don't. How did you find out about it? Did you speak to Kat?"

"No, the bastard left a message on my phone. Took great delight in letting me know about his visit and how he and Kat had enjoyed a little chat in which he just happened to mention my record."

Kevin shook his head. "That son of a bitch. That's low."

Jake couldn't help but agree. "You can say that again."

Silence fell between them. A while later, Jake looked across at Kevin. "Who do you think killed Shane?" he asked quietly.

Kevin contemplated the view outside the

darkened window. Lights from neighboring properties glowed in the distance. At last, his gaze returned to Jake.

"I don't know, but if I'd have to guess, I'd put my money on Holly. She's a wacko."

Jake frowned. "I thought you said she left at her usual time that night? The police haven't given me the official time of death, but I saw Shane's body in his office around eight-thirty the next morning, not long after Holly called. It didn't look like he'd been dead more than twelve hours."

"Yeah, well what if she didn't leave when she said?"

Jake shot him a dubious look. "Was she still there when you left?"

"I didn't see her."

"So…"

Kevin made an impatient sound in the back of his throat. "Okay, so I don't have all the answers, but one thing I do know is that Holly Greenwood's acting weird."

This time, Jake looked at him in astonishment. "The guy you told me she was in love with was shot and killed in his office and she was the one to find him. On top of that, one of her employers is dealing illegally in prescription drugs. She's twenty-two. It's a lot for someone so young to deal with. No wonder she's acting weird."

Kevin's jaw stuck out at a belligerent angle Jake knew all too well. "Say what you like, Jake. I know Holly. Something's out of whack."

Jake gritted his teeth and counted to ten. He was tired of feeling angry. It was late. He needed to go to bed and forget about the day. He stood and moved away from the couch.

"You need to go."

Kevin lifted his head and looked at him in surprise. "But—"

"Kevin, I need some time to myself, to get my head around all this shit. I want you to leave." Jake followed through with his request by heading down the corridor. He pulled open the front door and gestured for his friend to leave.

Kevin followed more slowly behind him, his expression a mixture of petulance and remorse.

"I thought we might be able to talk about this some more, work out what to do."

Jake stared at him. "Not tonight, Kev. Right now, I'm all out of suggestions."

"Okay. I guess I'll see you later then," Kevin mumbled and walked into the hall.

Jake shut the door behind him. It closed with a satisfying click.

Kevin pulled his car alongside the curb, outside the condominium complex that housed Mason and Isobel Alexander and their kids. Given that Jake had told him about the circumstances that had Kat packing her bags, it hadn't taken much working out that she would be here. Kat and her sister had always been close. She'd come here the night she left him. He knew that because he'd called Mason to make sure she was all right. Kat's brother-in-law had been short with him, but had grudgingly confirmed she was there.

After coming clean with Jake, it was time to do the same with his girlfriend. Ex-girlfriend. He hadn't told Jake about the affair with Holly, but he sure as hell had to tell Kat. If Holly followed through on her increasingly frequent threats, it was only a matter of time before Kat knew everything anyway. It would be better coming from him. Despite the fact she'd moved on with his best mate, he still didn't want her hurt unnecessarily.

With his mind made up, he opened the door and climbed out of the car, determined to confess before his courage gave out altogether. It was now or never. If he wanted to be able to hold his head high and call himself a man deserving of the title, he needed to see it done. He just hoped Kat would understand and forgive him. Then he could get on with working out what the hell he was going to do about the other messes in his life.

———————

Kat stared at the illuminated numbers of the alarm clock on the nightstand in her niece's room. Once again, the baby's cot had been moved into the room shared by her siblings so that Kat could use the daybed. Kat had been embarrassed to knock on her sister's door after only just moving out, but she was beyond relieved when Isobel welcomed her inside with only a few basic questions. Her sister had even let Kat go to bed without demanding an explanation this time, for which Kat was eternally grateful. The morning would be soon enough to face up to what had brought her there.

A knock on the front door snagged Kat's attention. She frowned. It was way past eleven. *Who would be calling on Isobel and Mason at that time of night?* Immediately, Kat's thoughts flew to her mother. Oh, God, did something happen to her mother, too? Kat had barely recovered from the emotional ordeal of burying her father. She couldn't face the thought of her mother passing so soon.

The knock came again. Kat heard footsteps pass her door and continue along the hallway. The sound of the door opening and a murmur of male voices reached her ears. She concentrated hard, but couldn't make out the words or recognize either of the voices, although she guessed one of them belonged to Mason. Curious, she climbed out of bed and pulled on her robe and made her way out of her room.

The light was on in the entryway. She rounded the corner and gasped in surprise at the sight of Kevin.

"What are you doing here?" she asked. He was the last person she expected to see. Mason stood beside the still-open door, frowning.

Ignoring her brother-in-law, Kevin strode forward. Kat took in his appearance. He was more disheveled than she'd ever seen him. He also smelled of alcohol. Her heart sank.

"Kevin, you need to leave," she said. "Whatever

it is, it will have to wait. It's late and I refuse to talk to you when you're drunk."

"I'm not drunk, Kat. I… I had a glass with Jake. One glass. I swear. And only one at home before then. I drove over here. Do you think I would have done that if I were drunk?"

Kat lowered her gaze. Kevin's brother had been killed by a drunk driver only a few years earlier. There was no way he'd drive under the influence. She gestured and moved into the living room. Kevin followed.

"Do you want me to stay?" Mason asked from the doorway.

Kat loved the fact his expression still displayed concern. Isobel had won the jackpot when she found and fell in love with this good man. Kat shook her head.

"No, I'm fine, Mason…but thank you. Please, go back to bed. I'll show Kevin out. He won't be staying long." The last she said directly to Kevin and her tone warned she wouldn't put up with an argument.

When Mason disappeared from view, Kat turned on her ex-boyfriend. "I'm going to ask you again and you'd better make it quick. What are you doing here, Kevin?"

"I'm sorry, Kat. I probably should have waited until morning, but I've just come from Jake's place and I was afraid if I didn't do this tonight, I'd lose my courage."

She frowned in confusion. "Do what? What are you talking about?"

"Can we sit down? It's been a long night."

Kat swallowed a surge of impatience and perched on the edge of the couch. Kevin followed suit and took a seat opposite. "Talk," she said.

"I don't know where to start."

Kat gritted her teeth. "I don't care where you start, Kevin. Just start."

"All right, all right. But you're not going to like it."

Kat stared at him. *What was he intending to reveal?* Several possibilities rushed through her mind, none of them comforting. She braced herself.

"For the past six months, I've been illegally dealing in prescription drugs, namely codeine."

She blinked. If he'd said he'd grown wings and flown to the moon and back, she couldn't have been more surprised. "I-I beg your pardon?"

"I'm a drug supplier, Kat. I've been selling codeine to people cooking meth. Is that clearer for you?"

Even having him say it again didn't make it any easier to accept. Shock rendered her almost mute. Her mind spun furiously. "Wh-where? H-how? W-why?"

Kevin ran a hand tiredly over his face. He looked like he'd aged ten years since she'd last seen him.

"Does it matter?" he asked.

"It does to me."

"Why?"

Anger replaced her shock. She glared at him. "You and I were together the whole time this was going on! I could have easily been caught up in it and I didn't have a clue! Did you bring it home with you? Did I come that close to it?"

"No. I stored the stuff at the clinic. It never came home."

"And what about your customers? Did you do business in our living room?"

Kevin shook his head. "No, Kat. I promise you. It never came into our home."

She stared at him and saw a stranger. She couldn't believe the man she thought she knew was someone she hadn't known at all.

"How *could* you?" she asked and her voice cracked with the strain.

Kevin looked at her, a helpless expression on his face. "I don't know. The opportunity just kind of presented itself one day and it just took off from there. By the time I'd made a few deals, I was lost. The money was great and it was so easy to come by. It wasn't long before I was approached by a bigwig—the owner of a number of meth labs. He wanted me to supply him exclusively and he was willing to pay exceptionally well for the privilege."

Kevin shot her a glance, as if reassuring himself she was still listening. Kat continued to stare at him in shock. She couldn't help it. He was speaking, but it was like he was talking in a foreign language—a language she never dreamed she'd hear coming from his mouth. *What did he need the money for? His life had held so much promise and his career was right on track...*

"Anyway, to cut a long story short," Kevin continued in a matter-of-fact tone, "Vlad's become more and more demanding. I can't keep up with the supply. He refuses to listen to reason. He puts in an order and he expects me to fill it. He's threatened me with dire consequences if I fail. The worse of it is, he won't let me out."

Once again, Kat shook her head in disbelief. The whole scenario was surreal. How could it be Kevin—the man she'd been in love with, shared her life with for the best part of the last three years—blithely confessing that he was conducting illegal drug deals practically right under her nose? It was beyond absurd and yet, apparently it was true. Why else would he be here, baring his soul?

She recalled he'd mentioned Jake and sat forward on the couch. "What did Jake say? I take it you've already told him?"

Kevin nodded. "Yes. He took it about as well as you."

CHAPTER 16

Anger flooded through Kat at Kevin's flippant remark. She surged to her feet. "How did you *expect* me to take it? You've just confessed to engaging in serious criminal activity! Did you think I was going to pat you on the back and congratulate you for being so enterprising? For seeing an opportunity and making the most of it? Or did you think I'd put my hand out and demand a share of the money? After all, it was going on during the time we were together. I'd be well within my rights."

Kevin chuckled condescendingly and the sound of it infuriated Kat further.

"Katrina, Katrina, Katrina. Now you're being silly. Only a little witch like little Miss Holly would think she was entitled to some of the rewards."

Kat frowned, momentarily distracted. "What are you talking about? What does Holly have to do with this?"

Kevin heaved a sigh. "Holly found out what I was up to. Now she's blackmailing me to handing over cash. One hundred thousand dollars, to be precise."

"You mean she's demanding you pay up or she'll go to the police?"

"No. Funnily enough, she hasn't made any mention of the police. She threatened to tell Jake about everything...and... And she also threatened to tell you about—"

He broke off suddenly and looked away. An uncomfortable expression crossed his face. Kat stared at him. *Something was off.* There was more to this... Kevin always squirmed when he was being dishonest. He was holding something back.

"Look at me, Kevin," she demanded and waited until he did. "What aren't you telling me?"

Once again, his gaze slid away and she gritted her teeth against a rush of irritation. "Don't look away!" she cried. "I want you to tell me the truth! What was Holly going to tell me?"

This time, Kevin held her gaze, his expression tortured.

"Kevin..." Her tone held a stern note of warning.

"You're right. There's something else I haven't told you."

Kevin's quiet words fell between them, hovering in the air. Kat tensed. Despite what she'd said, she didn't know how much more she could listen to that night. All of a sudden, she didn't want to know.

"Look, Kevin. Perhaps we should wait until tomorrow. I'm tired. I'm going back to bed." She took a step toward the door.

"I cheated on you."

Kat stopped cold. The words reverberated in her head. She spun on her heel. "You *what?*"

Kevin leaned forward and rested his elbows on his knees. "I cheated on you," he repeated just as quietly.

Kat shook her head and tried to clear it of her confusion. "You *cheated* on me?"

Kevin hung his head. "Yes."

"You bastard! With who?"

"Holly."

Kat blinked, convinced she hadn't heard right. "Did you say *Holly?*"

"Yes."

Kat's mouth gaped. Shock held her immobile. The meaning finally registered in her brain and with it came a torrent of rage. "*What?*"

"You heard me," he mumbled, his gaze now fixed to the floor again.

"Oh, I'm not questioning my hearing capabilities, just your ability to shock me over and over again. Who *are* you? Did I even know you at all? It doesn't feel like it. Just answer me this: Why?"

"I'm sorry, Kat. It just happened. She found out I was dealing and I wanted to keep her quiet. I thought if I charmed her a little and made her feel special, she'd keep her mouth shut. She said she'd fallen for Shane and wanted to make him jealous—it was a mutually agreeable arrangement."

"So you *slept* with her?" Kat whispered furiously, suddenly mindful of the sleeping children not far away.

"Yes."

"You worthless piece of dirt! How *could* you? How could you do that to me?"

She stood and strode to the far corner of the room, needing to put space between them. Her mind raced. *Kevin had an affair with Holly. How could that be?* He didn't even like Holly. At least, that's what he'd told her when she'd made an innocent comment, not long after Holly started at the clinic, about how cute and bouncy the young girl was, like a fresh-faced college grad.

From the corner of her eye, she saw Kevin come to his feet and make his way toward her. She turned to face him. His expression was solemn, his eyes begged her to understand.

"I didn't think you'd be so upset about it," he said. "After all, you were the one who broke things off. I assumed you'd fallen out of love with me. Isn't that the reason people choose to move on?"

"No! Yes! Oh, Kevin, I don't know." She sighed and some of the anger went out of her.

If she were honest, it was probably her pride that hurt over the admission he'd had an affair, rather than her heart. He was right. She had fallen out of love with him and it had been a gradual drawing away, over quite some time. *Had he sensed her fading interest? Was that the reason he'd accepted companionship elsewhere?*

She immediately dismissed the idea that his cheating had been her fault. Kevin was the one who had strayed. He was the one who hadn't found the courage to tell her he wanted to be with someone else. He was the one who'd tried to manipulate Holly by pretending to care for her, to silence her, while he was in a relationship with Kat. It was Kevin and only Kevin who was to blame.

She lifted her chin and stared him down. "How long did it go on?"

"The affair?"

"Yes."

"What does it matter?"

"It matters."

He sighed. "Five months, give or take a week."

Five months? How had she been oblivious to the fact her live-in boyfriend had been sleeping with someone else for so long? It seemed unbelievable and yet, if Kevin was to be believed, it was the truth.

"Why are you telling me this now?" she demanded. "As you say, we've already broken up."

He shrugged. "Ever since Shane's death, even before, my life was going to shit. The pressure to find enough codeine, the shit with Holly, guilt about you... I can't cope with it anymore. I needed to come clean; to bare my soul, if you like."

She contemplated him in silence. "You're seeking my forgiveness," she guessed. That's what this is all about, isn't it?"

A flush crept up from his neck and stained his cheeks. He nodded. Kat wondered why she felt even a modicum of surprise. Kevin's confession had nothing to do with her. It was all about him and trying to make himself feel better. To get things off his chest, as if that erased what he'd done. Well, she wasn't buying it. He'd gotten himself into the predicament all on his own. She refused to feel guilty about being unwilling to help him climb out.

All of a sudden, she felt an incredible weariness. It was way past late. She'd had enough for the night.

"Go home, Kevin."

He looked at her in surprise, as if expecting more. "What, that's it? You're not going to call me out, demand retribution, offer any suggestions on how I can fix the situation?"

"No, Kevin, I'm not. You did this all on your own. You can get yourself out of it. I suggest you start by attending the police station. You already have the name of a detective. In fact, I still have his number. He called around to see me this afternoon."

"Yes, Jake told me."

Kat frowned. "Jake knows about the visit from the detective?"

"Yes. The detective was good enough to tell him how he'd dropped around to Jake's condo looking for him. Instead, he found you." Kevin shot her a look that bordered on accusatory. Kat shifted uncomfortably.

"Yes, I'm sorry, Kevin. I was... I was going to tell you. Jake and I..." Her voice faded. *What could she say?* That she'd had mind-blowing sex with his best friend within days of breaking things off with him, but that now she was having second thoughts, playing it safe, taking things slowly, seeing where they led.

"It's all right, Kat," Kevin said, saving her from explaining further. "Jake told me. Don't worry, I'm fine. In fact, I'm glad for you both. A few days ago, I would have been gutted. I was determined to get my life sorted and win you back. Now, I can see you and I getting together again wouldn't be good for you. This stuff with Vlad isn't just going to go away. You deserve better. I'm sure you and Jake will make each other very happy."

Kat thought about what the detective had told her and wondered how Kevin could be so sure. Right now, she wasn't certain she even wanted to see Jake Alexander again, let alone contemplate making a life with him.

"Jake was brought up on charges relating to a serious domestic violence assault," she said bluntly.

She expected to get a reaction and Kevin didn't disappoint. What she didn't expect was him to regard her with such calm solemnity.

"What?" she said, with a sneer in her voice. "Nothing to say? He's a good friend of yours. You've known him for a long time. I would have expected you to warn me somewhere along the way."

"Warn you about what?" Kevin replied, his tone surprisingly mild.

"That Jake Alexander was an abuser of women! After everything my sister went through with her first husband, I would have thought that was the least you could have done!"

"You don't know what you're talking about. Jake didn't hurt anyone. Even if someone held a gun to his head, he wouldn't raise his fists to a woman."

Kat narrowed her eyes at him. Her anger once again rose to the surface. "You're wrong. Detective Grayson told me. Jake was charged with assaulting his girlfriend. Joanna-Marie—"

"Penberthy. Yes, I remember."

Kat stared at him in disbelief. "You *knew* about this? You knew he'd been involved in a case of domestic abuse? Were you going to keep something like that from me?"

Kevin advanced upon her, his gaze fixed on hers. "Like I said, Kat. You don't know what you're talking about."

"The detective told me—"

"I don't care what that detective told you. You don't know him from shit. He's trying to solve a murder and he's got me and Jake in his sights. He's fishing for clues, looking for cracks. Have you forgotten you're my alibi? You can sure as hell bet he hasn't. He's trying to get under your skin, Kat, and it looks like he succeeded."

"But—"

"Talk to Jake. Ask him about it. That's all I'm going to say."

Chapter 17

Dear Diary,

I can't believe Shane didn't care when I told him I was sleeping with Kevin! I was sure it would make him jealous. I was sure he'd see the error of his ways; how much I really meant to him.

Instead, he just laughed. He laughed at me! To think I was going to let him share custody of Chocolate. We'd talked about it more than once. Shane loved cats as much as I did. Maybe more. It was his mother who refused to have them in the house. And Shane loved his mother...

Just like my daddy loved my mom...

From the moment my mom had the accident, my daddy never paid attention to me. I tried so hard to please him, to get him to notice me, to get him to love me. I'd clean his guns so lovingly, I'd beg him to take me to the range... But it was no use. I was twelve years old and had become invisible.

I look back now and realize a lot of Daddy's obsession with my mom was because he was riddled with guilt. He'd been driving the car when she was injured. I overheard some nosy neighbor telling another he was drunk at the time.

My mom was paralyzed from her waist down. She spent the rest of her life in bed—or occasionally in a wheelchair seated on the porch. Daddy sat beside her, morning, noon and night. He stopped going to work and got a pension. He told me it was because he had to care for Mom. I lost both of them that fateful night. Things were never the same between us again.

And then I met Shane. He was all I ever dreamed of. Good looking, smart, funny. He was also a little bit shy. The way he used to peek at me over his glasses, or frown when some of his numbers didn't come out right...

I'm not sure why he became a doctor. He loved numbers most of all. I used to tease him about being in the wrong profession. He should have been an accountant, or maybe some kind of scientist. A nuclear physicist. I'm sure numbers are important to them, too.

But, it wasn't to be. He had a head for figures, but he couldn't figure out me. My heart longed for him. There was nothing I wouldn't have done for him. Hey, I slept with Kevin, didn't I?

No matter how hard I tried, Shane eluded me. He was tied to his practice...and to his mom. I knew all about the ties of loyalty; the hold a woman can have on someone. I'd lived through it for so many years, tiptoeing through their lives, like a ghost. I refused to be invisible again.

And so, I gave him an ultimatum. Either me, or his mom. I dangled Chocolate as an incentive, but in the end, even my precious cat wasn't enough. Shane laughed at me. I had no choice. Nobody laughs at Holly Greenwood and gets away with it...

Devlin stared at the whiteboard in front of him and wondered what he was missing. Enlarged photographs of Jake Alexander, Kevin Sutton, Vladimir Mikolaev and Holly Greenwood were taped to the board. In the middle was a picture of Shane Cannington. All four of the persons of interest—or POIs as they were known—had one link or another to the victim, but he couldn't point to any of them and categorically declare that they were the one who'd pulled the trigger.

Devlin groaned in frustration and squeezed his eyes shut. When he opened them again, Bryce was pushing his way through the squad room door, brandishing a USB stick.

"Have you seen this?" Bryce asked by way of greeting.

Devlin glanced at it and nodded. "Yeah. Lachlan brought it around a couple of days ago. Interesting stuff."

Bryce shook his head. "This didn't come from Lachlan. Warren Gregson dropped it off."

Devlin frowned. The name was familiar, but for the life of him he couldn't place it. "Who's Warren Gregson?"

"The head of Sydney Secure Solutions. They provide and monitor the CCTV footage of Cannington's building."

"At last. I've been chasing them for a more than a week. I hope you're going to tell me that's the footage from the night of the murder," Devlin said.

Bryce grinned. "Well, then. It looks like this is your lucky day."

Devlin's pulse leaped. Not having the footage had been another source of frustration. His initial calls to the company had gone unanswered. When he finally made contact, they'd told him they were having difficulty locating it. The next time he'd spoken to them, they were waiting permission from the landlord. He was relieved someone at Secure Solutions had finally come through.

"Have you seen it yet?" he asked.

"No. I was only just made aware of it by one of the constables downstairs."

Devlin acknowledged his partner's comment with a nod and pulled out his chair. Bryce grabbed one close by and pulled it up alongside. Devlin inserted the USB stick in his computer and together, they waited for the file to load.

The black-and-white screen was grainy, but Devlin made out the shape of the building that housed the offices of Doctors Alexander, Johnson and Cannington. The screen showed the date and time. Devlin had asked for footage for the twenty-four period leading up to the murder of the victim and would go through the entire film later. Right now, he wanted to focus on the few hours just prior to the time of Cannington's death.

Clicking on the fast forward button, he stopped it when the time stamp showed five o'clock. Most of the offices closed at that time and by six o'clock, the number of people coming and going from the building dwindled to a handful. By eight o'clock, there was no one.

Just before nine, the doors slid open and the

figure of a man appeared. Devlin sat forward and paused the image. Though it was far from clear, he was certain the man was Kevin Johnson. The doctor must have been working back. Funny, he hadn't volunteered that information in his first interview. Devlin wondered why.

Forty-five minutes later, he paused it again and this time, he frowned in confusion. Holly Greenwood was captured leaving the building, headed in the direction of the train station. Devlin turned to look at Bryce, who wore a matching frown.

"That looks like the little receptionist," Bryce murmured. "She was working rather late. Funny, when I spoke to her this afternoon, I'm sure she told me she'd left at her usual time."

Devlin compressed his lips and stared grimly at the image. "I seem to recall her telling me the same thing the first time we interviewed her."

Riffling through the files on his desk, Devlin found Holly Greenwood's statement. He scanned through the pages and finally found what he was looking for.

"There it is. Holly Greenwood told me she'd left the office on the evening of the murder at her usual time, a little after six. See, it's right here." He showed Bryce the statement.

Bryce's expression turned grim. "So, she lied. To both of us."

Devlin stared at the screen where he'd paused the image on the receptionist. "Yes, indeed she did. The question is, why?"

"At least Johnson's story appears to hold true.

He told us he left for dinner before nine. I think at the time I assumed he'd left from the hospital." Bryce looked uncomfortable. "I should have clarified that."

"Don't sweat it, Bryce. At least the footage backs up his departure time. Which means Katrina West was also telling the truth when she said he arrived at the restaurant shortly after that. Perhaps their breakup so soon after the murder was merely a coincidence; just an ordinary breakup, after all." Kevin Johnson was now at the bottom of his list.

"So, where does that leave Holly Greenwood?" Bryce mused.

Devlin stared at the grainy image of the receptionist. "I'm not sure, but there are only two reasons why someone would lie about something like this. Either she's covering for someone else, or—"

"She's covering for herself," Bryce finished.

"It's time we paid little Holly another visit."

Bryce glanced at the clock on the far wall of the squad room. Devlin followed his gaze. It was late. They both should have finished hours ago. He looked at his partner and noted the lines of fatigue that were etched on his face. They were both beat.

"Go home, Bryce. Get some sleep. This can wait until morning."

Bryce sighed and nodded. "Chanel will be thrilled to see me. Lately, we've been like two ships passing in the night. I can't remember the last time I said goodnight to the girls."

Devlin nodded. He was filled with a sudden pang of longing to have a significant other in his life. Someone to share his day with and keep the loneliness at bay through the night. Still, there was no point feeling sorry for himself. It would happen...one day.

In silence, the two men pushed away from the desk and with weariness dogging their footsteps, headed for the door.

———————

The sound of children squealing with laughter woke Kat way before she was ready to greet the day. After listening to Kevin's shocking bombshells the night before, she'd returned to bed, but sleep had been a long time coming. It felt like she'd barely nodded off when she was woken by Sophie and Ben. She could even hear Lizzie gurgling with laughter on the other side of the wall. With a groan, she rolled over and buried her head under the pillow.

It was just fortunate she didn't have to go in to work that day. The last thing she felt up to was chatting and smiling and soothing the nerves of injured patients and their anxious relatives. The sound of her phone indicating the delivery of a new text message caught her attention. Reaching over to the nightstand, she picked it up and checked the screen.

Jake.

Her heart skipped a beat. *Was she ready to talk*

to him about what she'd learned from the detective? She thought about what Kevin had said and frowned. Kevin had known Jake since college. He'd urged her to talk to Jake; had convinced her that she didn't know the full story. *But what more could Jake say?* What other explanation was there for him to have kept a charge for domestic assault from her?

She didn't know how much he knew about Isobel's first husband, Nigel, but as Mason's cousin and a guest at their wedding, surely Jake knew something of her sister's past and the horror she'd endured at the hands of her violent husband. Jake must have known that were Kat to find out he'd committed a similar crime, it would be the end of them.

With another groan, she rolled onto her back, the phone still in her hand. Despite her reservations, she slid her finger across the screen and opened his message.

Hi Kat, so sorry u had 2 find out this way. Not sure what that detective told u, but u wouldn't have left if he'd told u the truth. Please call me, Kat. Let me explain. I miss u. xx

Kat stared at the little crosses at the end of Jake's message and her resistance melted away. *How many times in the past had Jake shown her he was good and generous and kind?* He cared for those around him, from his patients to his friends. In the light of a new day, and after talking with Kevin, she couldn't imagine Jake was capable of the kind of violence her ex-brother-in-law had displayed.

Still, the detective wouldn't have made the whole thing up. And a little violence could escalate over time... She was sure there must be something to the story. The question was, was she willing to let Jake provide an explanation? Sitting up, she leaned back against the bedhead and typed a reply.

OK, but I'd rather do this in person. I'm off work 2 day. I can meet u somewhere.

She left off any hint of kisses. She might be willing to listen to his explanation, but that didn't mean she'd already forgiven him or condoned whatever it was he might have done. His reply came back quickly.

Unfortunately, I'm at the clinic. Will b here until late. Perhaps we can grab a bite 2 eat between my appointments?

Kat scanned the message and bit her lip. Isobel's condo was at least an hour from the hospital. Still, it was only early. She had plenty of time to shower and make herself presentable before lunchtime. She typed back a reply.

OK. I'll meet u at the clinic 4 lunch around 1.

A few moments later, she received Jake's reply.

Sounds good. Will make it happen. Can't wait. xx

She sent him two thumbs up emojis. Setting her phone aside, Kat drew in a breath and eased it out in an effort to settle the sudden rush of nerves that filled her belly. *Had she done the right thing by agreeing to meet him? Perhaps she should have talked to Isobel first? Or even Mason?*

As Jake's cousin, he probably knew the man

better than most. Still, it wasn't too late to do that. He might even know about the assault charges. She didn't know if both Mason and Isobel were at home, but at least one of them was with the kids. She could talk with them about what had happened and go from there. If need be, she could cancel her meeting with Jake. On the other hand, her sister and brother-in-law might just provide her with the information and reassurances she needed.

With that comforting thought in mind, she snuggled back under the covers and drifted back to sleep.

CHAPTER 18

Dear Diary,

I can still remember the day it happened, the day I found the note. It was hidden on his computer, still in draft form. It started out pleasant enough, congratulating me on how hard I worked, how pleasant I was to the patients. He moved on to include more intimate attributes, such as my soft blond hair, my generous boobs, my taut butt and the way he felt with me bent over his examination table, his cock deep inside me the nights I stayed back late. He also wrote about how much he looked forward to coming to work each day, knowing I was there, knowing how pleased I was to see him.

He was right about that. I would have done anything for him. Too bad he didn't feel the same way.

Then the letter turned meaner. The more I read, the more I was filled with disbelief. That's when the anger set in, first a trickle, then later a flood. By the time I'd finished reading, my entire body was engulfed in flames.

'I'm so sorry to break the news this way, Holly,' the letter went on. 'I know how much you love me and I'd give

anything to be able to spend time with your cat, but the truth is, I don't love you. At least, I don't love you enough. Not in the way I love my mother. She needs me and I need her. What you and I have at work will simply have to suffice.

I won't leave her like you want me to. Not even your tearful pleas will change my mind. She's my mother. She gave me life. I'm all she has. I'll devote myself to her care until the day I die.'

It was signed, 'love Shane,' but I knew better than that. He didn't love me. The only woman he loved was his mother.

From that moment, I realized I was wasting my time. A man who didn't have the courage to leave his mother for me was a man who deserved to die. It was lucky I had access to lethal weapons and I was more than competent in their use. The police would never imagine anyone would be so stupid as to kill someone they knew with their own gun...

Little did they know; that's what I counted on...

———————

Kat opened the door quietly and stepped inside the waiting room of the clinic where Jake and Kevin had their consulting rooms. She still found it difficult to accept that it was just the two of them now. Shane would never be part of the threesome again. Thinking about how his life had come to a sudden halt in these very rooms filled her with sadness.

"Oh, hi Katrina, I didn't realize you were stopping

by. I'm sorry, but Kevin isn't here. Oh, that's right...
You're not with Kevin anymore, are you?"

Kat's gaze fell on Holly where she sat behind
the reception counter, a smug expression on her
perfectly made-up face. But accepting what she
now knew about this woman sleeping with her
then-boyfriend... For the first time, Kat could see
past the beauty to the cold and calculating
woman beneath.

"Good afternoon, Holly. It's nice to see you
again," Kat responded smoothly, determined not
to let the woman see how much Kevin's
revelations had hurt.

Not that she was brokenhearted over the affair.
After a night of deliberation, Kat realized in that
regard, Kevin had been right. She'd moved on,
both literally and figuratively. Still, the knowledge
that he'd had an affair with his secretary right
under Kat's nose, stung.

All of a sudden, her plans to play it cool with
Holly went out the window. Anger surged through
her. She strode up closer and leaned over the
counter. Holly's eyes widened momentarily and
the girl instinctively pulled back.

"Kevin told me about the two of you." Kat's
voice vibrated with anger. To her surprise, Holly
merely raised her perfectly-plucked eyebrows and
smiled.

"Is that right? I must admit, I didn't think he had
the balls to do something like that. Who'd have
thought? Perhaps I've misjudged him, after all?"

The amusement in her tone did Kat's head in.
The woman had been sleeping with Kat's

boyfriend and she didn't even have the grace to look embarrassed or exhibit the slightest degree of remorse.

"This isn't a game, Holly, and you're old enough to know better. You ought to be ashamed of yourself."

Holly eyed her steadily, a smug smile playing around her lips. "It takes two, you know. I didn't have to force myself on him."

Kat shook her head, at a loss for words. She didn't know what she expected from Holly when she confronted her, but it wasn't this. She was wasting her time. The woman refused to acknowledge any wrongdoing and she was never going to apologize.

As the knowledge sunk in, Kat straightened and turned away. *Just leave it,* she remonstrated with herself silently. Getting upset over someone like Holly just wasn't worth her time.

"I used to wonder how you didn't know about us. How anyone could be that dumb," Holly said in a conversational tone.

Kat tensed and told herself to keep on walking. Holly was trying to goad her into losing her temper and both of them knew it. The sensible thing was to ignore her and hope like hell Jake was ready to go to lunch.

"Yes," Holly continued in the same casual way. "I mean, sometimes Kevin and I would fuck half the night. Surely you wondered where he was. If he were my boyfriend, I wouldn't have fallen for some lame excuse. Then again, not all of us are as trusting as you—or as stupid."

White-hot anger surged through Kat's veins and exploded in her head. Spinning on her heel, she strode back toward the desk.

"Listen here and listen well," Kat hissed. "You ought to be glad I broke it off with Kevin. The next time you steal another woman's boyfriend, she might not be so forgiving. Take a look around, Holly. The world's a dangerous place."

Once again, Holly merely looked amused. Kat gritted her teeth and fought for control. She refused to give the woman the satisfaction of knowing she'd gotten to her again. But there was one thing she *did* want to know and right now seemed the time to ask. After she spoke to Jake about what had happened, she hoped he'd fire the woman's ass.

"Tell me, Holly. Why Kevin? There were two other single men here, ripe for the taking. Why not Jake? Why not Shane? Or do you take a special sick pleasure in having sex with a man who's already taken?"

Holly merely smiled benignly until it was all Kat could do not to wipe the smug expression off the woman's face.

"How do you know I didn't?"

Kat recoiled as if Holly had struck her, aghast at the implications. *Surely Jake hadn't fallen for this woman's charms?* She wasn't so sure about Shane. After all, Kevin had taken Holly up on the promise in her baby blues and had enjoyed all she had to offer—and he had been committed to another. The other two men had been single.

"Kat! You're here! I didn't realize you'd arrived."

Kat turned to see Jake walking toward them from the direction of his office. She nearly collapsed with relief. He came closer and as if sensing her turmoil, he frowned.

"Kat? Are you all right?" He turned to Holly. "Why didn't you tell me Kat was here?"

"She only just arrived, Doctor Alexander. I was about to buzz you."

Jake looked at Kat for confirmation, but she steadfastly remained silent. There would be time enough to tell him about Holly—and to ask him if he'd also fallen victim to the beautiful receptionist's charms.

"Are you sure you're all right?" Jake asked again as he made his way back in the direction he'd come.

Kat managed a nod. "Yes. But... Do you mind if we go somewhere else to talk? Somewhere a little more private?"

Jake stared at her. A moment later, he nodded. "Of course. I know just the place."

Ten minutes later, Jake unlocked the door to one of the hospital rooms reserved for use by doctors. There were several of them spread through the floors of the hospital and they were usually occupied by medical staff who were doing double shifts and needed to catch a few moments' sleep in between emergencies.

Jake flipped a switch on the wall just inside the door and the room was filled with soft light. Kat looked around her. Though she'd known about the rooms, she'd never seen inside. This particular room was simply furnished with a single bed—

neatly made up—a bar fridge in one corner and a microwave that sat upon a small counter. Everything a tired doctor, too busy to go to the cafeteria to eat, could need.

Remembering all the things they had yet to discuss, her smile of approval was hesitant. "This is cozy. Do you come here often?"

He shook his head. "No. The days of doing double shifts are mostly behind me, thank goodness. Occasionally I stay back late for a patient, particularly if there's a chance they might not make it through the night, but other than that I try to get home."

Kat nodded, once again reminded of the good and caring man he was. Then she thought of Holly and some doubts crept back.

"I spoke to Kevin last night," she said quietly. "He told me he'd been having an affair with Holly. It might not be any of my business, but I just wanted to know if you'd been sleeping with her, too."

"*What?*" Jake's face reflected the shock that filled his voice.

Holly stared at him, trying to read the truth in his eyes. "Kevin's been sleeping with Holly for the past six months. He confessed last night. I mentioned it to Holly when I arrived at the clinic a little while ago. She implied he wasn't the only man who worked there that she'd had sex with."

Jake continued to look stunned. He shook his head slowly back and forth, as if Kat's words were only now sinking in. "That son of a bitch! I don't believe it! He *cheated* on you?"

Kat grimaced. Even though the knowledge didn't tear her heart in two, it still wasn't easy to talk about. "Yes."

"How *could* he? The bastard! To think he came over to my place last night purportedly confessing his sins and wiping the slate clean and he didn't once mention this! The coward! Next time I see him, I'm going to tell him exactly what I think."

Jake's anger soothed Kat's damaged pride. She was almost certain he hadn't been one of the men who'd fallen for Holly's seduction routine, but she needed to be sure. It wasn't that he cheated on her, but it was clear he was special to her, no matter how much she told herself she needed time. In fact, she was almost certain she was falling in love with him. It was important to clear the air.

"So... Were you one of the other men Holly referred to?" She lowered her gaze to the floor. Heat crept up her neck. The seconds while she waited for him to answer were almost unbearable.

"Kat, look at me."

The words were spoken softly, tenderly. They gave her the strength to lift her gaze to his.

"I've never slept with Holly. I've never even been tempted... Haven't even thought about it."

Kat looked at him a little skeptically. "Not even once?"

A faint blush stained his cheeks. "Okay, I'd be lying if I didn't admit I'd noticed her considerable assets, but she's a baby! She's like...nineteen or twenty! Like I said, a baby!"

A smile tugged at Kat's lips. "She's twenty-two,

actually. Only a couple of years younger than me."

Jake blinked in surprise. "Really? You're that young? You seem so much more mature. Are you sure she's only two years younger?"

"Yes. Kevin asked me to arrange a bouquet of flowers for her when her birthday came around a few months ago." She grimaced as she suddenly thought what the birthday gift had signified. "At the time, I thought he was being a sweet and thoughtful employer. Now I know what the bouquet really meant."

Jake pulled her into his arms and hugged her. Kat relaxed against him, enjoying the feel of his broad chest against her cheek. It seemed like a lifetime had passed since he'd held her.

"Kevin might be a complete and utter idiot, but believe me when I tell you, Holly never caught my interest."

Kat contemplated his words and frowned. "Then, she must have meant Shane," she mused.

Jake pulled away slightly and looked at her. "What are you talking about?"

"Holly, remember? She told me Kevin wasn't the only one in the clinic she'd slept with. If it wasn't you, it must have been Shane."

Jake pursed his lips in thought and then slowly shook his head. "You think you know someone. You go through college, med school, internships—you go through hell together and come out the other side. You trust each other, admire, respect and like each other. You go into business together and you make it work. And it *was* working. At least, I thought it was. Now I find out I didn't know either of my mates at all."

"Do you think any of this relates to Shane's murder?"

Jake heaved a heavy sigh. "No, I don't think so, despite what Kevin's been up to. Did he tell you about the codeine?"

Kat compressed her lips and nodded. "Yes."

"Last night Kevin rambled about some Russian drug dealer who has him in his sights. And then Kev even brought Holly into the mix, almost convinced she had something to do with Shane's death."

Kat frowned in concern. For all Holly's less-than-admirable qualities, Kat never imagined the receptionist was capable of murder.

With another quiet sigh, Jake brushed away a strand of hair from her eyes. The look he gave her was so tender, it stole her breath.

"You didn't come over here to talk about this," he whispered.

"No," she replied, her voice just as soft.

"You want to know about the assault charges and why I never mentioned them."

"Yes."

In silence, Jake took her hand and led her to the bed. She didn't read anything into it. There was simply nowhere else to sit. He perched on the edge and drew her down beside him. All of a sudden, she was tense, unsure about what he would reveal.

"Detective Grayson was right when he told you I had a criminal record and he was also right when he said the charges related to an allegation of domestic violence."

The butterflies in Kat's belly multiplied. Mason hadn't been available for her to speak to earlier and her sister hadn't known anything about Jake's possible unsavory past. She'd just warned her to be careful. Scared, Kat tried to pull her hand out of Jake's, but he was having none of it. Instead, he continued to speak, his voice calm and composed.

"I dated Joanna-Marie for a couple of years while I was in college. She was an under graduate studying sports science. She was outgoing, pretty and athletic. We got on well. At least, we did in the beginning. As time went on, I became more and more involved in my studies. We began to drift apart. We also became less and less compatible, sexually."

Kat shot him a curious look, wondering what he meant. Jake sighed and continued.

"Joanna-Marie had always liked it rough, even in the beginning. In the early days, I was surprised and excited by that. She was more than adventurous in bed."

Kat wanted to block her ears, but she knew Jake wouldn't be telling her this if it wasn't important. Instead, she kept her gaze focused on the floor and let him finish.

"Toward the end of our relationship, she seemed to want it rougher than normal. She wanted me to slap her, whip her, tie her up in chains." He shook his head. "I wasn't comfortable with it. It wasn't me. Probably because, to be honest, I'd lost interest. So, I broke up with her."

"Let me guess, she didn't take it well," Kat murmured.

Jake grimaced. "That's an understatement."

"What happened?"

"At first, not much. We argued; she cried, but eventually she appeared to accept we were over. She packed up her things and moved out. A week later, she turned up on my doorstep in the middle of the night with a black eye and two missing teeth. She told me she'd come from the police station. They were going to charge me with assault."

"*What?*" Kat gasped. There was no way she'd seen that coming. "What did you say?"

"I swore. I asked her what the hell she was doing and why she wasn't going after the person responsible. I told her I was going to march her right back down to the station and force her to tell them the truth."

"What happened?"

"She laughed in my face. Scoffed at me and asked me who I thought they'd believe. She play-acted a scene for the cops right in front of me and it was good. If I didn't know any better, I'd swear she was telling the truth."

"Oh, Jake!"

His expression turned grim. "Yeah. Anyway, the police arrived in due course and charges were laid. It was only because, on the night in question, I'd been rostered on duty and had a string of witnesses to prove it, that the charges were eventually dropped and I was free to go, but not until I'd made at least one appearance in court. It wasn't pleasant."

Kat stared at him, feeling his pain. She couldn't imagine what it would be like to be accused of something you hadn't done. It was a credit to the kind of man he was that he'd risen above it and had made a success of his life. Her heart swelled with love.

As if in tune with her thoughts, he turned to her and cupped her cheek with his hand. "I don't know all the details about your sister and her first marriage, but I know enough to understand how something like this would terrify you. I wish you hadn't heard it, but now that you have, I want you to know I could never hurt you—or any woman— like that. I hope you believe me."

The expression in his eyes was so raw and honest, it stole her breath. She tilted her head and parted her lips and brushed them against his mouth. It was the gentlest of kisses, but it set off an avalanche of emotion. Desire ignited inside her. Heat scorched a path to her core. Her arms came up around his neck and she held him as tightly as she could.

"Hang on a minute, babe," he whispered against her lips. He loosened her hold around his neck and pulled away.

"What...?" she asked, dazed with passion.

"The door. It isn't locked."

Chapter 19

Jake turned the lock with a decisive click and made his way back to Kat. She sat on the bed, watching him, a dazed expression on her face. Her lips were red and swollen and need shone in her eyes. He stared at her, hardly daring to believe she was his.

With hands that trembled, he framed her beloved face. His thumbs stroked her mouth. He heard her indrawn breath. His hands slid lower, down her neck and came to rest upon her shoulders. With infinite care, his fingers crept across her chest and slowly undid the buttons of her royal-blue blouse.

The color matched her eyes and turned them a deeper cobalt. The blouse was made from the finest silk. Softly, like butterfly wings, it slid over his hands like a lover's tender caress. At last, it came free and he spread it wide, staring at her perfect skin. Pale and creamy with a scattering of freckles, she was as beautiful as the first time he'd seen her.

Encased in black lace, her breasts were plump

and soft, swelling over the fabric. Testing the weight of first one and then the other in his hand, his fingers stroked their smoothness. She stared at him, motionless, her eyes huge and dark in the stillness, silently begging for more.

He loved that she wanted him to touch her and yearned to feel her skin against his. Reaching behind her, he unclasped her bra. As the fabric loosened and her breasts sprang free, they sighed simultaneously.

Jake smiled and rubbed the pad of his thumb across one dusky pink nipple. It puckered beneath his touch. He repeated the action with the other. He glanced up at Kat and noticed her pulse beat a frantic dance in her neck. A surge of satisfaction went through him that she was as turned on as he was.

As if unable to restrain herself a moment longer, she lifted her hands and loosened his tie and then went to work on his buttons. Working quickly, it was no time at all before she spread open his shirt and then tugged it off his shoulders. Like they had the first time, her fingers went to his tattoo and she traced the head of his heroic collie. The expression of reverence on her face was breathtaking.

Suddenly impatient for the feel of her, Jake stood and loosened his belt. Shucking off his suit pants, underwear, socks and shoes, he came back to her completely naked. In unspoken agreement, they removed Kat's clothes and lay down on the bed, skin to skin at last.

"You feel so good," he breathed, running his hands up and down the length of her, relishing the shape and feel of her. Her skin was petal-soft. She smelled divine. Her husky gasps of need only fueled his passion.

His lips found hers and fused in a mixture of love and tenderness and desire. Though neither of them had said the words, he could feel it in her every murmur, every movement of her body. She sung with passion, hummed with need and he saw it in her eyes. He looked at her in wonder, in awe that she was really his.

"I love you Katrina West," he breathed, no longer able to keep the words in.

Her eyes widened in surprise and then happiness flooded her face. "I love you, too, Jake Alexander. You're all I ever wanted."

Once again, their lips met and joined in a dance of passion. He opened his mouth; their tongues tangled; they kissed like there would be no tomorrow. Wanting the moment to last forever, but knowing his control was fast running out, Jake broke off the kiss, set her gently aside and rummaged in his pants for protection. Sheathing himself, he turned back to her and took her in his arms.

His cock was hard and throbbing. He was filled with burning need. She seemed to feel the same way, as silently, she lay on her back and let her legs fall open. Kissing his way across her chest, he moved lower down her belly. Pausing to dip his tongue in her navel, he continued on then buried his face in her center.

She was hot and moist and smelled amazing. She tasted even sweeter. His tongue swept along her heat.

"Jake! Please," she gasped. He knew exactly how she felt.

Positioning himself between her thighs, he slowly prodded her entrance. She lifted her hips and pressed against him and he gritted his teeth in an effort to maintain control. It was all he could do not to plunge headlong inside her.

"I want you, Jake."

It was as if she heard his silent pleadings. Needing no further encouragement, he thrust forward and seated himself to the hilt inside her. She gasped at the feel of him and he gasped alongside her, exhilarated by her nearness. He loved her with everything that he was.

He'd love her until he died.

———

Kat felt the full hard length of Jake nestled deep inside her. The feel of him, thick and hot, stretching her wide, was almost beyond description. They'd made love before, but it seemed so long ago, a far-off distant memory. Having him back in her arms again, she wondered why she'd insisted they wait.

In the past twenty-four hours, she'd endured one shock after another, but one thing had remained the same: Jake and the way he felt about her—and now she realized it was the same way she felt about him.

She loved him! This beautiful man with a heart so full of kindness and caring. She couldn't believe they'd found each other, or that the two of them had gotten so lucky. She thought of the years she'd spent with Kevin and a twinge of regret dampened her spirits. Resolutely, she pushed the feeling aside and concentrated on the man she was with.

On impulse, she rolled sideways, taking him with her until he was flat on his back and she sat astride his hips. Staring down at him, she shifted slightly forward and felt his cock, hard inside her.

"Is that the way it's going to be?" Jake teased and reached up and tweaked her nipples.

She gasped and moved her hips again and was satisfied with his answering growl. With her gaze on his, she rose and fell, loving the feel of his hardness. His thick cock stood proud and tall and remained buried deep each time she came flush against his body. Up and down, she moved in rhythm, and slowly the tension built. His fingers came back up to cup her breasts and she bit down on a surge of need.

"You like that, don't you?" he murmured.

Beyond words—it was all she could do to nod. Threading her fingers through his, she leaned forward and increased her pace. Faster and faster, she rose and fell, in time with Jake's murmurs of encouragement.

"That's it, Kat. Let it go. Come for me, babe. I want to hear you scream."

Distantly aware of their surroundings, Kat bit her lip against doing as he urged and instead fell over the pinnacle with a gasp.

A moment later, Jake flipped her over and

spread her legs wide and continued to pound into her. She clung to his shoulders; she heaved and gasped; she bit down again on a scream. Jake groaned low in his throat and thrust harder, once, twice…and finally it was over.

———————

Devlin made his way outside the building that housed the private clinic belonging to Johnson, Cannington and Alexander. He'd called ahead to check if Holly was in, but the phone had rung out. Eventually, it had been picked up by the answering machine and he'd irritably ended the call. Then he'd taken the elevator to the fifth floor to see for himself why no one was answering the phone. He'd found the door to the clinic locked and it looked very much like the office was deserted.

It was two in the afternoon. *Where was everyone?*

"How did you do?" Bryce asked from his position not far away, finishing off a jumbo-sized coffee and an iced donut.

"No good. The office is locked and there's no answer on the phone."

Bryce frowned. "Where is everyone?"

Devlin grimaced. "Exactly. The place looks abandoned and the phone just goes to a machine."

"Perhaps Holly's taking a later-than-usual lunch break? Have you tried Johnson's cell?"

"No," Devlin replied, scrolling through his contacts, "but I'm about to. Let's hope he answers. Unfortunately, I left Alexander's number back at the station."

The call dialed in and Devlin waited with the phone up to his ear. It rang once, twice, four times. Just when he expected voicemail to kick in, Kevin Johnson answered.

"Doctor Johnson, can I help you?"

"Doctor, it's Detective Grayson from the City of Sydney Police Station. My partner and I are outside your office building. We wanted to talk to your secretary, Holly Greenwood, but it appears she isn't in. At least, she's not answering the phone. Can you tell me where we might find her?"

Devlin could hear the confusion in Kevin's voice when he responded. "Holly? Why wouldn't she be answering the phones? It's only two o'clock."

"Perhaps she's on a break?"

"No. She takes her lunch break between half-past twelve and one and she doesn't leave until six. She should be there."

"That's what I thought," Devlin replied. "But here's the thing: She's not. I've already been up to the office. The lights are out and the door's locked. There's no one there."

"That's so strange," Kevin replied and once again Devlin heard his confusion. "Where could she be?"

"That's what I'd like to know," Devlin replied. "Do you think she might have called in sick?"

"Well, she didn't call me. It's possible she left a

message with Jake. And Jake should be in his office... Had a full day of appointments. Have you spoken to him?"

"No. I don't have his number on me."

"How about I call him for you? I'll call you right back."

Devlin opened his mouth to protest. He'd rather have the number himself, but before he could speak, Johnson ended the call. Devlin cursed and tossed the phone back in his pocket.

"I take it he didn't have good news?" Bryce asked mildly.

"He doesn't know where she is. He sounded as surprised as we are. He's checking with Alexander to see if he knows anything. Said he'd call back."

Bryce nodded and polished off the remains of his donut. Licking the pink icing off his fingers, he finally pulled out a handkerchief and wiped his hands clean.

A moment later, Devlin's phone rang and he tugged it back out of his pocket. The Caller ID was blocked, but he answered the call anyway.

"Detective Grayson."

"Detective," Kevin Johnson said, "I've just spoken with my colleague. He was at the clinic until a while ago. He says Holly was certainly there then. He had to leave for the hospital and has been caught up there. He's just as bewildered as I am that she isn't at the clinic during office hours. I can only assume she's come down ill and didn't think to call. Perhaps she's left a note on her desk. Leave it with me. I'll see what I can find out."

"You do that," Devlin said.

"Tell me, Detective. I'm curious as to why you need to speak with her?"

"We're following up some enquires in relation to the murder of your colleague. We think Holly can assist us."

"Really? In what way?" Johnson's tone had become even more curious.

"That's between the police and Ms Greenwood. But now that I have you on the line, you might like to answer some more questions I have for you."

Johnson blustered about having left patients waiting and how he needed to go. Devlin cut him off.

"What can you tell me about Vladimir Mikolaev and why does his number keep showing up in your phone records?"

Devlin had thrown the question out there with more curiosity than anything else. Given that Johnson had left the clinic on the night of the murder prior to the coroner's estimate of the time of death, Devlin was almost certain the man had nothing to do with the murder of his friend. Still, from the amount of coughing on the other end of the phone, Devlin's question had taken the other man by surprise.

"I-I don't know what you're talking about," Johnson wheezed.

"I think you do."

Devlin was met with a long moment of silence. His heart skipped a beat. When Johnson sighed heavily in defeat, Devlin's pulse took off at a gallop. He never expected a confession, but it sounded like that was exactly what he was going to get. He tensed in anticipation.

"Okay, you're right. Vlad is...a friend of mine."

"You have very poor choice in friends, Doctor. Mikolaev is the prime suspect in a criminal investigation into the manufacturing of methamphetamine. I'm surprised you're on a first name basis."

Once again, Devlin's comment was met with a bout of coughing. He waited for Johnson to finish before hitting him with the next blow.

"You know what I think, Doctor? I think you're mixed up with Mikolaev's little operation. It's the reason the two of you have such frequent conversations and why the lowlife was at your clinic the other week. He was there to collect his stash, wasn't he? Let me guess, you're supplying him with codeine."

"How... How did you know?" Johnson gasped.

Devlin's gut tightened on a surge of adrenaline. He never expected someone as smart as Johnson to crack so easily. The man must have been well and truly worked up over his involvement in criminal activity for him to confess with so little pressure. Or maybe he was on the stuff... Either way, Devlin was about to crack open a big case.

"I'll need you to come down to the station, Doctor Johnson. You'll need to participate in a formal interview, which will include your confession to supplying a prohibited substance. Where are you? I'll send someone around to collect you in the next thirty minutes."

Johnson's tone was subdued. It was like he

knew the game he'd been playing was up. "I-I'm at the hospital. I'm just about to start my rounds. I could present to the station straight afterwards. I assure you, I'll show. I'll tell everything you need to know about the Russian operation. I nearly came in last night of my own volition just to get it off my chest. The stress of what I've been involved in has been killing me. I should have come to you a lot sooner. I need to share what I know and cleanse my soul."

"I tell you what," Devlin replied. "I'll let you get on with your rounds, but I'm going to send one of my colleagues to the ward right now. It will probably be a plain clothes detective by the name of Lachlan Coleridge. He'll wait outside in the corridor and when you're done he'll escort you to the station. Does that sound reasonable?"

"More than reasonable, Detective, and more than I deserve."

"I'm counting on you to fill in some of the gaps with Mikolaev. We've been after him a long time. You never know, if you come up with the right kind of information and it leads to us making an arrest, I'll encourage the prosecutor to find it in his heart to go a little easy on you. Anyway, it's up to you. An officer will see you shortly. Right now, Detective Sutcliffe and I are going to locate Holly Greenwood."

"You might want to check if she went home," Johnson offered. "If she's not at work, it's probably the only other place she'd be. Either there, or the firing range. The other day, she mentioned some shooting competition she's involved in. I can't recall what day it was supposed to be on." At Devlin's request, Kevin rattled off Holly's home number.

"Thanks for the heads up, Doctor. Much appreciated. But this cooperation doesn't change anything. Be warned. Don't try any funny stuff. I know where you work and where you live. It will go a lot worse if we have to come and find you—and find you, we will. By the way, don't forget to pack your toothbrush."

———————

Holly unlocked the gun safe hidden inside her closet and carefully drew out the .22 caliber semi-automatic Buckmark Browning. It had cost her more than a month's wages and was her most prized possession. Running her hand over the shiny stock, she relished the smooth feel of the wood and metal. The gun had served her well in the past. She'd won many a gold medal. Just like she had with the Beretta.

Now that Kevin had spilled his guts to Jake and Katrina about the affair, she'd lost some of her leverage over him. God dammit! *Why couldn't he have simply paid her the money and kept his mouth shut?* It would have been better for everyone. It wasn't like she'd meant anything by it when she'd threatened him with the gun.

But no, he'd gone soft and confessed to his friends. For all she knew, he'd also told them about the drugs. If that were the case, his friends would be urging him to do the right thing. It was only a matter of time before the likeable fraudster found the courage to go to the police.

The detectives would scrutinize all of them more closely. They might even find the CCTV footage of her exiting the building nearly four hours after she'd told them she did. She owned guns of the same caliber as the murder weapon. If Kevin told them everything, they'd also know she was in love with Shane. If they recovered that letter on his hard drive, they'd know she'd been rejected.

It gave her motive. Once they worked that out, it would only be a matter of time before they came looking for her. She refused to let that happen. She hadn't made such a meticulous plan for all of it to fall apart now.

She'd arrived at work that fateful morning with the sole purpose of bringing an end to Shane Cannington's miserable life. She'd waited patiently, hour after hour, answering phones, greeting patients, carefully biding her time. And then, just as she'd resigned herself to waiting another day, she'd overheard the argument between Kevin and Shane.

Kevin was dealing in codeine. She'd known about it for some time, but Shane had been blissfully unaware. Until now, she hadn't really thought about how she could use the information to her advantage. Now, it seemed perfect. She could drop that little tidbit into the statement she would eventually give to the police. Just like she'd told them the day of the murder about the argument Jake had with his partners earlier the same week. It helped muddy the waters, shift the focus from her to the men. And it would have worked if Kevin hadn't lost his nerve. Now, if the police got wind of any of it, her careful planning would be for nothing.

A surge of determination went through her. Kevin Johnson would *not* ruin her life. And neither would Jake Alexander.

Slowly, as she caressed the barrel of her favorite gun, a plan formed in her mind. She'd return to work and pretend nothing was up. With a little luck, no one would realize she'd even been away from her desk. Kevin would be at the hospital for at least a couple of more hours. Jake had also disappeared—with Katrina. No guessing where they'd been headed. Probably to find a bed at the nearest hotel.

Jake had afternoon appointments at the clinic, so he was sure to return at some point. Holly would just have to make sure she got there before he did and if she didn't, she'd make up some excuse why she'd been away from her desk. She wasn't quite sure what she'd say, but she'd think of something on the way. She was sure of it.

For now, she best get ready for the final act in this play. She refused to go down without a fight. The only way to safeguard her future was to eradicate any and all threats. That put Jake Alexander and Kevin Johnson firmly in her sights.

With her mind made up, a sense of calm descended. Packing what she needed into an overlarge handbag, she pressed a kiss against

Chocolate's soft fur, collected her phone and keys and turned to head out the door.

Devlin pulled up alongside the curb and checked the address he'd gotten from the Internet. The poky cottage with stained fibro walls was set back on a good-sized lot. Devlin supposed there might have once been a garden. Remnants of dead stalks bordered a chipped concrete path, but the patchy lawn had long since turned yellow and there was now more dirt than grass.

"Is this the right place?" Bryce asked dubiously from his position in the passenger seat.

"Apparently. At least, that's what the online directory says."

"The place looks abandoned. Nothing like the home I expected for the glamor puss I interviewed at the clinic."

Devlin nodded. "Yeah. Still, none of us knows what goes on in the private lives of other people. We often only see the person they are at work."

Bryce shot him a sideways look. "What are you saying, Grayson? Is that comment directed at me?"

Devlin laughed. "Of course not. I count you and Chanel among my nearest and dearest friends."

"Don't forget the triplets," Bryce added. "Those girls love you to death."

Devlin smiled fondly and ignored the pang in

his chest. He looked across at his partner. "You ready to go in?"

Bryce nodded and his expression turned grim. "Yeah. Let's go and see what Holly Greenwood has to say about why she lied about her leaving time."

Devlin knocked loudly on the old wooden door that led to the front of the house. The peeling paint crumbled beneath his fist. No sound could be heard from inside. He waited a few moments and then knocked again. The second knock was also met with silence.

"I'm going around the back," Bryce muttered and Devlin gave him a nod.

Bryce disappeared around the corner. Moving over to the low front window, Devlin cleared a patch of the dirty glass with his hand and peered in. The place was simply furnished with cheap pieces that could be sourced from factory direct warehouse shops. A pale-colored cat with dark points on his ears lay on the sofa. The cat's large blue eyes remained fixed on Devlin's, curious and arrogant at the same time. Devlin was the first to blink.

A modest flat screen television sat on a wide pine bookshelf. The other shelves held a scattering of books and other knickknacks, many of which looked like ceramic statues of felines in all colors and sizes. It was clear Holly Greenwood was a cat lover.

Devlin was highly allergic. He couldn't stand the animals. Even from this distance, and with the protection of the glass and gauze window screen between him and the sofa, his eyes were watering and his nose had begun to itch.

"Ah...choo!"

"Bless you," Bryce said, coming around the side of the house.

Devlin turned to face him. "Find anything interesting?"

"No. The place is deserted. Wherever Holly Greenwood went from the clinic, it wasn't home."

"Yeah, deserted except for the cat." Devlin indicated with his head toward the front window and then braced himself for another sneeze.

"Ah...choo!"

"Allergic," Bryce chuckled.

"Chronically." Devlin grinned.

"Well, there's no point hanging around. It's obvious she's not here."

Devlin tugged a handkerchief out of his pocket and blew his nose just seconds before he sneezed again. "You won't get any argument from me."

"We might as well call in at the rifle range while we're out here, just in case she's there. After that, I'm out of options."

Devlin nodded and together, they headed back to the car and called in to get the address of the firing range.

Holly eased out the breath she'd been holding and tried to slow down the beating of her heart. Pressed hard up against the wall of the living room, she risked a peek out of the front window, relieved to see the detectives departing for their vehicle.

She'd been just about to open the door when she'd seen their car pull up to the curb. Though it was unmarked, its sleek, modern lines looked way out of place on her street. It hadn't taken her long to realize it was the detectives she'd talked to before. Thank goodness she hadn't bought a car that time she'd been tempted. If she had, they would have seen it in her driveway and would have tried harder to find out if she were home. No, the train suited her just fine.

She hadn't expected them to arrive so soon. *Had Kevin already betrayed her, or were they just there to ask more questions?* Either way, time was running out. She needed to put her plan into action—and fast.

Chapter 20

Jake ended the call from Kevin and dropped the phone back in his pocket. Pushing away from the bed, he began to pull on his clothes. Kat sat up and brought the sheet up around her. Jake hid a smile. It wasn't like he hadn't seen her naked.

"Who was that?" she asked.

"Kevin. The police are looking for Holly. Apparently, she's not at the clinic."

Kat frowned. "But we were there with her not long ago. Where could she have gone?"

"I don't know. But if Holly's not there, I have to get back even sooner than I thought. I'll have patients waiting."

Kat nodded and climbed out of bed. With no other choice, she dropped the sheet and began to dress.

"Why do the police want to see Holly, anyway?" she asked, turning her back on him and pulling on her panties.

Once again, Jake suppressed a grin. Her

shyness delighted him. He resolutely kept his gaze focused elsewhere and continued to dress.

"Kevin said they want to speak with her about Shane. Perhaps there's something to Kevin's speculation that she had something to do with Shane's murder."

Kat turned to face him, heedless of her nakedness. A frown marred the smooth skin of her forehead. "I remember you said something about that earlier. Do you really think Holly might be involved?"

Jake sat down on the bed and pulled on his shoes and socks. "I don't know. Last night, I thought Kevin was being overdramatic, especially after telling me about his drug-dealing mate. That Russian sounds like a real piece of work. I could tell he has Kevin spooked. I put his suspicions about Holly down to his paranoia with the dealer. Now, I'm not so sure."

Kat turned away again and hurriedly finished dressing. "Why would Holly want to kill Shane?" she mused. "What had he ever done to her?"

"Who knows? If she was sleeping with him, like Kevin said, maybe they had a lovers' tiff? Hell, I was oblivious to much of what's been going on right under my nose. Perhaps Shane and Holly really did have something going?"

"It doesn't mean she murdered him. It's quite a leap to go from a woman nursing a broken heart to wanting to kill someone out of revenge. Besides, I saw her at the funeral. She was beside herself with grief."

"Maybe that was all an act? Or perhaps she

only meant to frighten him?" Jake replied. "Kevin told me she drew a gun on him yesterday and threatened to use it if he didn't do as she said. Maybe she did the same thing to Shane and the gun went off by mistake?"

Kat frowned. "Isn't she a professional target shooter?"

"Yes. You're right. Shane was shot twice in the back of his head. Those bullets weren't fired by mistake."

Kat shot him a troubled look, but refrained from replying. After straightening the room, they collected their things and with a final hug, let themselves out of the room.

"We've missed lunch," Jake commented with a wry grin.

"That's okay. I'm more than satisfied with what we just shared. How about you? Are you still hungry?"

His gaze traveled over her in a slow once-over. "When it comes to you, I think I'm always going to feel famished."

She laughed softly and a blush stole across her cheeks. "I'll walk back to the clinic with you," she offered and Jake shot her a tender smile.

"The rest of the day's going to drag on forever," he said and took her by the hand.

"Oh, it will go by soon enough. Just know that I'll be waiting for you back home. In fact, I think I might run a bath—lots of bubbles and maybe even champagne. Yes," she said as if only just coming to a decision. "I think champagne is required. It's not every day you find the love of your life and are lucky enough to discover they feel the same."

She smiled and his heart swelled until he thought it might burst right out of his chest. All of a sudden, he was ten feet tall and bulletproof. There was nothing he couldn't do with Kat by his side. Life didn't get any sweeter.

"I don't know how I'm going to get through the afternoon without going mad, knowing you're wet and naked and a little tipsy in the tub."

She winked at him. "Then you'll have to hurry home, won't you?"

———————————

Kat dragged her heels as they approached the door to the clinic. After the past hour spent in Jake's strong arms, the afternoon stretched interminably ahead of her. She might just buy that champagne after all, and right now with the heat of the afternoon seeping through her blouse, a relax in a bathtub full of bubbles also sounded good.

Jake opened the door and stepped inside and Kat dimly registered that Holly was once again seated behind her desk. Kat tensed, bracing herself for another encounter with the receptionist.

"Holly! You're back," Jake said and walked further into the room.

Kat followed behind him, intent on making a quick escape. Her efforts were thwarted when Holly greeted her with a hearty hello.

"It's nice to see you again, Katrina. Did you enjoy your lunch?"

The question was so innocuous and Holly looked at her with such an innocent expression, Kat swallowed her irritation and answered.

"Thanks, Holly. It was lovely. How about you?"

"Oh, I had my lunch earlier, before you arrived. But I'm glad you're here."

Kat raised an eyebrow in silent query.

"Yes," Holly continued. "You see, I've been thinking about this a lot. With Shane gone and the police asking so many questions, I figured there's only one thing left to do."

Jake had stilled beside her, as if troubled by something in Holly's tone. He moved closer to Kat, his action eliciting a bark of laughter from the woman who sat behind the desk.

"How sweet! I think Doctor Alexander likes you, Katrina."

A shiver of foreboding went down Kat's spine at the unexpected malice in Holly's eyes. She was relieved to have Jake close by.

"What's going on, Holly?" Jake's tone was low and serious as he stared at his receptionist.

Her gaze swung to him. "What's going on? *This* is what's going on!"

Kat gasped at the sight of a deadly-looking pistol that now rested in Holly's hands. Then Holly swung it back and forth between Jake and Kat.

In that slow, shocking second Kat recalled what she knew of Holly and the numerous shooting accolades she'd received. All of a sudden, she knew Kevin's suspicions were more than mere paranoia: Holly had been involved in Shane's death. Kat was certain of it. And now the woman who'd put two bullets into the back of his head held them at gunpoint.

———————

Kevin thanked the nursing unit manager for her assistance on the ward rounds and turned the corner toward the elevators. The dark shape of the man Kevin presumed to be Detective Lachlan Coleridge stood quietly to one side, silently waiting.

Kevin was acutely aware it would be his last time in the hospital. Once news of his arrest was made public, he'd be stripped of his license to practice. Never again would he be allowed to work as a doctor. He was filled with sharp regret at all he'd risked and all he'd lost... *What the hell had he been thinking?*

At least he was prepared to do all he could to help the police with their investigations. He intended to come clean about Mikolaev; tell them everything. He'd even give them Petrov. And then there was Holly...

He was more and more convinced her strange behavior pointed to something sinister. In the last hour, in between patients, he'd managed to make calls to her known associates to try to locate her, but he'd come up empty. No one knew where she was. Still, he'd tell the detectives all he knew. It might save them some time, if nothing else.

Closing the distance between him and the detective, he came to a halt beside the man.

"Doctor Johnson?" Coleridge asked.

"Yes."

"I'm Detective Lachlan Coleridge. Detective Grayson called me and asked me to accompany you down to the station as soon as you're finished your rounds. Are you done?"

Kevin sighed quietly. "Yes, I'm done."

"Good. Then we can go." Coleridge strode over to the elevators and pressed the down button. Kevin waited beside him in silence. The elevator arrived at their floor with a *ding* followed by the soundless sliding open of the steel doors. They stepped inside. Kevin kept his gaze averted from the handful of other occupants. Once again, the knowledge that he'd never again ride this elevator as a doctor filled him with sadness.

When they were outside the hospital, the detective pointed out an unmarked squad car parked in an "emergency vehicles only" space. They headed toward it. Kevin remembered the calls he'd made and glanced at Coleridge.

"I... I wanted to let you know I haven't had any luck tracking down Holly Greenwood," he said. "I made some calls, talked to some of her friends, but nobody knows where she is."

"That's all right," Coleridge replied. "From what Detective Grayson told me, he and Detective Sutcliffe didn't find her at home, or at the rifle range. But I'm sure they'll find her. Thanks for trying to help."

Kevin detected a note of genuine gratitude in Coleridge's voice. It warmed him through. Yes, he'd made the right decision to come clean. This was the best he'd felt for months and he was on his way to jail. Go figure.

"Why do they want to see her, anyway?" he asked, filled with curiosity. He'd posed the question earlier to Detective Grayson, but the man had shut him down. He wondered if Coleridge would be more forthcoming.

There was a pause and then the detective sighed. "They found a discrepancy in your secretary's story. She told them she left work at six, but the CCTV footage shows her leaving much later than that. They want to talk to her about why she lied and what she was doing in the clinic all that time."

Kevin frowned. "No, that's not right. Holly left at her usual time. She even came in and said goodnight to Shane and me. We were still in our offices. I heard her talking to him in the room next door before she came in and told me she was leaving."

"I'm sorry, Doctor. I've seen the footage. It clearly shows Ms Greenwood leaving the building a little before ten."

Kevin stared blindly in the distance, filled with a growing sense of foreboding. *Holly hadn't left when she said she was going to. Why would she come in and say goodnight?* Past scenes whizzed through his mind in a kaleidoscope of motion and color. Holly telling him she wanted to make Shane jealous... Holly owned guns... Holly not only owned guns, she was an excellent shot... She'd even threatened him...

It was her. He was sure of it now. With his heart pounding, he told the detective as much and then explained his reasoning.

"We need to find her." The detective's voice was grim.

"I'll call Jake again," Kevin offered. "You never know, she might have turned back up at the clinic."

"Do it," Coleridge ordered.

Kevin pulled out his phone and keyed in Jake's number.

———————

Kat didn't dare take her eyes off Holly or the menacing pistol she waved back and forth in her hand. Fear held Kat immobile, yet she struggled to slow her thoughts long enough to come up with a plan. She needed a distraction, something to draw Holly's attention away from them. Frantically, she came up with and discarded several possibilities and then Jake's phone rang.

Both Holly and Kat turned to stare at him. Jake pulled out the phone. "It's Kevin," he said.

"Answer it!" Holly ordered.

Kat couldn't hide her surprise. *Why would Holly want anyone else knowing what was going on? Surely she had enough on her hands? Unless she intended to trick Kevin into stumbling into her deadly lair?*

Holly's next words confirmed Kat's worse fears. "Put the phone on speaker, Jake. I want to make sure he can hear."

Jake did as she asked and Holly moved closer. With the gun still trained on her captives, she shouted into the phone.

"I'm at the clinic with Jake and Katrina. Get over here now if you don't want the two of them to go the same way as Shane. It could be achieved very easily. I ought to know. And don't do anything stupid, like calling the cops."

Kat gasped in shock and her heart took off, fueled by a rush of icy terror. *Had Holly just confessed to murdering Shane? It very much sounded like it.* Now she held her and Jake at gunpoint. *Think, Kat! Think!* There must be something she could do! She was sure their lives depended on it.

––––––––––

Kevin's heart thumped hard and noise roared in his ears. Though he'd already come to the same conclusion, to hear Holly actually confirm she'd murdered Shane was devastating. He could only guess Shane had rejected her overtures, despite her claims she'd been sleeping with him—and that rejection must have pushed Holly over the edge. It was like something out of a horror movie. Images of rabbits boiling in pots on the stove came to mind...

Poor Shane! He hadn't stood a chance! If only

Kevin had checked the other rooms, to make sure they were alone. If only... *And what if he had found Holly?*

He wouldn't have thought it creepy. Strange, perhaps even unusual, particularly after she'd come to him three hours earlier and told him she was going home.

But, no doubt she would have had a suitable excuse and he would have left anyway. She must have gone in to see Shane some time after Kevin left. The police now claimed she exited the building almost an hour after he had. The knowledge that his friend had been shot in cold blood while Kevin was enjoying dinner filled him with pain. *Forgive me, Shane. I should have known... I should have seen something...*

Regrets would get him nowhere. What he needed to do was save the two friends he had left. In a daze, he shoved the phone back in his pocket and turned to Coleridge.

"What is it?" the detective asked.

"Holly. She... She's at the clinic. She's there with Jake and Kat. I think she just confessed to murdering Shane."

"Where's the clinic?" Coleridge demanded, tugging out his phone.

Kevin hurriedly gave him directions.

"Stay here. I'm going to call for backup," the detective said.

"No! It might be too late! You don't know Holly. She's gone mad. I think she might be armed and she's an excellent shot. I'm going to see what I can do to help."

Heedless of the shout from Coleridge, Kevin took off at a run. It was fortunate he was still outside the hospital. It wouldn't take him long.

He was puffing hard when he reached the intersection and gasped in relief when the lights stayed green. He tore across the road, over the pavement and straight into the foyer of their building.

He raced to the bank of elevators and waited impatiently for one to arrive. He thought briefly of the stairs and then dismissed that idea. The clinic was on the fifth floor. He was in no shape to take them at a run.

To his eternal relief, the elevator arrived and he threw himself inside. Screaming at the people waiting with him, he told them to stay clear. There was a shooter in the building. They best all head outside.

They didn't need to be told twice.

The doors slid closed on stunned faces and he frantically pressed the button for the fifth floor. The elevator inched slowly upwards, but way before he was ready, the doors slid open at his floor.

The corridors were all silent. It was like any other normal day. He strode past rooms that housed his colleagues—*Doctor Ava Wolfe, Psychiatrist; Doctor John Kennedy, Pediatrician; Doctor Duncan McClaren, Cardiac Specialist...*

The familiar names flashed past him as he hurried to the clinic rooms. With every step that brought him closer, his heart pounded harder. His breath came fast, his sides ached. His head ached even more. He prayed that he wouldn't be too late... And then he came to the door.

Through the glass, he saw all three of them in the otherwise empty waiting room and he was suddenly glad there was no one else involved. He couldn't imagine how much worse it would have been if Holly had gone psycho in front of their patients. He couldn't bear the thought of any other innocent people losing their lives to someone so unhinged. He strained to hear the sound of sirens, but heard none.

Where the hell was Coleridge?

Not knowing whether he was being foolhardy or courageous, with a deep breath, he opened the door and stepped inside. Holly noticed him immediately and her expression turned maliciously gleeful.

"Doctor Johnson, how nice of you to join us."

Kevin stared at her steadily. "Put the gun down, Holly. Let's talk about this. There's no need to be so melodramatic."

Her laughter peeled in the silence. She laughed long and hard. "Oh, Doctor Johnson, you always knew how to lighten any mood. What fun you used to be! It's too bad you got all serious and decided to find a conscience."

Her expression hardened and any trace of humor disappeared. "You went and told the others about me, didn't you? For all I know, you've even told the police."

"Of course not, Holly," he lied. "Why would I go to the police? You're not the only one who's been conducting illegal activities. We both know they'd throw me into the cell next to yours if I breathed a word. I can hardly tell them about you blackmailing me without revealing what kind of ax you're holding over my head, can I?"

Her expression turned calculating. "You're right. What I don't get is why you told these two. It could have been our little secret. Just the two of us. But you had to go and spoil it, just like Shane."

"How did Shane spoil things, Holly?" Jake asked, and Kevin could tell Jake did it in an effort to keep her talking. While she was talking, she wasn't thinking in a focused way about using the gun.

Holly turned her attention on Jake. Her lip curled up in a sneer. "He said he loved me. Every time he took my clothes off, he said I was the most beautiful girl in the world. But when I asked him to leave his mother and come and live with me, he laughed! He *laughed* at me and told me to leave and to never come near him again! When he turned away, I pulled out my gun and shot him twice in the head. *Bang. Bang.* No more Shane."

Ah, so that's what happened... Kevin compressed his lips at the knowledge. Poor Shane. He'd lost his life at the hands of a scorned woman. Kevin couldn't help but wonder if Shane had given any thought, had any clue about what the fallout would be from his actions. Knowing Shane, he probably hadn't. And he'd paid the ultimate price...

Jake looked in Kat's direction and Kevin followed his gaze. Tears rolled down Kat's cheeks. Kevin understood how she felt. To hear Holly speak so cold heartedly about how she'd done away with their friend—and all because he'd rejected her—Kevin shuddered, well aware he'd had a lucky escape.

"He passed me over for his mother!" Holly shrieked. "A woman of fifty-nine! A woman bound to a wheelchair! How could he! How could he do that to me?"

The rage in Holly's voice seemed to roll off her in waves. Kevin tensed. Any minute, the woman could lose complete control. He glanced at Jake and caught his eye and Jake gave him the faintest nod. Kevin steeled himself, dug deep for his courage and then returned it.

Without warning, Jake dived toward Holly and made a grab for the hand that held the gun. She screamed and tried to elude him, but Jake was fast and strong. He had Holly's wrist and was squeezing, but the woman held on fast. Kevin joined the fracas and prayed everyone would come out unscathed.

The roar of the pistol shattered the air and Kevin was almost deafened by Holly's guttural scream. Somehow, she pulled free of Jake's hold and once again, had the gun pointed at him, this time at much closer range.

Kevin's heart pounded so hard, he thought he might keel over and die right there on the floor of the waiting room. Before it could happen, he charged forward, right into Holly. Once again, the gun roared and this time, he felt a burning pain. He'd been shot! His shoulder was on fire.

Undeterred by the pain, he watched Holly

swing back toward him and aim the gun again. He tried to move—he swore he did—but his feet were no longer taking instructions. In desperation, he eyeballed Holly and it was like staring death in the face.

Like slow motion, the gun came up. All he saw was the barrel. It was sleek and silver and almost sparkled... *Or was that just his imagination?* Her finger moved on the trigger and he waited for the final blow. The roar happened like he thought it would, but he felt nothing.

Was he dead already?

The sounds of grunting reached his ears and he opened his eyes in time to see Jake wrestling Holly to the ground. Both of them were covered in blood. Kevin couldn't work out whose blood it was.

Kat stood back with her hand to her mouth, looking pale and terrified. A moment later, the gun went flying. Kat saw it, too. Kevin urged his feet forward, but they still refused to move. After a second's hesitation, Kat dived after it. When she picked it up, he sighed loudly in relief.

Just then, the door to the clinic burst open and he spied the grim face of Detective Coleridge. Detectives Grayson and Sutcliffe were right behind him. The pain in Kevin's shoulder intensified. He looked down and saw the blood pouring through his fingers. So much blood, pumping out...arterial blood. The significance of it hit him like a sledgehammer to the side of his head. Almost simultaneously, everything faded to black...

CHAPTER 21

Jake came awake slowly. Squinting against the light, he took in his surroundings: White walls, cream floors, white blankets. An IV tube was taped to his wrist. The smell of disinfectant reached his nostrils. He was in a hospital bed. The thought took root and he struggled to sit up. Pain, strong and immediate, stabbed through his side.

"Take it easy, Jake. You're not long out of surgery. You don't want the stitches to break."

It was Kat's voice, and Kat's soft cool hand that smoothed the matted hair back from his brow. He collapsed back against the pillows with an exhausted sigh.

"Surgery?" he croaked.

Kat came into focus. She bent over him and pressed a kiss to his cheek. He wanted to turn his head and taste her on his lips, but he didn't have the energy.

"Yes. You were shot during the struggle with Holly. Thankfully, it was only a flesh wound. The bullet went through the lower part of your abdomen and passed out your lower back. You were lucky it didn't hit anything vital. The doctors repaired the torn muscle and have prescribed a few days' bed rest. They've started a course of IV antibiotics as a precaution to combat infection."

Jake looked at her, grateful for the recount. And then he remembered his friend.

"What about Kevin?"

Kat's expression turned grim. "His wound was far more serious. He's come out of surgery and the doctors are quietly confident, but he's still in the ICU. I called down there a little while ago, while you were still asleep. He lost a lot of blood, but the nurses said he had a good night and his vitals are strong. He's going to pull through, Jake. I'm sure of it."

"What happened to Holly?"

Kat grimaced. "She escaped unscathed. The only one who deserved to be shot and she walked away unharmed. The police have her in custody. No doubt they'll be along to ask some questions now that you're awake. I've given them a statement. They said they already had their suspicions about her. They told me it was Kevin who tipped them off. If he hadn't arrived and distracted her... If he hadn't brought the police..."

Her voice faded away and she shuddered. Jake reached for her hand. "It's okay, babe," he whispered. "Don't think about it. It's over. We're safe."

Tears pricked her eyes, but she nodded and offered him a tremulous smile. "I'm just so glad. When I think of what she did to Shane... What she intended to do to us... She'd gone home and retrieved the gun. She planned to kill all of us." The memory of what had nearly happened overwhelmed Kat. She gasped on a sob and buried her face against the sheets.

Jake stroked her hair and murmured words of comfort. He knew exactly how she felt. When Holly drew the gun and started waving it around, his life had flashed before his eyes. He suddenly realized how much he had to live for and how he longed to spend it with Kat by his side. He'd loved her from afar for so long, but now his dream of calling her his own was about to come true.

"I love you, Kat," he whispered and tightened his hold on her hand.

She lifted her tear-stained face to his. "I love you, too," she sobbed.

He smiled, knowing her tears were happy tears. His heart swelled with tenderness and love.

A knock on the door caught their attention and they both looked up. Detective Grayson filled the doorway and Kat hastily swiped at her eyes.

"I hope I'm not interrupting anything," the detective said.

Jake lifted his hand in greeting and Grayson and his partner came further into the room.

"I'm glad to see you're awake," Grayson said to Jake.

"Me, too," Jake said.

The detective looked from Jake to Kat and then back to Jake again. "I wanted to come here and tell you how grateful we are for what you did yesterday. It was very brave of you—both of you."

"You should thank Kevin," Jake replied. "He's the one who provided the distraction. It's unfortunate Holly got off those shots before I could restrain her, but we all could have easily died. That was her plan. She told us. Right after she admitted to killing Shane."

Grayson's lips compressed into a thin line. "Yes. She confessed to everything down at the station." He shook his head. "It never ceases to amaze me how warped some people's thinking can get."

"What's going to happen to Kevin?" Jake asked quietly, needing to know. He was the one who'd encouraged his friend to go to the police. He was filled with dread at the thought of Kevin going to jail, even after all he'd done to help.

The detective nodded in acknowledgement of Jake's question. "Doctor Johnson will be formally interviewed as soon as he's well enough to speak with us. In the meantime, we all wish him a speedy recovery. Nobody's excusing what he did and I have no doubt it will mean the end of his medical career, but he also confessed voluntarily and has agreed to assist us in our evidence gathering with the dealers he came into contact with. He's playing a dangerous game by turning informant. I'll make sure the judge gives him credit for that when it comes to his sentencing."

"Do you think he'll do jail time?" Jake asked.

"Of course," Grayson replied. "And so he should. But I'm sure once the prosecutor knows of the assistance he's promised us, things will go easier for him. That's how these things usually work."

Jake nodded, satisfied. Kat's fingers tightened around his hand. He could tell she also accepted Kevin needed to be punished, but they hoped the legal system would give some weight to the fact he'd done his best to redeem himself and help others.

"Well, I guess we'd better get moving," the detective said. "We'll come back a little later to take your statement. While your doctor confirmed you were conscious, he did ask us to give you some space. Rest up, Doctor Alexander and take care."

The detectives exited the room as quietly as they'd arrived. Jake looked at Kat. "I guess that's it, then."

She sighed sadly. "Yes. I guess it is. Poor Kevin."

"Yeah. Let's hope he's out in time to be best man at our wedding."

Kat's eyes widened in surprised delight. A grin stretched her lips wide. "Is that a proposal, Doctor Alexander?"

He shrugged and grinned back at her. "Call it whatever you like."

She pulled a face and picked up a spare pillow and tossed it at his head. He ducked instinctively and the sudden movement caused pain to run up his side. "Ouch," he cried in genuine alarm. Kat was immediately by his side, her face filled with remorse.

"Oh, Jake! Your wound! I'm sorry. Please, tell me you're all right."

He drew in a deep breath. The pain eased. He smiled at the woman he loved more than his life.

"I'm fine. And it's my own fault. I should have known better than to think an offhand proposal would suffice." Once again, he reached for her hand and brought it to his lips.

"I'd get down on bended knee, but... Katrina West, would you do me the honor of becoming my wife?"

EPILOGUE

Six months later

Kat nervously smoothed down the white-beaded satin of her dress. Her hand shook slightly as she thought of the hours ahead. Jake was already at the church, waiting for her to arrive.

"Are you all right, Katrina?" her mother asked anxiously. "You're not having second thoughts?"

Kat tossed her a soft smile. "No, Mom. I'm fine. Perfectly fine. It's nothing more than last-minute nerves. I love Jake with all that I am. I can't wait to become his wife."

Her mother's eyes sparkled with tears. She stood and gave her daughter a gentle hug, careful not to crush her dress. "You look beautiful, honey. He's a very lucky man."

"We're both lucky, Momma. Just like you and Daddy. Isobel and Mason. Every now and then, a person finds their soul mate. I'm just glad I recognized him in time."

"The limo is here," Isobel announced, coming into the room. She took one look at her sister and mother and tears sprang to her eyes.

"You two need to stop crying," Kat protested, carefully wiping the corners of her eyes. "We'll all be a mess before we get to the church. Come on, let's go. I don't want to be late."

The soft sounds of the string quartet greeted Kat and her small wedding party as they stood outside the church. Isobel walked down the aisle ahead of her and then it was Kat's turn. She turned to her mother and took her hand. Her mother leaned up to kiss her on the cheek.

"It's a shame Daddy wasn't here to see this," Kat whispered.

Her mother smiled. "Oh, he's here all right. He's watching down on you right this moment and I know he's thinking exactly what I'm thinking: I've never seen a happier or more beautiful bride."

Tears stung Kat's eyes and she hurriedly blinked them away. She looked toward the front of the church and was pleased to see Kevin standing proudly by Jake's side. They'd delayed the wedding until Kevin's release date. In return for giving evidence against Vladimir Mikolaev and Anatoly Petrov which had ultimately helped the prosecutors secure convictions on numerous drug charges, Kevin had received a much reduced sentence. As of yesterday, he was a free man.

Thankfully, the same couldn't be said for Holly. She'd pleaded guilty by reason of insanity, but the jury hadn't bought it. She was currently serving a fifteen-year sentence without any chance of parole for the murder of Shane Cannington.

Forcing the sad thoughts aside, Kat walked beside her mother and headed down the aisle, past friends and relatives and work colleagues, to the man who would soon become her husband; the man she would love for the rest of her life.

NOTE TO READERS

I do hope you have enjoyed reading Jake and Katrina's story. If you've enjoyed this book, please feel free to leave a review for The Likeable Fraudster at Goodreads and your favorite digital retailer. Every review is very much appreciated.

Receive a free book when you sign up for my newsletter at www.christaylorauthor.com.au. You will also receive news on upcoming stories, release dates, book launches and other snippets. I love to receive feedback from my readers. Please feel free to contact me at chris@ christaylorauthor.com.au.

An Accidental Murderer is the first book in my next series, The Sydney Legal Series.

Turn the page for a sneak peek:

AN
Accidental
MURDERER

BOOK ONE OF
THE SYDNEY LEGAL SERIES

CHRIS TAYLOR

PROLOGUE

Nurse Jiao Zheng squinted in the dimness at the label on the medicine bottle and did her best to decipher the words. Tugging a small flashlight from the pocket of her uniform, she adjusted the beam so that it better illuminated the writing and once again concentrated on the letters and numbers

She was almost certain the bottle contained the cough serum the doctor had prescribed for the elderly patient who moved restlessly in the bed. After all, it looked similar to the bottle she'd found on the woman's nightstand earlier in the evening. She was also nearly certain the medication chart required that she administer two tablespoons of the stuff. She checked the label and the medication chart again and frowned. Was that two tablespoons, or two teaspoons? The words looked so much the same, especially in the dark.

Did it matter so much if she got it wrong? It was only cough serum, after all. Surely a little extra couldn't hurt? It might even do some good. Poor

Mrs Eveleigh had been coughing something awful for the best part of a week. Perhaps she needed something stronger?

Still, it wasn't Jiao's place to question the doctor's orders. She was only a second year nurse. She wasn't experienced enough to make treatment suggestions to members of the medical fraternity and she wasn't brave enough, either. She was just happy to have a job. It didn't matter that she worked in the Lady of Lourdes Nursing Home. The pay wasn't as good as it would have been if she'd been employed in a busy Sydney hospital, but it was better than what she could have earned back home in China. Her family were depending upon her fortnightly wage for their survival. She sent them nearly everything she made. It was never enough, but it was something and more—much more—than they would have received if she'd stayed in her hometown, uneducated and unemployed.

Yes, she'd made the right decision to come to study in Australia. Not only had she obtained her university credentials at the reputable Richmond University and secured a job straight after graduation, she had a far better life in Sydney than she could have ever dreamed while living in Shenzhen, a large city of more than ten million people situated in the southern part of China, just to the north of Hong Kong. Her family's life had improved, too.

Besides, she loved nursing, despite the challenges she faced. The English words were the worst, although she couldn't complain. She read better than many of her fellow students, especially those who had arrived in Australia from non-English speaking parts of the world.

Setting aside her flashlight, she poured liquid into a measuring cup. One tablespoon measured about twenty milliliters, give or take. She remembered the conversion rate from college. She filled the cup to the fifty milliliter mark. A little extra couldn't hurt. Leaning closing, she gently nudged the shoulder of her patient.

"Mrs Eveleigh? Are you awake? It's Nurse Zheng. I have some medicine for you."

The woman struggled to open her eyes. She looked up at Jiao, her gaze unfocused in the dimness.

"Nurse? Is that you?" the old woman croaked.

"Yes, Mrs Eveleigh. It's time to take your medicine."

"Oh, all right."

Jiao moved closer and put her hand beneath the woman's head. Gently, she raised her patient up until the woman could drink the medicine from the cup. Almost immediately, the woman pulled a face.

"What is that, Nurse? It doesn't taste so good."

"It's cough mixture, to help your chest," Jiao replied. "The doctor prescribed it for your cough."

In response, Mrs Eveleigh started coughing. The sound of it broke Jiao's heart. She'd seen enough chest infections in the past two years to know this one had taken a strong hold. So many of their residents died from pneumonia and it always started out like this: a hacking cough that just didn't get any better. It saddened her to know that Mrs Eveleigh might not survive.

Still, she'd administered the treatment as prescribed. There was nothing more she could do.

"What time is it, Nurse?" the old woman said around a gasp.

Jiao squinted at the second-hand nurse's watch pinned to her uniform. "It's going on for two o'clock."

"In the morning?"

"Yes, Mrs Eveleigh, in the morning. You try and go back to sleep."

"All right, Nurse. I'll try. Goodnight."

The woman struggled to turn onto her side and Jiao helped her, making sure she was comfortable.

"How's that, Mrs Eveleigh?" she asked.

"That's good. Thank you, Nurse."

"I'll see you in the morning," Jiao said. Taking the measuring cup with her, she quietly left the room.

CHAPTER ONE

Six weeks later

Ben Fitzgerald's fingers moved lightning-fast over the keyboard. It was always this way when he was in the homeward stretch of drafting his closing arguments. The witnesses had taken the stand, the evidence had been presented; documents had been tendered by either side. As the lawyer for the plaintiff, Ben got to make his closing arguments first. It was his favorite part of any trial, especially one like this, a trial he was confident he would win.

His client had been in a collision with another vehicle and had suffered permanent injuries. Sam Redding was barely nineteen and now he'd spend the rest of his life in a wheelchair. There was no question the woman who'd caused the accident was liable. She'd been texting on the phone and had run a red light. The only thing up for discussion was the damages. Sam had registered a low range prescribed concentration of alcohol. It was a question of contributory negligence.

Still, even if the jury accepted that Sam must bear a proportion of the blame, Ben was confident their award for damages would be far more generous than the offer put forward by the defendant. That was what he was betting on.

A sharp rap on his office door caught his attention. He looked up from the computer screen and smiled.

"What are you up to, Ben?" Blake Harton Junior asked, closing the door behind him.

Ben greeted his friend and colleague and then returned his attention to the words in front of him.

"I'm writing my closing arguments. Tomorrow's the last day of the Anderson trial."

"How's it going?" Blake asked and took a seat in one of the two matching leather high-backed chairs that stood opposite Ben's desk.

Ben shrugged. "It's going well, I think. The jury seems comfortably sympathetic. Eight of the twelve are middle-aged women. I got lucky."

"Hopefully they all have sons around Sam's age."

"Yeah. That's what I'm aiming for and of course, they're very aware the damages will be coming from that big old insurance building on the corner. It's not like it's coming out of the defendant's pocket." Ben typed in a few more words and then paused to look at Blake.

"Are you here for any reason in particular, or are you just chewing the fat?"

Blake tried to look affronted. "And here I

thought you'd be pleased to see me! Didn't I agree to take that Jennings matter off your hands? By the way, the man's an asshole, just like you said. You owe me big time."

"Yeah, right." Ben grinned, not in the least remorseful. He'd been flat out with the Anderson trial. He hadn't had a moment to give to the Jennings case. Besides, he'd done work for the man before. Brian Jennings was rude and arrogant and thought all lawyers were scum, especially those he was forced to call upon to get him out of his latest financial fix. Ben had lost count of the number of times the man had declared his company bankrupt. It didn't seem to matter to Jennings. He'd have a new company set up before the ink was dry on the bankruptcy papers and in the blink of an eye was already back in business. Ben had no time for sharks like Jennings.

It was too bad Ben didn't get to call the shots. Despite the fact he billed more hours than every other associate, he still hadn't made partner. That would all change when the Anderson judgement was handed down. He was sure of it. At least, he hoped things would turn out that way. He had no intention of remaining an associate for the rest of his days. It was easy for Blake. His grandfather had started the firm. Blake's father was a senior partner. Nobody was surprised when Blake was offered a junior partnership the year before last.

Not that Ben begrudged him. Blake worked hard and he was one of the best criminal defense lawyers there was. Ben was proud to call him a friend. Glancing back at the man, Ben noticed Blake's expression had turned serious.

"So, what brings you here?" Ben asked. "It's too early for drinks."

His attempt at a joke fell flat. Blake stared at him somberly and leaned closer toward Ben's desk.

"I want to tell you about a client of mine."

Ben groaned and rolled his eyes, trying hard to suppress a grin. "I knew there'd be a payback somewhere. Can't it wait until after the Anderson trial? We'll finish closing arguments tomorrow. The jury won't take more than a day or two to decide and then I'll be all yours."

"I guess it can wait a few days," Blake replied and pushed away from Ben's desk.

Ben saw him turn and head toward the door and he was flooded with guilt. Blake had helped him out more than once. Repaying the favor was the least he could do.

"All right, Blake. I'm sorry. Sit down again. Tell me about your client."

With a sigh, Blake returned to his seat and opened the file he held in his hand. Ben hadn't noticed it earlier.

"Jiao Zheng is a Chinese nurse who studied at the Richmond University. Six weeks ago, a patient by the name of Dulcie Eveleigh died from poisoning while under Zheng's care. Two weeks ago, Nurse Zheng was charged with murder."

"Wow. Is there any evidence Zheng intended for the woman to die?"

Blake compressed his lips and shook his head. "No, but you can't blame the police. Dulcie

Eveleigh was the mother of the leader of the Upper House. George Beckwith is complaining to anybody who will listen that Zheng's a murderous foreigner in the guise of a nurse, intent on spreading evil."

Ben shook his head in disgust. "Where the hell are we going with all this? I thought we were supposed to be more accepting of our international visitors, not less."

"Blame Donald Trump, I guess," Blake said dryly. Ben refrained from offering a reply and Blake continued.

"Unfortunately for Jiao, she made a number of admissions in the police interview."

Ben frowned in disbelief. "She admitted to murder?"

"No, but she confessed to not knowing what was contained in the medicine bottle and being unable to decipher the doctor's handwriting. She wasn't sure of the correct dosage, but she administered the medicine, anyway."

Ben stared at Blake in surprise. "Hell. Who does that?"

Blake ignored his muttered question and continued. "Yes. Not only did Jiao Zheng administer the incorrect dosage, she also gave Dulcie Eveleigh more than two tablespoons of antibacterial hand sanitizer.

Ben swung around to face Blake, his body flooding with shock. "Holy shit! What did she think she was giving the poor woman?"

Blake regarded him solemnly. "She thought it was cough medicine."

"Fuck."

Blake nodded. "Yeah."

Ben stared down at his desk, his thoughts far away from the closing arguments. He couldn't imagine how the victim's family felt. No wonder her son was screaming murder. It was a terrible mistake. A truly terrible mistake.

"How did she come to be your client?" he asked quietly.

"I got a call from a buddy at Legal Aid. She qualified for assistance, but he didn't think he had anyone capable of helping her out. She's in a fix, that's for sure."

"You've got that right."

"Yeah, well, like I said, the police had no evidence of intention and the poor woman's beside herself with remorse. The best I could do was get her to plead guilty to manslaughter. The prosecution's agreed to a ten-year non-parole period."

Ben nodded. "You did well. Particularly given the media attention this case is going to attract. I'm surprised I haven't heard about it already. Then again, I've been caught up in this Anderson trial for the past fortnight. It's taken all my focus."

"Yeah, I know how that is," Blake replied with a brief smile. "I'm glad I caught you at the end of it. I thought you might like to help."

Ben frowned at his friend in confusion. "You've already negotiated a great deal. How can I help?"

"I'm not talking about my client. I'm talking about the Lady of Lourdes Nursing Home and Richmond University."

Ben shook his head. "Okay, now I'm totally

confused. What do the Lady of Lourdes Nursing home and Richmond University have to do with anything?"

Once again, Blake leaned forward in his seat. His gaze burned into Ben's. "Two years ago, Jiao Zheng graduated from nursing at Richmond University. She was immediately employed by the Lady of Lourdes Nursing Home in Strathfield. The reason why she administered the incorrect dosage and medicine wasn't because she meant to cause harm or that she was negligent."

He paused and Ben was filled with a surge of impatience. "So, what was the reason?"

"Jiao Zheng administered a lethal dose of hand sanitizer to her patient because she couldn't read."

"What?" Ben exclaimed. "I thought you just said this woman was a college graduate? You're not making sense."

"She is a college graduate, hence my reference to Richmond University. But despite her college degree, she was unable to properly read both the label on the medicine bottle and the medication chart written by the doctor. These unfortunate circumstances lead to the death of Dulcie Eveleigh."

"Hell," Ben muttered, still trying to get his head around it. "How the hell did she graduate from an Australian university without being able to speak English?"

Blake smiled. "That, my friend, is the question I want you to answer. A woman is dead because her nurse was unable to read. A nurse who was apparently qualified. Someone fucked up somewhere along the way and they should pay. I want you to look into it. File a lawsuit against the university and while you're at it, add the nursing home to the claim. Someone, somewhere must have known about this and yet, they let Jiao Zheng loose on unsuspecting patients. Frankly, I can't believe she hasn't had a hand in more deaths. We're lucky she was caught the first time."

"You can say that again," Ben murmured.

"We're lucky she—"

"Ha! Everyone's a comedian," Blake interrupted with a roll of his eyes. He followed it with a quick smile.

Ben threw up his hands in surrender. "Hey, what can I say? I can't help it if I'm a funny guy."

"Yeah, you're real funny, Fitzgerald. A word of advice: Don't go giving up your day job."

This time, Ben laughed and Blake joined him in his mirth. Finally, the two men sobered.

"So, you'll do it?" Blake asked.

Ben thought about all Blake had told him and nodded solemnly. "Yeah, I'll do it."

Blake's face broke out into a smile. "Thanks, Ben. I really appreciate it. I told Jiao Zheng that somehow, we'd make whoever's responsible pay for sending her out into the world ill equipped to handle the challenges of her profession." He paused and shook his head, as if overcome anew at the enormity of what had happened. "Graduating her from nursing knowing full well she was unable to read English... For Pete's sake, what's this world coming to?"

"That's if they did know," Ben murmured.

Blake's expression turned fierce. "Yeah. They want to hope like hell they didn't." With that, he stood and headed toward the door. Before he reached it, he swung back around to face Ben.

"Oh, by the way, the big boss is calling a meeting at five. He wants everyone to be there."

"What's that about?" Ben asked, curious. It wasn't often the senior partner called a firm-wide meeting.

"I don't know, but if you want any chance of making partner, I suggest you show." With a final wave, Blake was gone.

CHAPTER TWO

It was a couple of minutes before five when Ben exited the elevator on the fifteenth floor of the building that housed the offices of Harton & Wentworth. He'd managed to finish his closing arguments and had even had enough time to do a little research on Richmond University. Blake's account of what had happened to his client intrigued Ben and he was determined to discover how such a thing had come about. How did a nursing student graduate without being able to properly read English? It still didn't make sense.

Ben rounded the corner and pulled up short. The boardroom was nearly full to bursting. The room was noisy with chatter. Whatever the managing partner, Frederick Wentworth, had to say, it had to be important. Ben spied Dimitri Gianopoulos on the far side of the room and made his way toward him.

"Dimitri! How are you doing?" he greeted his friend and colleague with a hearty slap on the back.

"Ben! Where have you been? I've barely seen you around these past weeks."

Ben grimaced. "I've been flat out fighting for a decent award of damages on a motor vehicle case."

Dimitri grinned. "Let me guess. Another sad tale of a plaintiff who's been screwed over by their insurance company and who can't afford a legal bill. You're doing it *pro bono*, right?"

Ben laughed, taking the gibe in the spirit it was intended. "No, mate. This one's paying his way. Or at least, his mom and dad are. He's a Sandringham from Vaucluse."

Dimitri gave a low whistle, looking impressed. "Well done! That's sure to keep the partners happy. How much are you talking?"

"The kid's a paraplegic. He was T-boned by a woman who ran a red light. I'm going for millions."

"It sounds like a done deal. What's the insurance company even fighting about?"

Ben compressed his lips. "My guy was over the limit. Only a little, but he was a provisional driver. Zero tolerance."

Dimitri nodded in understanding. "Contributory negligence."

"You got it in one."

They fell silent and Ben surveyed the crowd. He glanced back at Dimitri. "What's going on here?"

Dimitri shrugged. "Your guess is as good as mine."

Ben elbowed his friend in the ribs. "Maybe old man Wentworth's going to announce your partnership. It's about time they made that call."

Dimitri looked embarrassed. "After all that stuff that went down with my father...and my mother warming her butt in jail... I don't think so."

He looked so sad, Ben couldn't help but feel sorry for him. Dimitri's legal career was going from strength to strength. He'd been a shoe in for junior partner. Everyone had guessed it would happen before the end of the year. Then Dimitri's father, a senior partner at the same law firm, had come out as a gay man and his wife had been charged with a number of murders. It was a bizarre time for everyone, most especially Dimitri. Ben admired the man for holding his head high and continuing to work there. It couldn't have been easy.

"Yeah, somehow I don't think it has anything to do with my name and a partnership."

Once again, Ben felt a stab of sympathy at the sad resignation in his friend's eyes. Ben couldn't imagine what it would feel like to sit back and watch your dream die. He yearned for a partnership. Every waking hour was spent working toward that goal. He was sure it would happen for him one day and hopefully one day soon. Winning the Anderson case with a multi million dollar award for damages would go a long way to helping him achieve it.

"All right, everybody, listen up."

The order for attention came from the managing partner, Frederick Wentworth. Even at seventy-six, the man stood tall and stately. He exuded calmness and authority and it was no surprise he'd been a formidable opponent in a court room. His thick white hair was neatly styled and framed an equally handsome face. Ben hadn't known Frederick in his younger days, but he could imagine he'd been a man to be reckoned with.

Wentworth's deep baritone rumbled across the room. "Thank you for coming together at such short notice. I know you're all busy and I appreciate you giving me a little of your time."

Ben hid a wry smile. Only a fool would ignore an order that had come directly from the managing partner. Besides, like him, everyone in the room was curious about why they were gathered there.

"I'm sure you're all wondering why we're here," Wentworth continued, as if reading Ben's mind. "Well, let me put your minds at rest." The man cleared his throat and continued.

"We've had a little excitement in the firm recently. I'm sure you've heard about it. Facts, rumors, half-truths—it doesn't take a genius to realize they've all done the gamut of the office. Well, I'm here to set the facts straight and thereafter, it will never be referred to again.

"The truth is, one of our senior partners, Alexei Gianopoulos, has had some personal troubles. His wife was charged with several murders and is currently awaiting trial. Alexei also came forward with a...revelation...

"Suffice it to say, the ensuing publicity has been far from positive and Alexei was only too happy to take an extended leave of absence. He remains a senior partner in this firm and we will do all we can to support him during these difficult times. He's also entitled to his privacy and I'd like to remind you that you're all under a gag order insofar as the media are concerned. No interviews, no sound bites, no opinion pieces. Period. I don't care if it's a two-bit rag or the Sydney Morning Herald. Those of us at Harton & Wentworth pride ourselves on taking care of our own and that includes keeping out inquisitive reporters and anyone else who is of a mind to sully our good name."

Wentworth's steely eyed glare moved around the room. "Do I make myself clear?"

A low murmur of assent echoed across the floor. Ben was only too happy to join in. In his experience, loyalty was something that was often in short supply in the real world. He was all for the show of support now.

Wentworth nodded his approval. "Good. That's what I expect to hear. Now, there's something else. Though some of you might question the timing, the truth is the senior partners and I have been thinking about this for some time. It's important to stay current in this fast moving world of ours and one way we're going to do it is to change our name."

There was a collective gasp of disbelief. Ben was as surprised as the rest. The name Harton & Wentworth went almost as far back as the colonial days. It enjoyed an outstanding reputation and was synonymous with wealth and privilege. Only the cream of the crop worked there. Ben had worked his butt off to secure the marks at college to even begin to dream of applying for a job. He'd been stunned when he'd been offered a position. That had been six years ago and every day, he worked harder than the last in his quest to be the next junior partner.

Wentworth lifted one hand in an effort to quieten the room. The murmur of voices faded away.

"I understand that this might come as a shock to some of you, but we've taken a vote and the result was unanimous. From now on, Harton & Wentworth will be known as Sydney Legal."

"Like the TV show, Boston Legal?" someone asked and there was a titter through the crowd.

"Exactly," Wentworth beamed. "I've always had a soft spot for James Spader and William Shatner. I mean, what can I say?"

Once again, a ripple of amusement filled the room. Ben glanced around him, not sure whether to join in. He caught Dimitri's eye and leaned in close, pitching his voice low.

"Is Wentworth hinting at Shatner's sexuality?"

"Who knows? The show ended with Denny and Alan getting married." Dimitri replied out of the side of his mouth. "But Wentworth's been with his wife for more than fifty years. Dad and I attended the golden anniversary bash. It was held at the Hilton." He shrugged. "Hell, I'm as confused as you."

Ben returned his attention to the managing partner. If the man did have a soft spot for homosexuals, it boded well for Dimitri and his father. Ben was glad. Both men were fine lawyers. They deserved to be judged for that alone, not on their personal lives and who they chose to sleep with.

"And one more thing before we go," Wentworth added, interrupting the murmur of voices. He turned slightly to one side and ushered a young woman forward. Her navy-blue suit hugged her curves and looked like it had been made her for. *Perhaps it had?* Her five-inch heels made her long slim legs appear even longer. Long blond hair hung straight past her shoulders. Her face was turned away from Ben as she directed her attention to his boss.

"I'd like to welcome our latest staff member. This young lady is a fourth year lawyer. We've snatched her away from Pearce and Kew. She has a reputation for having a fine legal mind and I'm proud to be able to say she will now be joining our team of associates. She specializes in children's court cases and will be working under Malcolm Pring. Please put your hands together and welcome Abby Brown."

The room filled with the sound of polite applause. The woman turned to face the crowd. Ben focused on the perfect features of her face and froze.

Abby Brown? What the hell? It couldn't be.

Seemingly unfazed by the introduction before several hundred lawyers, the woman surveyed the room calmly with a smile on her face. Her gaze drifted over to Ben and he wanted to turn away and hide. Instead, he braced himself against the impact of her eyes.

Even from this distance, he could tell the cobalt orbs were as brilliant as they had been fifteen years ago. He did his best to look away, but found himself snagged by her gaze. Her eyes flared in recognition and her smile widened. It felt like a sucker punch to his gut...

And then she looked away and the moment was over.

Ben sucked in a breath on a harsh gasp and tried hard to slow his racing heart. Abby Brown was a lawyer. Abby Brown was a lawyer in his firm. He couldn't believe it! How had it happened? How had Abby Brown not only become a lawyer of some repute, but she'd also managed to snag a job in the most prestigious firm in town. It didn't seem possible, and yet it was. He shook his head in silent disbelief. The last time he'd seen Abby Brown she was a sixteen-year-old homeless junkie living on the streets.

Chapter Three

Abby stared at the unmistakeable features of Ben Fitzgerald and her heart skipped a beat. Stumbling slightly from the unexpectedness of coming up close and personal with a ghost from her past, she clutched at the arm of the managing partner. He shot her a look of concern, coupled with a disapproving frown and she blushed and hurriedly dropped her hand. She'd impressed a lot of people on her way into a job at the reputable Harton & Wentworth—Sydney Legal, now—and she wasn't about to let all that hard work and effort dissolve into nothingness because of the presence of a certain man.

So what if she'd been madly in love with him? She'd been a teenager. He was her first love. It didn't mean she still had feelings for him. No, she was a mature thirty-year-old, now. She knew better than to fall for a pair of smiling eyes and a warm heart. Ben Fitzgerald was her past and that's where he would stay. Nothing good could ever come of anything else.

Despite her silent pep talk, she couldn't help peeking at him once again. He looked good. Tall and broad shouldered, he'd filled out over the years. His chest looked as wide as the Mississippi, encased in a tailor-made suit. His dark brown hair was cut shorter than he'd worn it at seventeen. Then again, he'd been living on the streets. A barber was the last thing on his mind. The dark, closely cropped beard was new and it suited him. It gave him a mature, sophisticated air. Her gaze wandered over the rest of his face. Unable to help herself, she looked into his eyes. Her gaze was immediately captured by his.

The green eyes that stared back at her were wide with surprise and disbelief. He looked just as shell shocked as she felt. *Good.* At least she wasn't the only one affected by their chance meeting. Idly, she wondered at the vagaries of life and the sheer coincidence that they'd both ended up as lawyers. It was the last thing she would have expected from him fifteen years ago. She was sure he was thinking exactly the same thing.

"Is everything all right, Abby?"

Abby blinked and forced her attention back to the man who continued to frown down at her.

"Yes, Mr Wentworth. I'm sorry. I guess... Being presented to such a big crowd in such a way... All those things you said... I'm a little overwhelmed."

The old man chuckled. "Don't be silly. I meant every word. You're a real catch for our firm. Edgar Pearce used to brag about your success rate in the court room. If I didn't know any better, I'd have thought the old bugger was in love with you. He'd sit at the bar in the gentlemen's club night after night and sing your praises." The managing partner's voice dipped lower and his eyes filled with a possessive gleam. "I've stolen you away from him. Now, you're mine."

Abby squirmed a little under the brilliance of his regard. She wasn't anybody's, although she felt a pang of wistfulness at the mention of her old boss. Edgar Pearce had been the father she'd never had. He'd employed her as a legal clerk while she'd still been at college and had encouraged her every step of the way. He saw something in her that no one else had. He gave her a chance. It was all she needed.

But all of that now seemed so long ago. Edgar was involved in a car accident that left him in a semi-vegetative state and just like that, life as she knew it was forever changed. It hadn't taken long for the piranhas to circle. Edgar's fellow partners had always resented the hold she had over their colleague. Abby was actually grateful when Frederick Wentworth had called her office and invited her out to lunch. She'd been taken aback at his generous offer and had barely hesitated to accept it. Moving across to Harton & Wentworth was exactly what she needed. Today, she was starting afresh. As long as she stayed out of the way of Ben Fitzgerald.

Ignoring Wentworth's comment, she politely excused herself and blended into the crowd, moving purposefully in the opposite direction to where she'd spied her nemesis.

"Abby! Over here!"

Abby looked through the press of bodies and heaved a sigh of relief. Her one and only friend, Chinese born Sally-Ann Li, waved to her, smiling widely.

"Congratulations!" Sally-Ann gushed, throwing her arms around Abby's waist in an enthusiastic hug. "I had no idea I was in such esteemed company. You never said a thing."

Abby felt heat rise from her neck and creep across her cheeks. She ducked her head, embarrassed by the praise. Sally-Ann was also a fourth year associate and worked on the same floor. In the three days since Abby had started employment there, the two of them had become fast friends.

"Don't be silly," Abby responded. "Wentworth's just being...Wentworth."

"Now who's being silly?" Sally-Ann replied. "You haven't been here long enough to know Wentworth doesn't praise anybody. Not like that, out in the open. Trust me, he's much more a behind-closed-doors kind of guy."

Abby nodded and then changed the subject in an effort to divert the attention away from herself. "What happened with Alexei Gianopoulos?"

Sally-Ann heaved an exaggerated sigh and then her lips turned up in a conspiratorial smile. Her voice lowered to a loud whisper. "He came out to everyone and his wife was sent to jail. All at the same time. You should have been here. It was hilarious!"

Abby shook her head in bemusement. It didn't

sound hilarious. "Came out? As in, decided he was gay?"

Sally-Ann nodded then shrugged. "He's been married for more than thirty years, so I guess you'd technically call him bi. Whatever. It provided good fodder around the water cooler, let me tell you."

"When did this happen?" Abby asked.

"About a month ago."

"Wow, and people are still talking about it?"

"Well, Alexei was a senior partner and his gay lover did proclaim to anyone who would listen that Alexei was the love of his life. I wasn't there, but from all accounts, it was quite a spectacle. Then factor in the bit about his wife being sent to jail for multiple murders and that his son, Dimitri, still works here..." Sally-Ann shrugged. "It's good gossip material."

"Alexei's son works here?" Abby asked in surprise.

"Yes. He's been here for years. We all expected that he'd make junior partner this year, but after what happened with his parents... Still, you can't blame someone for another person's mistakes. Perhaps Dimitri will make partner, after all. He certainly deserves it. He's a good lawyer."

Abby nodded absently and cast her gaze around the room. About half of the occupants had wandered off, but there were still plenty of suits in the room. "Which one is he?" she asked, curious.

Sally-Ann made a show of looking around her. It wasn't until she turned right around that she spied him. "Oh, there he is. Standing against that wall. He's the short one with the dark hair, wearing the charcoal-gray suit. The guy next to him is—"

"Ben Fitzgerald," Abby interrupted. Sally-Ann turned to look at her in surprise.

"Yes, it is. How do you know Ben? He's awfully cute, isn't he? He's single, you know. I've asked around. He doesn't seem to date anyone from work. I wonder if it's that, or if he's gay?"

Ben looked across at them and his gaze locked on Abby's. Sally-Ann's chatter receded, a mere echo in Abby's ears. Her heart pounded, her palms grew damp. She licked her lips that were now as dry as the desert. And still Ben stared at her.

She tried to drag her gaze away and couldn't. Her chest went tight. Her breathing quickened. All of a sudden, she couldn't get enough air. With a gasp, she wrenched her gaze away, turning her back on him. Sally-Ann shot her a strange look and then almost immediately, her friend's expression morphed into a wide smile.

"Oh, my God! Abby! He's coming over here!"

Abby barely had time to register the words before Ben's deep, familiar drawl sounded in her ears. He might have grown older and matured, but his voice was exactly the same. It whispered down her spine and it was all she could do not to shiver from the low, sexy sound of it.

"Abby Brown. I don't believe it. Fancy meeting you here."

Abby tensed and then forced herself to turn and face him, unwilling to make a scene. The last thing she wanted to do was have her colleagues wondering what was going on between her and Ben. She shot him a tight smile that had barely formed before it disappeared.

"Ben. It's nice to see you again. It's been awhile."

Lips that she'd kissed so many times curved up into a humorless smile. "You can say that again."

Though the words he spoke were innocuous, the expression in his eyes remained hard. Abby's stomach tightened with tension.

"Ben, is it? I don't think we've met. I'm Sally-Ann Li. I work with Abby."

To Abby's relief, Ben was forced to switch his attention to her friend. He shook the hand Sally-Ann held out to him and offered her a smile. His face relaxed into laugh lines. His teeth showed white against the tan of his skin and the darkness of his beard. Abby caught her breath at the sheer sexiness of it.

"Sally-Ann, it's nice to meet you."

He gave her a slow once-over that had Abby gritting her teeth. The petite Asian woman with the curtain of long, glossy black hair, full red lips and high cheekbones turned heads wherever she went. It irked Abby to know that like most of the men Sally-Ann came across, Ben wasn't immune.

"How long have you worked here, Ben?" Sally-Ann tittered.

"Six years."

"Same as me," Sally-Ann replied. "I can't believe in all that time we've never met!"

"I work in litigation," he replied, offering her a casual shrug.

"I guess that explains it," Sally-Ann giggled. "I spend all of my days in the children's court, mostly out at Parramatta. No wonder I haven't run into you before."

Desperate to bring the conversation to an end, Abby cleared her throat. "Yes, well speaking of children's court, I'm before the judge first thing in the morning." She looked over in Ben's general direction, not feeling brave enough to meet his eyes. "It was nice to see you again, Ben. Sally-Ann, I'll catch you in the morning."

Without waiting for their response, she turned and took a step in the direction of the exit. A warm hand grasped her firmly by the arm. Even through the thickness of her jacket, she felt his heat. She swallowed a gasp.

"Actually, Abby. I was hoping you might have a few moments. I'd like to speak with you in private."

Ben's low rumble sounded in her ears and once again, her heart took off in a gallop. She looked frantically toward Sally-Ann, but the girl merely shrugged, offered a slight wave and then disappeared into the crowd. As if sensing victory, Ben moved closer. His gaze narrowed. All of a sudden, his air of civility dissolved.

"What the hell are you doing here, Abby?" he snarled.

She took a step back, surprised at the venom in his eyes. "W-what do you mean?" she stammered, hating the traitorous beat of her heart at his nearness.

"You know exactly what I mean. Of all the law firms to target, you chose mine. What a coincidence."

His voice dripped with sarcasm. She stared at him coldly, refusing to be intimidated. "What's your point, Ben?"

"You know exactly what my point is! You're here to stir up trouble! There's no other reason you'd target this firm."

She shook her head at him, unable to believe the extent of his arrogance. "It was always all about you, wasn't it, Ben? After all these years, nothing's changed."

The anger didn't lessen on his face. His eyes glinted green steel. "Look, I don't know what game you're playing, Abby, but you can forget about it. I've worked damn hard to get where I am. I'm not having you come in and ruin it."

She stared at him, at a loss. "Why would I do that?"

"Because you can," he snarled.

An Accidental Murderer will be released on 30 April, 2017 and is available for pre-order from your favorite digital retailer.

About the Author

Chris Taylor grew up on a farm in north-west New South Wales, Australia. She always had a thirst for stories and recalls writing her first book at the ripe old age of eight. Always a lover of romance and happily-ever-afters, a career in criminal law sparked her interest in intrigue and suspense. For Chris to be able to combine romance with suspense in her books is a dream come true.

Chris is married to Linden and is the mother of five children. If not behind her computer, you can find her doing the school run, taxiing children to swimming lessons, football, ballet and cricket. In her spare time, Chris loves to read her favorite authors who include Richard North Patterson, Sandra Brown, Kathleen E Woodiwiss and Jude Devereaux.

You can find out more about Chris and sign up for her newsletter at her website:

http://www.christaylorauthor.com.au